A NEW WAY TO DIE

"The silverslith will follow us easily," Losting said, "Follow us forever!"

"If the beast follows, I am going down . . . down to whatever is there," Born said.

"Death is there."

"True, but we know what the silverslith will do when it catches us. At the very least we may now find a new way to die . . ."

THERE WERE TWO LEVELS TO HELL BELOW AND FOUR LEVELS TO HELL ABOVE. THE ALIENS KNEW NOTHING AND DIDN'T CARE. BUT THE PEOPLE OF MIDWORLD KNEW EVERYTHING AND CARED A LOT . . . CARED ENOUGH TO KNOW THEY WOULD SHOW THEIR VISITORS THE DEADLIEST WAY OUT!

A Gripping New SF Adventure by the Author of *Icerigger*

Alan Dean Foster
MIDWORLD

BALLANTINE BOOKS • NEW YORK

Library of Congress Catalog Card Number:
75-35865

SBN 345-25364-7-150

Book Club Edition: November, 1975

First Printing: February, 1976

Cover art by H. R. Van Dongen

Printed in the United States of America

BALLANTINE BOOKS
A Division of Random House, Inc.
201 East 50th Street, New York, N.Y. 10022
Simultaneously published by
Ballantine Books of Canada, Ltd., Toronto, Canada

This book is dedicated to:
    Saturn
    Mittens
    Calathea insignis
    JoAnn
    and all the rest of the breathren
    who inspired . . .

". . . where highest woods impenetrable to star or sunlight, spread their umbrage broad."
—Milton, *Paradise Lost*

"Who hears the fishes when they scream?"
—Thoreau

". . . . . . ! ! ! . . ? ? . . . O ! !"
—*Calathea insignis*

I

World with no name.

Green it was.

Green and gravid.

It lay supine in a sea of sibilant jet, a festering emerald in the universe–ocean. It did not *support* life. Rather, on its surface life exploded, erupted, multiplied, and thrived beyond imagining. From a soil base so rich it all but lived itself, a verdant magma spilled forth to inundate the land.

And it was green. Oh, it was a green so bright it had its own special niche in the spectrum of the impossible, a green pervasive, an everywhere-all-at-once, omnipotent green.

World of a chlorophyllous god.

Save for a few pockets of rancid blue, the oceans themselves were green from a surfeit of drifting plant life that nearly strangled the waters. The mountains were green until they blended into green froth; only at the heights did lichens battle with creeping ice as on most worlds waves warred with the land. Even the air had a pale green cast to it, so that looking through it one would seem to be staring through lenses cut from purest peridot.

There was no question of the planet's ability to support life. Rather, it was a question of it's supporting too much life, too well.

Even so, in all the life that grew and flew and fought and died on the most fertile globe in the heavens, there was not a single creature that thought—not in the manner in which thought is usually and comfortably defined.

It must be considered that that which inhabited the world with no name regarded the universe in a fashion other than usual . . . if anything did so at all. Oh, there were the furcots, of course, but they had not even a name that could be called a name until the people came.

They arrived, these people did, on the way to some place else. To the commander and officers of the colony ship, who studied and cursed and ranted at their controls and coordinates, it was a clear case of a malign accident. This was not the planet to which their automatic pilot should have brought them. Now they were in orbit, with no fuel to go anywhere else, without proper equipment to settle on this world, without time or way to call for help. They would have to make do with this calamitous landfall.

The colonists voted a Soviet ballot and set about the matter of bringing civilization to this world. They were tired and desperate and overconfident, but unprepared.

They put down in that green hell. It filtered out the preponderance of human chaff from the seed grain right quick and neat, and ate them alive. And it changed those it did not.

Mankind in those early days was used to controlling the universe, by force if necessary. Those who held to such practice did not beget a second generation on the world with no name. A few, less constrained by pride and more resilient, survived and had children. Their offspring grew up with no illusions about the supremacy of humankind or anykind. They matured and observed the world around them through different eyes.

Roll the log.

Give and take.

Bend with the wind.

Adapt, adapt, *adapt . . . !*

II

Born watched the morning mist rise and dreamed of the sun. He snuggled deeper into the cranny in the thomabar tree and wrapped his cloak of green fur more tightly about himself. Thoughts of the sun cheered him a little. Hard work, much climbing, and courage had gifted him with that sight three times in his modest lifetime. Not many men could boast of that, he prided himself.

To see the sun one had to climb to the top of the world. And crawl to the crown of one of the Pillars or emergents that were the world's buttresses. To ascend to such places was to court death from the host of ravenous shapes that drifted and soared in the Upper Hell.

He had done it three times. He was among the bravest of the brave—or as some in the village insisted, the maddest of the mad.

The damp mist thinned further as the rising sun sucked moisture from the Third Level. He shivered. It was dangerous as well as uncomfortable to rest comparatively exposed so early in the day, when all sorts of unpleasant things roamed the canopy world. But dawn and dusk were the best times for hunters to hunt, and Born counted himself their equal. A good hunter did not hide away safe while others took the best game.

He thought of calling to Ruumahum, but the big furcot was not close by, and a yell now would surely scare away potential kill. For the moment he would have to do without the comfort of his companion's hulking warmth.

That Ruumahum was within calling distance Born did not doubt. Once a furcot was joined to a person

3

it never strayed far until that person died. When he died . . . Born angrily shrugged off the thought. These were useless musings for a man engaged in a hunt.

Three days out from the village now and he had encountered nothing worth taking. Plenty of bushackers, but he would walk the surface itself before he would return to the village with only a bushacker or two. He burned with remembrance of Losting's return with the carcass of the breeder, remembrance of the admiration and acclaim accorded the big man. Small things, frivolous things, but nevertheless he burned.

The breeder had been as big as Losting, all claws and pincers, but it was those threatening claws and pincers that were filled with the best white meat, and Losting had laid them at the feet of Brightly Go and she hadn't refused them. That was when Born had stormed out of the village on his present, and thus far futile, hunt.

He had never been able to match Losting in size or strength, but he had skill. Even as a child he had been clever, faster than his friends, and had taken every opportunity to prove it. Though none questioned his abilities now, he would have been appalled to learn that everyone considered him a bit reckless, a touch crazy. They wouldn't have understood Born's constant need to prove himself to others. In this one way, he was a throwback.

Now he was soloing again, always a dangerous situation. He concentrated on shutting himself off from the world, blended with the foliage, became a part of the prickly green, virtually invisible in the meandering pathway of the cubble.

The mist had fled, rising into the Second Level. The air was clear although still moist. Born's view of the big epiphytic bromeliad several meters down the vine was unobstructed. The huge parasitic blossom grew from the center of the cubble, parasite feeding on parasite. Broad spatulate leaves of olive and black backed the green bloom. Thick petals grew tightly together, curving out and up to form a water-tight basin. As was usual following the evening rain, it was now

4

filled with fresh water a meter deep. Eventually, something worth killing would come to partake of it.

Around him the forest awoke, the hylaeal chorus of barks, squeaks, chirps, howls, and screeches taking up where less loquacious nocturnal cousins had left off.

He was discouraged enough to consider trying another place, when he detected movement in the branches and lianas above the natural cistern. He risked edging forward, momentarily breaking the camouflage of his wavy green cloak. Yes, a definite rustling, still well above the cubbleway, but traveling downward.

Moving as little as possible, he shifted the snuffler from its resting place. The meter-and-a-half-long tube of green wood was six centimeters around at its back end, narrowing to barely one at its tip. Gently he slid it out on the hump of wood in front of him. It rested there motionless, like a leafless twig. He sighted it on the cistern. Reaching into the quiver slung across his back under the cape, he pulled out one of the ten-centimeter-long thorns it held. Holding it carefully by its fan-shaped tail end, where it had been snapped from the parent plant, he slid it into the open back end of the snuffler.

The sack slung next to the quiver produced a tank seed. It was bright yellow, veined with black and slightly bigger around than a man's fist. Its leathery surface was taut as a drum. Born eased it into the back of the snuffler, then latched the backblock in place. Above, the rustling had become a crashing and bending of thick branches.

Wrapping his right hand around the pistollike trigger and using the other to steady the long barrel, he settled himself on the weapon, still as a statue. Concentrating on the bromeliad, he strove to reach out and become one with the plant.

See what a fair resting place I offer, he thought tensely. How spacious this cubble limb, how broad and tasty its companions, how clear and fresh and cool the water I have caught so patiently just for you. Come down to me and drink deep of my well!

A lost breeze blew, riffling leaf tips on the bromeliad. Born held his breath and prayed it would not carry

5

his scent to whatever was making its ponderous way downward.

A last loud crunching of parted vegetation, and the vertical traveler showed himself—a dark brown cone shape, covered with stubby brown fur. At the flat end of the cone two long tentacles reached out. Red-irised eyes tipped them. Evenly spaced around the cone-shaped body of the grazer were four thickly-muscled arms, which held it suspended between upper and lower branches with the aid of the prehensile tail that extended from the point of the cone.

Nearly two meters of bulk, five times Born's weight, the grazer would be difficult to kill. The thick, close-matted fur would be hard to penetrate, but only a thin bristle covered the flat base of the cone. To strike there Born would have to wait until the creature turned toward him. The tiny round mouth set in the center of the base was harmless, lined with four opposing sets of flat grinding teeth. But those arms could reduce the cubble path to splinters. A man would come apart much more easily.

One arm shifted its grip, grabbed a lower branch. The tail curved down to grip the same support. Then the upper and left arm let go and the grazer swung lower still. Born wished he had prepared a little more thoroughly, setting out a second tank seed and jacari thorn. Now it was too late. A single slight movement from him and the grazer would be gone in a blur of arms and tail. It could travel up, down, or sideways through the forest with tremendous speed. It could also circle behind a man almost before he had time to turn.

It paused on the liana directly above the cistern. The tail and double-handed grip rotated it slowly as it looked in all directions. Once, it seemed to Born that the weaving eyes stared straight at his hiding place, but they neither stopped nor hesitated and swung on past. Apparently satisfied with the state of the neighborhood, the grazer dropped to the cubble. Three arms supported it in a semistanding pose on the outer edge of the bromeliad. It leaned forward, the broad flat face dipping down to the water. Born could hear slurping sounds.

6

The real problem was: when he whistled, would that massive head turn left or right? If he guessed wrong, he would lose precious, perhaps decisive, seconds. Making his choice, Born slid the tip of the snuffler slightly in the grazer's direction. He pursed his lips and let go with a low, stuttering whistle. The grazer wouldn't touch meat, but flowerkit eggs were a delicacy.

At the sound of Born's imitation of a female flowerkit's danger call, the big head came up and around and stared directly at him. Letting out a short, nervous breath, the hunter pulled hard on the trigger. Inside the barrel a long, sharpened sliver of ironwood shot backward, punctured the tank seed's stretched skin. There was a soft bang as the gas-filled seed exploded. The compressed gas was further compressed by the narrowing barrel of the snuffler. Thus propelled, the jacari thorn shot outward and hit square center of the grazer's flat, bristly face, just above the mouth and between the two eye stalks.

All four jaws dilated. There was a horrid choking shriek. The aural catalyst set off the surrounding forest, and the panicked howling and crying continued for long moments.

The grazer took a hopping, threatening jump toward Born, shook briefly as it landed barely two meters away, and collapsed down off the cubble. But the paralyzed hands and tail held it firm to the big vine. Those powerful, multidigited fingers would have to be cut or pried open.

He watched the creature steadily. Grazers had a way of playing dead until their attacker came close, when they would unexpectedly reach out to clutch and rend with limb-tearing violence. But this one didn't even quiver. The thorn had pierced its brain and killed it instantly.

Born sighed, put the snuffler down and stood up, stretching cramped muscles. The green fur cloak fell freely from his neck. Taking his bone skinning knife from his belt, he stepped free of the sheltering crevice and walked down the broad vine toward the limp shape.

Easily five times his mass, Born mused, and almost

7

all of that edible! But tasting it in one's mind and cooked over a hot fire were two different things. There was now the small matter of getting the prized carcass back to the village and dealing with hungry scavengers along the way. The sooner they left here, the better.

Bending over the edge of the cubble, he got busy with the knife. Muscle and tendon parted as he cut at the hands and tail which held it fast. The grazer fell into the foliage just below.

A voice like an idling locomotive sounded suddenly behind him. Born leaped instinctively, sailed out and down before grabbing a branch of the cubble and jerking to a muscle-biting stop. Panting, he turned and looked back up. He had recognized the rumbling even as he jumped, but too late to stay the reflex action.

Ruumahum stood looking down at him from the main bole of the cubble. The furcot moved closer, all six of his thick legs gripping the wood. The ursine face peered at him, the three dark eyes set in a curve over the muzzle staring down mournfully. Great claws scratched at the branch.

Born shook his head and swung himself onto the vine.

"I've told you often, Ruumahum, not to sneak up on me like that."

"Fun," Ruumahum protested.

"*Not* fun," Born insisted, making use of a herbaceous stalk to return to his former level. A short jump and he was back on the cubbleway. Grabbing Ruumahum by one of his long floppy ears, he pulled and shook by way of making his point.

The furcot was as long as the grazer, though not quite as massive. He was also incredibly powerful, quick, and intelligent. A furcot pack would be the scourge of the canopy world were it not for the fact that they were lazy beyond imagining and spent most of their lives engaged in fulfilling a single passion—sleep.

"Not fun," Born finished, with a last admonishing yank. Ruumahum nodded, walked around the hunter, and sniffed down at the grazer below.

8

"Too old not," he rumbled. "Good eating . . much good eating."

"If we can get it back Home," Born agreed. "Can you manage?"

"Can manage," the furcot replied, without a moment's hesitation.

Born bent over the edge, studied the corpse. "It struck a pretty solid branch, but it could easily slip off. Do you want to pick it up, or circle beneath and catch it when I shove it free?"

"Circle, catch."

Born nodded. Ruumahum started downward, making a wide circle to take him below the grazer. Once positioned, Born would move directly down until he could push it off. Neither of them wished to descend after a tumbling carcass to unpredictable depths, to levels unknown.

There were seven levels to the forest world. Mankind, the persons, preferred this, the Third. So did the furcots. Two levels rose above this one, to a sun-bleached green roof and the Upper Hell. Four lay below, the Seventh and deepest being the Lower and True Hell, over four hundred and fifty meters below the Home.

Many men had seen the Upper Hell. Born had seen it three times and lived. But only two legendary figures had ever made their way to the Lower. To the surface. To the perpetually dark swamp, a moist land of vast open pits and mindless abominations that crawled and swam and ate.

Or so they had claimed. The first had not been of whole mind when he returned and had died soon after. The second had returned with several important parts of himself gone, but had confirmed the ravings of his companion, though he, too, screamed almost every night.

Not even the furcots, hunting back through ancestral memories, could tell of one of their kind who had ever descended below the Sixth Level. It was a place to be shunned. Understandable, then, that neither man nor companion desired to go hunting there for fallen prey.

Ruumahum appeared beneath the grazer and

9

growled. Born shouted an answer and started down. The grazer was still hanging from the branch when he reached it, but a single shove was enough to dislodge it. Bracing himself, Ruumahum dug the claws of rear and middle legs into the hard wood of the cubble. Reaching out slightly, he slammed both forepaws, either of which could crush a man's skull with much less effort, deep into the body of the grazer, just below the tail.

With Born's aid, the grazer was then balanced evenly on Ruumahum's back. Forepaws steadied the dead weight while Born tied it securely with unbreakable fom from the loops at his waist, passing the line several times round the carcass and under the furcot's two bellies. He knotted it and stood aside.

"Try it, Ruumahum. Any shifting?"

The furcot dug all three pairs of claws into the wood and leaned experimentally to the left, then right. Then he shook deliberately, raised his head, and lowered his hips. "Shift not, Born. Good rest."

Born studied the huge bulk with concern. "Sure you can make it all right? It's a long way Home, and we may have to fight." The load was considerable even for a mature furcot as big as Ruumahum.

The latter snorted. "Can make . . . not sure of fighting."

"All right, don't worry about it. Kill or no kill, if we get into any real trouble I'll cut you free." He grinned. "Just don't go to long sleep on me halfway between here and Home."

"Sleep? What is sleep?" Ruumahum snorted. The furcots possessed a peculiar sense of humor all their own that only occasionally coincided with that of persons. As Born was a bit peculiar himself, he understood their jokes better than most.

"Let's go, then."

Back to the hiding place to retrieve the snuffler and sling it snugly across his back. Then there was only one more thing to do. Born walked back past the heavily laden Ruumahum and stopped at the brim of the bromeliad which had attracted such excellent prey. He ran his hands caressingly over the broad leaves and strong petals. Hands cupped, he

10

bent to drink deeply from the clear pool that the unlucky grazer had sought. Finishing, he shook the droplets free and wiped wet palms on his cloak. He stroked the nearest leaf again in silent tribute to the plant, and then he and Ruumahum started the arduous trek Homeward.

It was a green universe, true; but its stars and nebulae were brilliantly colored. Cauliflorous air-trees growing on the broad branches of the Pillars and emergents bristled with fragrant blossoms of every conceivable shape and color, some exuding fragrances so pungent they had to be avoided lest olfactory senses be smothered forever. These perfumed blooms Born and Ruumahum avoided assiduously. Their localized miasmas were as deadly as they were sensuous. Vines and creepers put forth flowers of their own, and in places aerial roots bloomed with their own flowerings. There were color and variety to make Earth's richest jungles seem pallid and wan in comparison.

Although plant life held dominance, animal life was also abundant and lush. Ornithoid, mammaloid, and reptiloid arboreals glided or flew through winding emerald tunnels. They were outnumbered by creatures that swung, crawled, and jumped along gravity-defying highways of wood and pulp.

The steady cycle of life and death revolved around Born and Ruumahum as they made their way over crosshatched tuntangcles and cubbles and winding woody paths back toward the village. A drifter with helical wings pounced upon an unwary six-legged feathered pseudolizard, was swallowed in turn when it chose to land on a false cubble. The false cubble looked almost identical to the thick wooden creepers Born and Ruumahum strode across. Had Born stepped on it he would have lost a foot at the least. The false cubble was a continuous chain of interlocking mouths, stomachs, and intestines. Both drifter and pseudolizard vanished down one link of the toothed branch.

It was close to noon. Occasional shafts of light reached the Third Level, some digging even deeper

11

to the Fourth and Fifth. Mirror vines shone everywhere, their diamond-shaped reflective leaves bouncing the sun and sending life-giving light ricocheting hundreds of meters down green canyons to places it otherwise would never reach. Noontime was the crescendo of the hylaeal symphony. Comb vines and resonators formed a verdant vocal background for the songsters of the animal kingdom. They would have astonished a curious botanist, as would the mirror vines.

Born was no botanist. He could not have defined the term. But his great-great-great-great-great-grandfather could have. That knowledge had not kept him from dying young, however.

Eventually the damp night mist slid about them with feline stealth. The cheerful raucousness of the creatures of light gave way to the sounds of awakening nightlings, whose grunts were darker and deeper, their cries closer to hysteria, the booming howls of the nocturnal carnivores a touch more menacing. It was time to find shelter.

Born had spent much of the last hour searching for a wild Home tree. Such trees were rare and he had encountered none this afternoon. They would have to settle for less accommodating temporary quarters. One such lay ten meters overhead, easily reached through the interwoven pathways of the forest canopy.

What disease or parasite had caused the great woody galls to form on the branch of the Pillar tree neither Born nor Ruumahum could guess, but they were grateful for their presence. They would serve to gentle the night. Six or seven of the globular eruptions were clustered together on the branch. The smallest was half Born's size, the largest more than spacious enough to accommodate man and furcot.

He tested the biggest with his knife, found it far too tough for the sharpened bone—just as he had hoped. If his skinning blade could not penetrate the woody gall, the chances of some predator coming in on them from behind were small. He untied the dead grazer—it was already beginning to smell—from Ruumahum's back, slid the hulk onto the branch.

Ruumahum stretched delightedly, fur rippling as the muscles in his back popped. He yawned, revealing multiple canines and two razor-sharp lower tusks.

Under Born's direction, the furcot went to work on the gall with both forepaws, ripping open nearly all of one side. Together they wrestled the carcass into the cavity. Working carefully and smoothly, Born tied his remaining jacari thorns into the length of vine until they formed a crude barricade across the opening. Any scavenger who tried to sneak in now risked a fatal pricking. The barbed thorns crisscrossed the opening neatly. An intelligent scavenger could work around them easily, but they would stop anything that was not a man.

Their kill safely secured for the night, Ruumahum went to work on the gall next in line, cutting a smaller opening in it for them to enter. Born knelt, peered inside. It was long dead—dry and black. As he entered, he pulled a packet of red dust from his belt; Ruumahum was already scraping some of the dust-dry gall lining into a pile near the opening they had made. Born poured a little of the red powder on a thin scrap of wood and pressed his thumb into it. A few seconds of contact with his body heat was enough to cause the dust pile to explode in flame just as the hunter withdrew his thumb. The incendiary pollen served as a especially effective form of defense for a certain parasitic tuber. Born's people had discovered its usefulness the hard way.

He built the tiny blaze into a modest fire that burned freely on the smooth, dead floor of the gall. Its dance and crackle was a great comfort in the blackness of night. Only one more thing to do. He had to shake Ruumahum violently to awaken him long enough to cut a tiny hole two-thirds of the way up the far side of the gall. Circulation and smoke exit assured, Born took a piece of dark jerky from his belt pouch and chewed at the spicy, rock-hard meat.

The evening rain began. It would rain all night—not an occasional downpour, but a steady, even rain that would cease two hours before dawn. With few exceptions, it had rained every night Born could re-

13

call. As sure as the sun rose in the morning, the rain came down at night. Water drummed steadily on the roof of the gall, flowed down its curved sides to drip away to depths unseen. Ruumahum was fast asleep.

Born studied the fire for several minutes. Putting the rest of the jerky away for the next night, he nestled himself into Ruumahum's flank. The furcot stirred slightly in sleep, pressing against the inner wall of the gall, his head curved into his chest. Born sighed, stared at the solid wall of blackness beyond the fire. He was satisfied. They had met no scavengers on this first day of return, and Ruumahum had handled the massive load of the great grazer without falling asleep even once. He stroked the furcot's fur appreciatively, running his fingers through the thick green coat.

A warm, dry shelter for the night, too. Many nights spent in wetness made him appreciate the dry gall. Pulling the green fur cloak tightly about him, he turned on his side. His knife was close to his right hand, the snuffler ready at his feet. Relatively content and more or less confident of not waking up in the belly of some nightcrawler, he fell into a sound, dreamless sleep.

It had been a fairly hard rain, Born reflected as he stared out through the hole cut in the gall. Behind him, Ruumahum slept on oblivious. The furcot would continue to do so until Born woke him. Left to his own devices, a furcot would sleep all but a few hours a day.

Droplets still fell from the green sky above, though the rain had long since ceased. A couple struck Born in the face. He shook the tepid moisture away. Walking would be slippery and uncertain for a while, but they would start immediately anyway. He was anxious to be Home. Anxious to see the look on Brightly Go's face when he dumped the grazer at her feet.

Rising, he booted Ruumahum in the ribs a couple of times. The furcot moaned. Born repeated the action. Ruumahum got to his feet two at a time, grumbling irritably.

"Already morning . . . ?"

"Long day's march, Ruumahum," Born told him. "Long rain last night. There should be red berries and pium out before midday."

Ruumahum brightened at the thought of food. He would have preferred to sleep, but . . . pium, now. A last stretch, extending forepaws out in front of him and pulling, digging eight parallel grooves into the alloy-tough dead base of the gall. Persons, he had to admit, were sometimes useful to have around. They had a way of finding good things to eat and making the very eating more enjoyable. For such rewards Ruumahum was willing to overlook Born's faults. His triple pupils brightened. Humans flattered themselves with the idea that they had done an awesome job of domesticating the first furcots. The furcots saw no need to dispute this. The reality of it was that they had stuck with the persons out of curiosity. Human persons were the first beings the furcots had ever encountered who were unpredictable enough to keep them awake. One could never quite predict what a person might do—even one's own person. So they kept up the pact without really understanding why, knowing only that in the relationship there was something worthwhile and good.

Keeping hearts of pium in mind enabled Ruumahum to arrange the grazer carcass on his back without falling asleep more than once in the process. So Born lost little of his precious time.

Either no scavenger had blundered into their camp, or else they had elected not to risk those deadly interlocking thorns. Born recovered all the vine-entwined jacaris, reset the poison darts in the bottom of his quiver, looped the vine around his belt, and started off again.

"Close Home," Ruumahum muttered that evening, pausing to send a thick curving tongue out to groom the back of a forepaw.

Born had been recognizing familiar landmarks and tree blazes for over an hour. There was the storm-treader tree that had killed old Hannah in an unwary moment. They gave the black and silver bole a wide berth. Once they had to pause as a Buna floater drifted by, trailing long stinging tentacles. As they

15

waited, the floater let out a long sibilant whistle and dropped lower, perhaps to try its luck on the Fourth Level where scampering bushackers were more common.

Born had stepped out from behind a trunk and was about to remove his cloak when above them sounded a shriek sufficient to shatter a pfeffermall, more violent than the howl of chollakee hunting. So sudden, so overpowering was the scream that the normally imperturbable Ruumahum was shocked into a defensive posture, backing up against the nearest bole despite the restrictive mass of the grazer, forepaws upraised and claws extended.

The scream dropped to a moan that was abruptly subsumed by an overpowering, frightening roar of crackings and snappings. Even the branch of the nearby Pillar tree shook. Then the branch they stood on rocked fiercely. With his great strength, Ruumahum was able to maintain his perch, but Born was not so secure. He fell several meters, smashing through a couple of helpless succulents before he hit an unyielding protrusion. He started to bounce off it before he got both arms locked around the stiff fom. The vibrating stopped, and he was able to get his legs around it, too.

Shaking, he pulled himself up. Nothing felt broken, and everything seemed to work. But his snuffler was gone; its restraining tie had snapped, sending it bouncing and spinning into the depths. That was a severe loss.

The crashing and breaking sounds faded, finally stopped. As he had fallen, Born thought he had seen in the distance through the green an impossibly wide mass of something blue and metallic. It had passed as swiftly as he had fallen. As he stared that way now there was nothing to be seen but the forest.

Peepers and orbioles came out of hiding, called hesitantly into the silence. Then bushackers and flowerkits and their relatives joined in. In minutes the hylaea sounded and resounded normally again.

"Something has happened," Ruumahum ventured softly.

"I think I saw it." Born stared harder, still saw

16

only what belonged. "Did you? Something big and blue and shining."

Ruumahum eyed him steadily. "Saw nothing. Saw self falling to Hell and gone. Concentrated on staying *here* with grazer weight pulling *there*. No time for curious-looking."

"You did better than I, old friend," Born admitted, as he climbed up toward the furcot. He tested a liana, found it firm, and started off in the direction of the murderous sounds. "I think we'd better—"

"No." A glance over his shoulder showed the furcot with his great head lowered and moving slowly from side to side in imitation of the human gesture of negation. Three eyes rolled toward the path they had been following.

"So far, lucky be we, person Born. Soon though, others grazer to smell will begin. We will fight have to every step to Home. To Home go first. This other"—and he nodded in the direction of the breaking and crashing—"I would talk of first with the brethren, who know such things quickly."

Born stood thinking on the woody bridge. His intense curiosity—or madness, if one believed many of his fellows—pulled him toward the source of the sounds, however threatening they had been. For a change, reason overcame. Ruumahum and he had been through much in the killing and carrying of the grazer. To risk losing it now for no good reason was unsound thinking.

"Okay, Ruumahum." He hopped back onto the bigger branch and started toward the village again. A last look over his shoulder still showed only speckled greenery and no unnatural movement. "But as soon as the meat's disposed of, I'm coming back to find out what that was, whether or not you or anyone else comes with me."

"Doubt it not," Ruumahum replied knowingly.

III

They reached the barrier well before darkness. In front of them, the hylaea seemed to become a single tree—the Home-tree. Only the Pillars themselves were bigger, and the Home-tree was a monstrously big tree for certain. Broad twisting branches and vines-of-own shot out in all directions. Air-trees and cubbles and lianas grew in and about the tree's own growth. Born noted with satisfaction that only plants which were innocuous or helpful to the Home-tree grew on it. His people kept the Home-tree well and, in turn, the Home-tree kept them.

The vines-of-own were lined with flowers of bright pink, with pollen pods which sat globelike within them. These pods were akin to the yellow tank seeds that made the snufflers such deadly weapons, but far more sensitive. A single touch on the sensitive pink surface would cause the paper-thin skin to rupture, sending a cloud of dust into the air that would kill any animal inhaling it, whether through nostril, pore, or other air exchanger. The vines entangled and crossed the tree in the middle of the Third Level—the village level—forming a protective net of deadly ropes around it.

Born approached the nearest, leaned over and spat directly into the center of one of the blossoms, avoiding the pod. The blossom quivered, but the pod did not burst. The pink petals closed in on themselves. A pause, then the vines began to curl and tighten like climbing vines hunting for a better purchase. As they retracted, a clear path was formed through which Born and Ruumahum strode easily. Even as Ruumahum was through, the outermost vines were already relaxing once again, expanding, coming together and

18

shutting off the pathway. The bloom into which Born had spat opened its petals once more to drink the faint evening light.

A casual observer would note that Born's saliva had disappeared. A chemist would be able to tell that it had been absorbed. A brilliant scientist might be able to discover that it had been more than absorbed— it had been analyzed and identified. Born knew only that carefully spitting into the bloom seemed to tell the Home-tree who he was.

As he walked toward the village proper he tried to whistle happily. The song died aborning. His mind was occupied with the mysterious blue thing that had come crashing down into the forest. Rarely, one of the greater air-trees would overreach its rootings, or overgrow its perch, and fall, bringing down creepers and lesser growths with it. But never had Born heard such a smashing and shattering of wood. This thing had been far heavier than any air-tree. He knew that by the speed with which it had fallen. And there was that half familiar, metallic gleam.

His thoughts were not on his expected triumph as he entered the village center. Here, the enormous trunk of the Home-tree split into a webbing of lesser boles, forming an interlocking net of wood around a central open space, before joining and growing together high above to form once more a single tapering trunk that rose skyward for another sixty meters. With vines and plant fibers and animal skins the villagers had closed off sections of the interweaving trunklets to form homes and rooms impervious to casual rain and wind. For food, the Home-tree offered cauliflorous fruits shaped like gourds, tasting like cranberry, which sometimes grew within the sealed-off homes themselves.

Small scorched places lay within the houses and beneath the canopy in the central square. These minute burns did not affect the enormous growth. Each home also possessed a pit dug into the wood itself. Here, many times daily, the inhabitants of the tree offered thanks for its shelter and protection, mixing their offerings with a mulch of dead, pulpy plants gathered for the purpose. The mulch also served to

19

kill strong odors. When the pits were full they were cleaned out. The dry residue was thrown over the side of the Home-tree into the green depths, so that the pits could be used again. For the tree accepted and absorbed the offerings with great speed and matchless efficiency.

The Home-tree was the greatest discovery made by Born's ancestors. Its unique characteristics were discovered when it seemed that the last surviving colonists would perish. At that time no one wondered why a growth unutilized by native life should prove so accommodating to alien interlopers. When the human population made a comeback, scouts were sent out to search for other Home-trees, and a new tribe was planted. But in the years since Born's great-great-great-great-great-grandfather had settled in this tree, contact with other tribes had first dwindled and then stopped altogether. None bothered to reopen such contact, or cared. They had all they could do to survive in a world that seethed with nightmare forms of death and destruction.

"Born is back . . . look, Born has returned . . . Born, Born!"

A small crowd gathered around him, welcoming him joyously, but consisting entirely of children. One of them, ignoring the respect due a returning hunter, had the temerity to tug at his cloak. He looked down, recognized the orphan boy Din who was cared for in common.

His mother and father had been taken one day while they were on a fruit-gathering expedition, by something that had coughed once horribly and vanished into the forest. The rest of the party had fled in panic and later returned to find only the couple's tools. No sign of them had ever been found. So the boy was raised by everyone in the village. For reasons unknown to anyone, least of all to Born, the youngster had attached himself to him. The hunter could not cast the youth away. It was a law—and a good law for survival—that a free child could make parents of any and all it chose. Why one would pick mad Born, though . . .

"No, you cannot have the grazer pelt," Born

20

scolded, as he gently shoved the boy away. Din, at thirteen, was no longer a child. He was no longer pushed so easily.

Following at the orphan's heels was a fat ball of fur not quite as big as the adolescent. The furcot cub Muf tripped over its own stubby legs every third step. The third time he tripped, he lay down in the middle of the village and went to sleep, this being an appropriate solution to the problem. Ruumahum eyed the cub, mumbled disapprovingly. But he could sympathize. He was quite ready for an extended nap himself.

Born did not head directly for his home, but instead walked across the village to another's.

"Brightly Go!"

Green eyes that matched the densest leaves peeked out, followed by the face and form of a wood nymph supple as a kitten. She walked over to take both his hands in hers.

"It's good that you're back, Born. Everyone worried. I . . . worried, much."

"Worried?" he responded jovially. "About a little grazer?" He made a grandiose gesture in the direction of the carcass. Beneath its great mass Ruumahum fumed and had unkind thoughts about persons who engaged in frivolous activities before considering the comfort of their furcot.

Brightly Go stared at the grazer and her eyes grew big as ruby-in-kind blossoms. Then she frowned with uncertainty. "But Born, I can't possibly eat all that!'

Born's answering laughter was only slightly forced. "You can have what you need of the meat, and your parents, too. It's the pelt that's for you, of course."

Brightly Go was the most beautiful girl in the village, but sometimes Born found himself thinking unflattering things about her other qualities. Then, he would eye her thin wrapping of leafleather and forget everything else.

"You're laughing at me," she protested angrily. "Don't laugh at me!" Naturally, that encouraged him to laugh even more.

"Losting," she said with dignity, "doesn't laugh at me."

That shut him up quickly. "What does it matter what Losting does?" he shot back challengingly.

"It matters to me."

"Huh . . . well." Something had suddenly gone wrong somewhere. This wasn't working out the way he had imagined it would, the way he had planned it. Somehow it never did.

He looked around the silent village. A few of the older people had stared out at him when he had returned. Now that the novelty of his survival had worn off, they had returned to their household tasks. Most of the active adults, naturally, were off hunting, gathering edibles, or keeping the Home clear of parasites. The anticipated adulation had never materialized. He had risked his life, then, to return to a cluster of curious children and to the indifference of Brightly Go. His earlier euphoria vanished.

"I'll clean the pelt for you, anyway," he grumbled. "Come on, Ruumahum." He turned and stalked angrily off toward the other side of the village. Behind him Brightly Go's face underwent a series of contortions expressing a broad spectrum of emotions. Then she turned and went back inside her parent's compound.

Ruumahum let out a snort of relief when the dead-weight was finally untied and he could shake it from his back. Whereupon he walked directly to his corner in the large single room, lay down, and entered that region most beloved of all furcots.

Muttering to himself Born unpacked his hunter's pouch-belt, removed his cloak, and set about the business of preparing the grazer. He wielded the bone knife so angrily he almost cut through and ruined the skin several times. The layer of fat beneath the skin was next. Turning the carcass was a laborious job, but Born managed without having to wake Ruumahum. The fat was slung into a wooden trough. Later it would be melted down and rendered into candles. Then he was at the meat, cutting away huge chunks to dry and preserve. Organs and other nonedibles went into the pit at the back of the room. This he covered with the ready mulch mixture, adding water from a wood cistern. The Home would be pleased.

The hollow backbone and the huge flaring circular ribs he separated, cleaned and scoured, and set outside where the sunlight would dry them. The thick bone would make tools and ornaments. The teeth were valueless, not worth wearing, unlike those of the carnivórous breeder Losting had killed. He would make no necklace of these flat, grinding molars to wear at ceremonies. But he would eat well.

Once the grazer had been reduced to its useful components, Born cleaned his hands and arms. Moving to a corner he pulled aside a curtain of woven fiber. Rummaging behind it he found his other snuffler. He would have to secure a second one now. He studied it and thought over the problem. He would get Jhelum to make one. His hands were far more skillful at working the green wood than Born's, and quicker. He smiled slightly. He would lose most of his grazer in trade for the new snuffler, but he would still have good eating for a time. Jhelum, who did not hunt and who had two youngsters and a wife, would be appreciative of the meat.

"I am going to see Jhelum, the carver, Ruumahum. I'll—"

A long low whistling came from the furcot's corner. Born uttered an angry word. It seemed no one cared whether he lived or died. He ripped the leafleather screen aside and marched off toward Jhelum's place.

Most of the remainder of the day was taken up in working out the arrangements of the exchange. In the end, Jhelum agreed to prepare the new snuffler in return for three-fourths of the grazer meat and the whole skeleton. Ordinarily Born would never have gone so high. He had worked nearly a week to get the grazer, and taking such prey involved uncommon risk. But he was tired, frustrated by the indifferent reception, and confused by Brightly Go. Besides, Jhelum showed him an exquisite section of green wood pipe, almost blue in spots, that could be used for the weapon. It would make an exceptionally handsome snuffler. He would not be cheated, but neither would he get a bargain.

23

He climbed alone into the upper reaches of the village, to where trunklets started to rejoin to form a single bole. From there he could look back at the village and out at the forest wall.

The village center was the largest open space he had ever seen in his life, save for the Upper Hell, of course. Here he could relax and study the world without fear of attack. As he watched, a glass flitter touched down alongside a pink vines-of-own blossom. Red and blue wings fluttered lazily, the sun shining through the transparent organic panes.

This was another thing that prompted some in the village to call Born a little mad. Only he sat and wasted his time watching things like flitters and flowers, which could neither nourish nor kill. Born himself did not know why he did such things, but something within him was gratified when he did. Gratified and warmed. He would learn all there was to know about everything.

Reader, the shaman, had tried numerous times to exorcise the demon that drove Born to such wastefulness, and had failed as many times. Born had submitted to such ministrations only at the urgings of the worried chief couple, Sand and Joyla. Eventually, Reader had given up, pronouncing Born's aberrations incurable. As long as he harmed no one, all agreed to let Born alone. All wished him well.

All save Losting, naturally. But Losting's dislike had its roots not in Born's aberrations, but in one of his obsessions.

A drop of lukewarm rain hit Born on the forehead, trickled down his face. It was followed by another and more. It was time to join the council.

He made his way back through the trunklets into the village. The fire had been lit in the center of the square on the place scorched tough and black by many such fires. A broad canopy of woven leafleather kept the rain off and there was room beneath for all the villagers. Already most of the people were assembled, Sand, Joyla, and Reader foremost among them.

As he trotted down through the now steady rain, he spotted Losting. Entering the circle, Born took his place among the men opposite his rival. Losting had apparently learned of Born's return and his offer of the grazer pelt, for he glared with more venom than usual across the fire at him. Born smiled back pleasantly.

The steady patter of warm rain falling on the leafleather and dripping to the wood-ground murmured in counterpoint to the sounds of the assembled people. Occasionally a child laughed, to be shushed by his elders.

Sand raised an arm for silence. Beside him, Joyla did likewise. The people became quiet. Sand, who had never been a big man—perhaps about Born's size— now, shrunken and bent with age, appeared even smaller. Nevertheless, his presence was still impressive. He was like a weathered old clock that spent all its time patiently, solemnly ticking, but struck startlingly loud and clear at the necessary moment.

"The hunting was good," someone reported.

"The hunting was good," the assembly echoed approvingly.

"The gathering has been good," Sand intoned.

"The gathering has been good," the chorus agreed readily.

"All who were here last are here now," Sand observed, staring around the circle. "The sap runs strong in the Home."

"The faring of the ready pod," announced one of the women in the circle. "The seed of Morann and Oh ripens. She will ripen within the month." Sand and everyone else nodded or murmured approval.

Somewhere far above, thunder pealed, echoed down cellulose canyons, rolled off chlorophyllous cliffs. The evening litany droned on: how much and what kinds of fruit and nuts gathered; how much of what kinds of meat killed and cured; the experiences and accomplishments and failures of each member of the tribe for that day now past.

There was an appreciative, admiring murmur from the crowd when Born announced the taking of the grazer, but it was not as strong as he had wished. He did not take into account the fact that there was

25

something else paramount in everyone's mind. It was for Reader to bring it up.

"This afternoon," he began, gesturing with his totem of office, the holy axe, "something came out of the Upper Hell into the world. Something gigantic beyond imagining—"

"No, not beyond imagining," Joyla interrupted. "It must be assumed the Pillars are greater."

Appreciative mutters sounded in agreement.

"Well considered, Joyla," Reader admitted. "Something for its size, *heavy* beyond imagining, then," and this time he looked satisfied as Joyla remained silent. "It entered the world northwest of the stormtreader and passed on to the Lower Hell. Probably it was a denizen of that Hell visiting its cousins in the Upper, and it has returned now to its home."

"Might we not be wrong about the demons of the Upper?" someone in the crowd ventured. "Might they not in truth grow as large as those below? We know little enough of both Hells."

"And I for one," someone else put in, "have no desire to know more!" There was sympathetic laughter.

"Nevertheless," the shaman insisted, gesturing with the axe at the dweller who had preferred his comfortable ignorance, "this particular demon chose to descend near to us. What if it has not returned to its home in the depths? It has made no sound or movement since its arrival. If it remains near us, who can say what it might do?" There were nervous stirrings in the crowd. "There is a chance it might be dead. While the opportunity to inspect a dead demon would be interesting, so much meat would be more valuable."

"Unless its relatives come around to claim its corpse," someone shouted, "in which case I'd rather be elsewhere!" There were mutters of agreement.

Lightning crackled above the tallest emergent, and thunder rolled down to them again. To his amazement Born found himself suddenly on his feet, speaking. "I don't think it was a demon." There was a mass shifting of bodies as all eyes came to focus on him. The abrupt attention made him acutely uncomfortable, but he held his ground.

"How do you know? Did you see the thing?"

26

Reader finally asked, recovering from Born's unexpected pronouncement. "You said nothing of this to anyone."

Born shrugged, tried to sound casual about it. "No one rushed to ask me about it."

"If it was not a demon, this thing you say you saw, then what was it?" asked Losting suspiciously.

Born hesitated. "I do not know. I had but the briefest glimpse of it as it fell through the world—but see it I did!"

Losting sat back in his place, his muscles rippling in the firelight, and smiled at those near him.

"Come, Born," prompted Joyla, "either you saw the thing or you didn't."

"But that is exactly it," he protested. "I was falling myself. I saw it, yet did not. As the breaking sounds and shaking of the world reached its peak, I saw a flash of deep blue through the trees. Shining bright blue, like that of an asanis."

"Maybe that's what you saw, a drifting asanis bloom," Losting said with a smirk.

"No!" Born spun to glare angrily across at his rival. "It was that color, but brilliant, deep, and too . . . too sharp. It threw back the light."

"Threw back the light?" wondered Reader. "How could this be?"

How could it? They were all staring at him, half wanting to believe he had seen something that was not a demon. He struggled to recall that instant of falling, that glimpse of alien blue among the branches. It caught the light like an asanis leaf—no, more like his knife when it was polished. His eyes roved absently as he thought furiously for something to compare it with.

"Like the axe!" he blurted, pointing dramatically to the weapon dangling in the shaman's hand. "It was like the axe."

Everyone's gaze automatically shifted to the holy weapon, Reader's included. Soft whispers of derision sprang up. Nothing was like the axe.

"Perhaps you are mistaken, Born," Sand ventured gently. "It did, as you say, happen very fast. And you were falling when you saw it."

27

"I'm positive about it, sir. Just like the axe." He wished he was as certain as he tried to sound, but he could not back down on his story now without sounding like a complete fool.

"In any case," he found himself saying, to his horror, "it is a simple enough matter to prove. We need only go and look."

The mutterings from the crowd grew louder; they were no longer derisive, but shocked.

"Born," the chief began patiently, "we do not know what this thing is or where it has gone. It may have already returned to the depths from which it probably came. Let it stay there."

"But we don't know," objected Born, leaving his place to stand close by the fire. "Maybe it hasn't returned. Maybe it's down only a level or so, sleeping, waiting to catch the scent of the Home to come seeking us one by one in the night. If it is such a monster, then we would do better to seek it out first and slay it as it sleeps."

Sand nodded slowly, stared around at the people. "Very well. Who will go with Born to sniff out the trail of this demon?"

Born turned to look at his fellow hunters, silently imploring. Long silence, defiant stares. Then, startlingly, a response came from an unexpected quarter.

"I will go," Losting announced. He stood and stared smugly across at Born as if to say, if you're not afraid of this thing, then there can be nothing to be afraid of. Born did not meet the other man's eyes.

Reluctant assent came from the hunter Drawn and the twins Talltree and Tailing. The other hunters would eventually have given in and agreed out of fear of appearing cowardly, but Reader raised the axe. "It is enough. I will go, too, despite my better judgment. It is not appropriate that men should visit one of the damned without an authority on damnation."

"That's for sure," someone muttered. The laughter this provoked was a welcome release from the solemnity of the proceedings.

Sand put a hand over his mouth delicately to hide an unchiefly chuckle. "Now let us pray," he intoned forcefully, "that those who seek out the demon shall find him sickly and weak, or not find him at all, and return to us whole and sound." He raised both hands, lowered his head, and commenced a chant.

No Earthly theological authority would have recognized that chant. No minister, priest, rabbi, or witch doctor could have identified its source or inspiration, though any bioengineer could. What none of them could have explained was why this chant seemed so effective there under the crying night sky and leafleather canopy.

Triple orbs glowed like hot coals, reflecting the dance of the distant flickering fire. Ruumahum lay in the crook in the branches and stared down doubtfully at the gathered people. His muzzle rested on crossed forepaws. A clumsy scratching and clawing sounded on the limb alongside his resting place. A moment later, forty kilos of awkwardly propelled fur and flesh crashed into his flank. He growled irritably and glanced back. It was the cub who had attached itself to the orphan young person, Din.

"Old one," Muf queried softly, "why are you not at rest like the others of the brethren?"

Ruumahum turned his gaze back to the distant leafleather canopy and the chanting humans beneath. "I study Man," he murmured. "Go to sleep, cubling."

Muf considered, then crept up close to the massive adult and likewise stared down toward the fire. After a pause, he looked up questioningly. "What are they doing?"

"I am not certain," Ruumahum replied. "I believe in some ways they are trying to become like the brethren . . . like us."

"Us? Us?" Muf coughed comically in the rain and sat back on his several haunches. "But I thought we strive to become like the persons?"

"So it is believed. Now, go to sleep, shoot!"

"Please, old one, I am confused. If Man is trying to become like us and we are trying to become like Man—then who is right?"

"You ask many questions, cub, you do not fully understand. How can you expect to understand the answer? The answer is . . . That-Which-Is-Sought, a

29

meeting, a conjoinment, a concatenation, an inter-woven web."

"I see," whispered Muf, not seeing at all. "What will happen when that is achieved?"

"I do not know," Ruumahum replied, looking back to the fire. "None of the brethren know, but we seek it anyway. Besides, Man finds us interesting and useful and believes himself master. The brethren find Man useful and interesting and care not about mastering. Man thinks he understands this relationship. We know we do not. For this contented ignorance we envy him." He nodded in the direction of the as-sembled persons below. "We may never understand it. Revelation is never promised, only hoped for."

"I understand," murmured the cub, not understand-ing at all. He struggled awkwardly to his feet and turned to go, then paused to look back. "Old one, one more question."

"What is it?" Ruumahum grumbled, not turning his gaze from the prayer gathering.

"It is rumored among the cubs that we neither spoke nor thought till the persons came."

"That is no rumor, budding, that is truth. Instead, we slept." He yawned and showed razorlike teeth and tusks. "But so did Man. We wake together, it is thought."

"I know," Muf admitted, not knowing at all. He turned and rambled off to find a sleeping place for the night.

Ruumahum turned his attention to the persons once more, considered how fortunate he was to have a person as interesting and unpredictable as Born. Now there was this new thing they would go out to find tomorrow. Well, if the world was to change tomorrow, he thought as he yawned, it was better to face change having had a good night's sleep. He rolled over on his side, tucked his head between fore- and midpaws, and went instantly and peacefully to that country.

Born was all for starting before the morning mist had lifted, but Reader and the others would not hear of it. Losting viewed the originator of such a pre-posterous, dangerous idea with pity. Anyone who

30

would even consider moving about the world in mist, when a man could not see what might be stalking him from behind or above until it was right on top of him, had to be more than a little crazy.

There were twelve in the party—six men and six furcots. The men traveled in single file through the treeways, while the furcots spread out above, below, and on both sides, forming a protective cordon around the persons. Born and Reader shared the lead, while Losting, by choice, guarded the rear. The big man had mixed feelings about this expedition and was striving to stay as far away from its originator—Born —as possible. Besides, as much as he disliked Born for the other's interest in Brightly Go, Losting was not so stupid that he failed to recognize Born's skills. As such, Born belonged in the lead. But then, Losting told himself comfortingly, the mad are always clever.

Their progress through the sunny Third Level branchings was rapid and uninterrupted. Only once did distant warning growls, from the left of their course and below, cause the party to pause and set snufflers. Taandason, who had made the warning sounds, appeared a short while later on the cubble running parallel to the persons' path. He was panting slightly and puffing with anger.

"Brown many-legs," the furcot reported. "A mated hunting pair. Saw me and the she spat, but her mate turned her. Gone now." The furcot turned, leaped to a lower branch, and disappeared in the undergrowth. Reader nodded with satisfaction and waved the column forward. Thorns were returned to quivers, tank seeds to pouches.

A single brown many-leg wouldn't hesitate to charge two or three men, Born reflected. A mated hunting pair would take on almost anything in the hylaea. But a group of man and furcot in such numbers would cause even the greater forest carnivores to think twice before attacking. Whether a demon would think likewise remained to be seen.

They must be nearing the place. Born recognized a distinctive Blood tree, its pitcherlike leaves filled with crimson water caused by the plant's secretion of tannin. Soon after passing the Blood tree they found themselves walking into a steady breeze. A responsive murmur sprang up among the marchers. Within the forest world the wind rarely blew steadily in any single direction. Instead, gusts of air came and went like wraiths, darting and curling around branches and boles and stems like living things. But this breeze was steady and purposeful and warm. Warm enough, Born reflected, to come from Hell itself.

Reader brandished his axe, defying any evil spirits in the area who would dare to come near. Each man pulled his green cloak more tightly and protectively around him.

Born motioned the party to slow and spread out. Ahead of him the world seemed suddenly to change perspective. He took another couple of steps along the cubble, pushed aside a drooping whalear leaf, and cried out at what he saw, one hand tightening convulsively around a supporting liana. Similar cries sounded nearby, but he was momentarily paralyzed, unable to look for his companions.

Not a hand's breadth away the thick wood of the cubble he stood on had been shattered like a rotten stem, as had that of other lesser and greater growths nearby. A vast well had been opened up in the world. Born looked up, up, to a circle of strange color two hundred meters overhead. A patch of deep blue flecked with white cumulus—the blue of the Upper Hell.

Below—he gripped the liana ever tighter—below and down an equally great distance, somewhere at the Fifth Level, lay a brilliant blue object that caught the sun like the axe. In its center was something even more shiny, something that made rainbows from sunlight, an uneven half-globe of material like a flitter's transparent wings. Its top was ragged and open to the air.

Already vines, creepers, cubbles, tuntangcles, and other growth were destroying the smooth sides of the well, pushing outward in furious competition for the wealth of unaccustomed sunlight.

Born studied the spreading epiphytes and rampaging growers and estimated that in another twice seven-days the new vegetation would cover the well completely. They would have to avoid this area for some time, however, until some denser growth filled it in.

"Here, Born!" a voice called.

He turned to see Reader standing on the broken-off limb of a Pillar, leaning out as far as he dared and gesturing with the axe. It flashed like lightning in the greenish light. In a few minutes every member of the party had assembled on the meters-wide broken branch. The furcots had gathered to themselves and sat silently on one side to see what the persons would do.

"It is a demon for sure, and it sleeps," began one of the twins—Talltree, Born noted.

"I still do not think it is a demon," Born countered firmly. "I believe it is a thing, an object that has been fashioned," and he nodded toward Reader, "like the axe."

Various exclamations greeted Born's blasphemous opinion. Reader held up a hand for quiet. "People, this is no place for loud noises. The demons of the Upper Hell could surely come down to this place through the hole the larger demon has made. We will discuss this matter further, but I say, quietly." Conversation and argument continued, but in whispers. "Now then, Born," continued Reader, "what makes you so certain this blue thing below us is not a demon, but an object made like the axe?"

"It has the look of it," Born replied. "Notice how regular are its outlines and the way it throws back the light."

"Might not a demon do this as well? Does not the skin of the orbiole throw back the light? Are you certain, Born?"

Born found himself looking away. "There is no way to be sure, shaman, save," and he stared across at the older man, "to go down to it and see for oneself."

"But if it is a demon?" Drawn wondered loudly, "and it sleeps, and our pokings awaken it?" The hunter rose from his squatting position, holding his snuffler firmly. "No, friend Born. I respect your guessings and honor your skill, but I will not go with you. I have a mate and two children and I'm not ready to go knocking on the skull of a demon to see if anyone is home. No, not I." He paused, thinking. "But, I will consider what the shaman and my brothers say."

"Whay say the hunters, then?" asked Reader.

The other twin spoke. "Truly, it may be as Born says. Be it only a made thing, with no life in it, then it seems to me no threat to the Home. Or it may be, as Drawn says, a sleeping demon waiting only for some careless person to stumble blindly in and waken it. If we leave it alone it may sleep forever, or go peacefully on its way. Myself, I think it is a demon of a new kind, one injured in its fall from the Upper Hell. We must leave and not disturb it, but let it die in peace, lest it arise in anger and destroy us."

Tailing and Talltree rose together and offered further opinions. Sometimes one of the twins would begin a sentence and the other would finish it. They did this without looking at one another, which was not surprising, for in the forest does one branch of a tree have to consult with another before putting out leaves? Some thought the twins were more of the forest than of Man.

"Whatever it is, shaman," Talltree concluded, "it seems we have nothing to lose by leaving it undisturbed and everything to gain by returning Home quietly the way we came."

"Don't you care about it at all?" Born asked openly. "Aren't you at all curious? Do you not care if it is a benign demon?"

"I've never heard of a helpful demon and I care only about surviving," Drawn responded. The others listened attentively. After Born, Drawn was the most skillful hunter in the village. "As it lies"—he nodded toward the world-well—"it threatens us not, nor the Home. I do not see a close inspection improving that. I vote to return Home."

"I also . . . and I . . . and I . . ."

The word passed around the little circle of persons in the trees, and it was all against Born. Always against Born, he thought, furious.

"Go back, then," he shouted disgustedly, moving

34

from the circle to a higher branch. "I'll go down alone."

The other hunters muttered. Reader and Drawn, the eldest among them, looked sympathetic, but they agreed that Born had not yet acquired caution to match his other abilities. The village would miss him if he failed to return. If he would go, then let him go, but do not match madness with him.

So Born crouched alone on his higher limb and pouted while his companions made themselves ready. Their furcots fanning out around them, they started down the cubble toward the Home.

Despite his feelings, he was half tempted to join them and try further talk. Only Losting's barely veiled grin steeled him. Nothing would please that overripe pium fruit more than to see Born vanish forever, leaving him a clear path to Brightly Go. But Born would not vanish so conveniently. He would learn the truth of the blue monster below and return to tell of it to all. The others who had left would be ashamed, and Brightly Go would smile favoringly on him.

Still, it was to be considered that there had been only brave men in the little group, and that wise Reader was not an idiot. There still existed the chance he was wrong and everyone else was right. He put aside this unpleasant possibility and whistled once, softly.

Ruumahum appeared in a minute, the small branch sagging under their combined weight. The furcot eyed him expectantly, promptly crossed all four front paws and went to sleep. Born studied the massive form absently before turning his attention to the right. There, past a few thick fronds and several dangling vines, lay the pit open to the Upper Hell. At the bottom of the pit lay an enigma he would have to resolve alone. Well, not quite alone.

He whacked Ruumahum along one side of his head, a blow that would have jolted a large man. The furcot merely blinked, yawned, and started preening itself with a forepaw.

"Up and out," Born said firmly.

Ruumahum stared at him drowsily. "What to do?"

"Come, good for nothing. I want a close look at the blue thing."

Ruumahum snorted. Didn't the person have two perfectly good eyes of his own? But he conceded that Born was right. Someone would have to watch the open spaces above and to the sides while Born was exposed in the clearing.

Born crawled, alone, without loaded snufflers to back him up, without ironwood spears to reinforce his confidence, to the edge of the pit and stared downward. The glistening blue circle lay as before. It had not moved and showed no sign of moving. Even as he watched, a loud crackling sounded, and the object appeared to drop a little lower. The well it had made was ample testament to its great weight, and it seemed to be sinking deeper, branch by shattered branch, cubble by overstressed cubble. It might continue to sink, falling to the Sixth Level and eventually to the Lower Hell itself. Born would not seek it at that depth for all the meat in the forest, not even for Brightly Go. He had to proceed now, before the chance was forever denied him.

He leaned out further over the abyss, tightening his grip on the seemingly unbreakable liana nearby. The liana might have been unbreakable. His grip wasn't. Something clutched him around waist and neck and yanked hard. The yell in his throat turned to anger as he disengaged himself from the gentle grasp of Ruumahum.

"What the—?"

Ruumahum glanced significantly upward, rumbled softly. "Devil comes."

Born peered up through a crack in the well wall. At first he did not see the dark speck against the sky, but it grew rapidly larger. When the shape became recognizable, Born retreated another meter into the forest and loaded the snuffler.

The sky-devil had a long streamlined body suspended between broad wings. Four leathery sacks, two to a side, inhaled air and expelled it out rubbery nozzles near the monster's tail. It moved in gaspy jerks as it circled lower and lower. A long-snouted reptilian head weaved atop a snakelike neck.

Two yellow eyes stared downward, and needlelike teeth flashed in the pale green sunlight. Ideally equipped for skimming silently across the treetops hundreds of meters above and picking off careless arboreals, the sky-devil found itself drawn to something deep in the well. Three-meter wings left it little room for maneuvering within that crude cylindrical gap, but it managed, circling, spiraling lower and lower in tight circles, examining each section of the green wall as it dropped.

Born sat very still on his branch, concealed behind a broad leaf taller than Losting, wrapped tight in his green cloak. The devil reached his level, circled, and passed on. Staying close to the branch, Born edged his way to the precipice once again. Far below he saw the scaled back and wings winding down toward the blue object. Eventually it reached bottom, folded its wings, and stopped. The devil walked clumsily on the blue surface, making its way awkwardly to the half-dome at the object's apex. It poked at the globe with its toothed beak, stabbed again. Born could hear it yelling, a distant, muffled croak.

Another sound drifted up to him. One that penetrated above the normal din of comb vines and resonators and chattering chollakees. It was a human scream, and it came from somewhere near or in the object!

IV

Born started downward without thinking, plunging recklessly from branch to branch, shoulder muscles straining at the shock, taking meters at a jump. Ruumahum followed close behind. They were making enough noise to attract half the afternoon forest predators, and the furcot told him as much. Wrapped

37

in other thoughts, Born ignored the furcot's warnings.

Once he nearly dropped square onto the back of a Chan-nock, the big tree-climbing reptile's knobby back the perfect imitation of a tuntangcle vine as it lay stretched between the boles of two air-trees. Born's foot hit the armored back. Instantly he was aware he had met flesh and not wood. But he was moving so fast he was meters below as the Chan-nock whipped around to crush the interloper. Furious at missing its prey, the blunt snout swung round for a stab at Ruumahum. Not even pausing in his down-ward rush, the furcot stuck out a paw in passing and crushed the flat, arrowhead-shaped skull.

If Born had stopped to think about what he was do-ing, he might have fallen and hurt himself seriously. But he was traveling on instinct alone. Unhindered, his reflexes did not fail him. Only when Ruumahum put on an extra burst of speed, got in front of him, and slowed down, did Born become conscious of how fast he had been moving. He nearly dislocated a shoulder as he slowed to a halt behind the furcot. Both were panting heavily.

"Why stop now, Ruumahum. We—"

The furcot growled softly. "Are here," he mut-tered. "Air-devil is near. Listen."

Born listened. He had been so excited he had nearly shot past the level at which the blue thing lay. Now he could hear the horrible half-laugh, half-coughing of the devil and a scratching sound, a sound similar to the one Reader produced by running his nails over the axe blade during the invocations. Then he was right about the composition of the blue thing! He had no time to bask in his own brilliance. A moan sounded now, not a scream; but it was no less human.

"There are people there and the sky-devil is after them," Born whispered. "But what people live on the Fifth Level? All persons known live on the Third or Second."

"I do not know," Ruumahum answered. "I sense much strangeness here. Strangeness and newness."

"*It* needs killing."

"Air-devils die slowly, Born person," advised Ruum-ahum. "Go carefully."

Born nodded and they backed deeper into the brush. "The air-devil may not be able to penetrate here. It is too big and clumsy on the wood. But if it does . . ."

He started searching, working around the well circumference, always staying well back from the open pit where the nightmare-in-life scratched and clawed at the blue thing. He found what might serve—a certain epiphytic orchid that nestled in the crotch formed by the great lower limbs of an emergent. The bottom of the plant overreached the limbs on both sides, the great ball of self-made soil sending long air-roots downward in all directions. Above, long thick petals of dark chalcedony color curled toward the sky. A wonderful limelike fragrance issued from the huge flower's depths, its creamy petals many meters long.

Keeping a careful distance from the gigantic bloom, Born moved cautiously back toward the well.

"Softly," Ruumahum urged anxiously. Born looked back at the furcot and made quieting motions, but he took the advice. There was more open space here where the light did not penetrate as well. There were fewer places to hide, fewer webs of vines and lianas to lose a big meat-eater in. Surely there was nowhere near enough open space for the sky-devil to spread its wings. But it had thick clawed legs and just maybe could scramble through the open places.

Hence his enlisting of the orchid as a silent ally.

Born reached the edge of the well bottom. A cluster of shattered wood and herbaceous growth bordered it. Everything here was sticky and slippery from spilled sap. He would have to watch his footing. Then suddenly he was staring at the sky-devil from between the leaves. It battered and dug in frustration at something deep within the blue metal disk. The moaning, Born now was sure, came from somewhere inside. Taking a deep breath and wishing for a more stable footing, he lined up the end of the snuffler with the skull of the demon, a difficult target that was bobbing and weaving on a long flexible neck.

Born jerked the trigger. There was a tiny explosive puff as the tank seed popped. The jacari thorn hit the devil just behind the left eye. It quivered, its slow nervous system reacting dully to the poison, then it spun to look in the direction of the shot. At the same time Born yelled, "Be strong!" at the top of his lungs, to alert those within the blue metal, then he turned and raced back along the branch.

A tremendous thrashing sounded immediately behind him as the sky-devil, showing unexpected strength, smashed through the outer wall of branches and vines in its drooling desire to get at him. Born fancied he could feel its fetid breath hot on his neck. The giant orchid loomed ahead.

That crawling leathery horror was at his spine. At any second long teeth might close on his neck and snip his head off. There was no time to look back, no time to think or consider. He dove past the soil ball of the flower, reaching out with the end of the snuffler so that the green wood pipe brushed several of the dozens of dangling rootlets.

Born fell another couple of meters before landing with a jolt in a bed of hyphae below. Above him, the tiny rootlets he had brushed and everything around them curled protectively inward against the bulk of the plant. The sky-devil burst through the undergrowth, reaching with claws and jaws for Born, who stared up in helpless fascination at that descending abomination.

Too quick to see, the thick white petals of the pseudo-orchid thrashed in blind fury in all directions. Three of the petals struck the rampaging devil, curled shut about it and contracted. The devil seemed to explode, eyes shooting like ripe seeds from the skull, wings crumpling, guts and innards shooting in all directions. The plant continued thrashing about for several minutes before the petals began to relax.

As it returned to its normal shape and form, the orchid released the mangled pulp that had been the sky-devil. The shattered corpse fell bouncing into the depths. Born sat up and watched it fall, his heart beating fast. The devil had died too quickly to scream, never knowing what had hit it.

Using his snuffler as a brace, Born pulled himself

erect and climbed over to where Ruumahum lay, watching him quietly. "I think," he said, trembling slightly, "we can go help the people now." The furcot nodded silently.

They started back toward the world-well, once again giving the now quiescent pseudo-orchid—known in Born's village as "Dunawett's plant"—plenty of room.

Born parted the broken stems and walked out into something he had experienced only a few times in his life. Something few people ever experienced—the open air. He stared upward, but from here the sky was a distant circlet of blue pasted against an otherwise green heaven.

"Will watch Upper Hell," Ruumahum announced, sitting himself down by the edge of the well. His head inclined and he studied the distant blue disk stolidly.

Born extended a cautious foot, set it down easily on the deep blue surface of the object. It was cool and hard, just like the axe blade. Reassured, he walked out onto the curving surface, making his way toward the half-dome in the center. As he neared it, he saw it covered a circular cavity in the metal. Looking down at the broken, jagged edges of the dome he saw tangles of tiny vines and roots inside, which were also made of some shiny, hard substance.

An inspection of the interior of the disk showed one side made of more metal that was filled with dents and abrasions from the claws and probing beak of the sky demon. Born thought he heard a slight moaning coming from behind it.

"Hello. Is anyone alive here? It is safe to come out. The devil has gone to its cousins in Hell."

The moaning ceased abruptly and was followed by clicking, metallic sounds. Then the section of rectangular metal began to disappear inward, on hinges.

A man peered out and up at him uncertainly. Something small and reflective shone in his hand. Born caught his breath. It was an axe—No, no . . . a knife made of the same material as the axe, only far cleaner and smoother. After a long stare the man's gaze went around the open cavity in the metal. When he satisfied himself that Born's words were true and the sky-devil was safely gone, he emerged into the open space and commenced a detailed survey of the mass of tangled instrumentation and components while keeping a watchful eye on Born.

Born studied the giant. Though he was only a normal-sized man by normal man standards, he towered a good twenty-five centimeters over Born. He displayed other surprising characteristics, as well. He was undeniably a person, but the differences were striking. His hair was orange-red instead of brown, his eyes blue instead of green, and his skin—his skin was so pale as not to be believed, though among his own people he was considered moderately well tanned. His build was slim and his face freckled and friendly.

"Jan?" A second voice, slightly higher. "Is it clear to—?" Then the speaker caught sight of Born, standing quietly on the surface of the skimmer. She was a couple of centimeters taller than the man. Her body beneath the torn single-piece jungle suit was bony and athletic. Short hair the color of tarnished silver indicated she was somewhat older, as well. Strong, long legs showed from the beige shorts and their color was also, to Born, unbelievably pale. She seemed less nervous than the man, a little more assured.

"Who the hell is that?" she asked with a jerk of her head. The man she had called Jan continued picking disgustedly at the crushed remnants of the skimmer's controls.

"The man who just saved our lives, I think. For the moment." He stared up at the sky uneasily.

"The sky-devil is dead," Born informed him. "It went too near a stimulated Dunawett's plant. It will not trouble you again."

The man digested this information, grunted something noncommittal, and turned back to his discouraged probing. "Board's shot to hell and gone, Kimi," he finally declared. "What didn't come apart in the touchdown, that flying carnivore pecked to shreds. This skimmer isn't going anywhere except the scrap yard."

The woman sat down in the ruins of a swivel chair, bent now at an angle its designers had never intended. Born stared curiously at her. She suddenly became conscious of his attention and looked up at him.

"What are you staring at, short stuff?"

Born bristled, more at her tone than the words. "If my presence makes you uncomfortable . . ." He hefted the snuffler, turned to go.

"No, no, wait a minute, fellow." She rested her head in crossed arms for a minute. "Give me a second, will you? We've just been through a pretty rough time." She looked up again, locked fingers. "You've got to understand, when our drive went . . ." She noticed Born's questioning frown and tried again. "When the thing that powered our skimmer . . ." The frown deepened. She patted the metal wall next to her. "When this thing which carries us through the air . . ." Born's face showed an expression of disbelief, but she pressed on. ". . . crashed here, we thought we were already dead. Instead we crawled out of what was left of our chairs and found we were still alive. Shaken, but alive."

She gestured at the surrounding green walls. "This incredible planet—three-quarters of a kilometer of stratified rain forest—cushioned our fall just enough." Her voice dropped. "Then that long-necked horror landed on top of us. We barely got through the engine-access hatch when it started working on the door. I thought we were dead all over again. Now you show up and insist some local vegetable has slaughtered something it would take an arm's-length laser to discourage. And then there's the matter of yourself, which is no small shock to us, either."

"What about myself?" queried Born, unaccountably self-conscious.

She made a fluttering, tired gesture. "Just look at you." Born declined to do so. "You're an anomaly, you don't belong here, according to what we've been told," she added hastily. "This is supposed to be an unreported, barely surveyed, uninhabited world known only to—"

"Careful, Kimi," the man said warningly, glancing back over his shoulder.

She waved him off. "What for, Jan. This"—and she nodded toward Born—"*native* obviously knows noth-

43

ing that could complicate our presence here." She looked back at Born as she got to her feet. "As I said, this is supposed to be an uninhabited world. All of a sudden, on the heels of a series of rather disconcerting events, we're faced with accepting your presence. I presume you're not a solitary freak? There are others of your kind?"

"The village supports many," Born told her, in what he hoped was an adequate answer. These giants were fascinating.

"I said native, but what kind remains to be determined." She studied Born openly. He bore her examination because he was engaged in one of his own. "You're nearly a whole foot shorter than an average adult, but you've got the arms and shoulders of a weight-lifter." Her gaze lowered considerably. "And what look like awfully long, probably prehensile toes. You're dark as old redwood and with hair to match . . . but green eyes. Altogether, the most remarkable specimen I've seen in a long time. Though not," she added in an odd tone, "for all that, unappealing." The man made a sound which Born interpreted as one of distaste, though for what reason he could not imagine.

Strange and fascinating these giants! Yet it was they who were calling him strange.

"If your people developed here," the woman was concluding, "despite your coloring and size and grabby toes, it has to be the most unlikely case of parallel evolution on record. And you speak Terranglo. What do you say, Jan?"

The man looked up briefly at Born, then sighed and made a gesture of helplessness toward the board he had been working on. "I don't know why I'm fooling with this. It's hopeless. Even if we could fix the drive without the aid of a full machine shop, that flying beast chewed up the controls like so many worms in a paper bag. We're stuck here. The tridee's in no better shape. And all that talk about dying's probably still appropriate."

"You give up too soon, too easily, Jan," she admonished him. She looked at Born. "Our small friend here appears to have unpredictable resources. I don't see why he couldn't—"

The man whirled, confronting her with outrage barely held in check. "Are you crazy? It's hundreds of kilometers to the station through this impenetrable morass . . ."

"*His* people seem able to negotiate it," she said quietly.

". . . and if you're thinking of hoofing it, guided by some ignorant primitives—!" he continued.

The language of the giants was peculiar, high and distorted, but Born could make out the meaning of many of their words. One word he recognized clearly, despite the twisted accent, was "ignorant."

"If you are so much the smarter," he interrupted sharply, "how come you to be here like this?" And he kicked the blue skin of the skimmer.

The giant called Kimi smiled. "He's got you there, Jan." The man uttered another disgusted sound and made a related gesture. But he didn't call Born ignorant again.

"Now then," the woman said formally, "I think introductions are in order. First off, we'd like to thank you for saving our lives, which you most surely did." She glanced at the man. "Wouldn't we, Jan?"

He made a muffled sound vaguely intelligible as "yes."

"My name," she went on, "is Logan . . . Kimi Logan. This sometimes buoyant, occasionally depressed associate of mine is Jan Cohoma. And you?"

"I am called Born."

"Born. That's a fine name. A fitting name for one so brave, for a man who'd tackle a meat-eater like that winged monster single-handed."

Born expanded with pride. Strange the giants might be, but this one at least could be properly admiring. Maybe one day Brightly Go would regard him as well as this peculiar giant did.

"You mentioned a village, Born," she continued.

He turned, pointed up and southwest. "The Home lies that way, a fair walk through the forest and two levels higher. My brothers will greet you as friends." And admire the hunter who had braved the sleeping blue demon and killed a sky-devil to rescue them, he thought to himself.

45

He jumped up and down several times on the blue metal, then noticed that both giants had drawn away and were watching him. "I'm sorry," he explained. "I mean you no harm. Of all who came here only I had the courage to descend and find you out. I guessed this . . . thing . . . was not alive, but something carved."

"It's called a skimmer," Cohoma told him. "It carries us across the sky."

"Across the sky," Born repeated, not really believing the words. It seemed impossible that anything so heavy could fly.

"We're glad you did, Born. Aren't we, Jan? Aren't we?" She nudged him and he muttered assent. His initial antagonism toward Born was weakening rapidly as he realized that the small native posed no threat to them. Quite the contrary, it seemed.

"Yes, it certainly was a brave act. An extraordinary act, now that I think of it." He smiled. "You've come this far, Born. Maybe you could help us at least try to get back to our station—our home on this world."

"We got a last fix before we went down," Logan told him. She hesitated, then pointed in a direction toward the Home tree. "It's in that direction, about . . . let's see, how can I get some idea of the distance across to you?" She thought a moment. "You said something about levels in the forest?"

"Everyone knows the world is made of seven levels," Born explained, as though lecturing a child, "from the Lower Hell to the treetops."

"Figure the average height of one of the big emergents," she murmured. "Say a little over seven hundred meters." She engaged in some mental computation, translating meters into levels, and told Born how far away the station lay.

Now it was Born's turn to smile; he was too courteous to laugh. "No one has ever traveled more than five days' journey from the Home," he told them. "I myself only recently went two, and that proved dangerous enough. Now you are talking of a journey of many seven-days. It cannot be done, I think."

"Why not?" Cohoma objected. "You're not afraid, are you? Not," he added quickly as Born took a step toward the bigger man, "an exceptional hunter like yourself?"

Born relaxed slightly. He had already decided that of the two giants, he liked the man far the less.

"It is not a question of fear," he told them, "but of reason. The balance of the world is delicate. Each creature has its place in that balance, takes what is needed, and returns what it can. The further one moves from one's own niche, the more he disrupts the order of things. When the balance is upset severely, people die."

"I think what he's saying, Jan," Logan said to her companion, "is that they believe the further they go from their home village, the more the chances of successfully returning to it are reduced. An understandable feeling, but the explanation is interesting. I wonder how they came to that world-view way of thinking. It's not natural."

"Natural or not," Cohoma objected, "I still don't see why—"

"Later," she cut him off. He turned away, muttering to himself. "I think the first thing we should do," she suggested, "is get out from under this open space before a relative of the monster you so smoothly dispatched, Born, gets curious and comes round to investigate."

That was the first sensible thing the giants had said. He beckoned for them to follow. Cohoma filled his pockets with small packages from various compartments, then let Born lead the way into the trees.

Despite the comparative openness of this level and the absence of accustomed vines and branches, Born was startled to see how clumsy the giants were and how hesitantly they advanced. He inquired about their obvious difficulty as tactfully as possible and was glad when neither seemed offended.

"On the world we come from," Logan explained, "we're used to walking on the ground."

Born was shocked. "Can it be that you live in Hell itself?"

"Hell? I don't understand, Born."

He pointed downward. "Two levels below us lie the Lower and True Hell, the surface Hell of mud and

47

shifting earth. It is the abode of monsters too horrible to have names, so it is said."

"I understand. No, Born, our home's not like that. It's solid and open and light—not full of monsters. At least," she said with a grin, "not any monsters we can't live with." Like the Church Bureau of Supra-Commonwealth Registry, she reflected.

Born's head was swimming. Everything the giants said seemed to go against all reason and truth, yet their very presence and the solid evidence of their sky craft hinted that yet greater wonders might exist.

For now, though, he must restrain his curiosity in favor of more immediate concerns. "You both look tired and hungry, and you must be exhausted by your ordeal."

Cohoma added a heartfelt "Amen!"

"I will take you to the Home. We can talk further there, and more easily."

"One question, Born," asked Logan. "Are the rest of your people as receptive to strangers as you are?"

"Think you we are not civilized?" Born asked. "Any child knows that a guest is as a brother and must be so treated."

"A man after my own heart," sighed Cohoma. "I've got to apologize, friend Born. I had some wrong ideas about you, at first. Lead on, short stuff."

Born pointed upward. "To the Home level first— a fair climb." Both giants groaned. Judging from what he had seen of their climbing ability thus far, Born could understand their reaction. "I will try to find an easier route. It will cost us some time—"

"We'll risk it," said Logan.

Born located a spiraling branch root, descending in a tight double helix from an air-tree somewhere far above. They would have several dozen meters of simple ascent. He started upward, and as he did a scream sounded behind him. He reached for the snuffler, relaxed when he saw it was only Ruumahum. The fear displayed by the two giants at the sight of the affectionate furcot was amusing.

"It's only Ruumahum," he informed them. "My furcot. He'd no more harm you than me."

"Persons," grunted Ruumahum sardonically, sniffing

first at the waist of a frozen Logan, then Cohoma. Neither giant moved, relaxing only when that great fanged head moved away.

"My God," Logan muttered, staring in awe at the massive form as it bounded into the canopy overhead, "it talks. That's two sapient forms Survey missed." She looked at Born with new respect. "Carnivorous hexapod—how'd you ever tame *that?*" she asked wonderingly.

Born considered in confusion, then understanding dawned. "You mean," he said in amazement, "you have no furcots of your own?" He looked from a stupefied Logan to Cohoma.

"Furcots of our own?" echoed Logan. "Why should we?"

"Why," Born recited without thinking, "every person has his furcot and every furcot its person, as every flitter its blossom, every cubble its anchor tree, every pfeffermall its resonator. It's the balance of the world."

"Yes, but that still doesn't explain how you tamed them," pressed Cohoma, staring after the departed carnivore.

"Tame." Born's expression twisted. "It's not a question of taming. Furcots like persons and we like the furcots." He shrugged. "It is natural. It has always been so."

"It talked," noted Logan aloud. "I distinctly heard it say 'persons.'"

"The furcots are not very bright," Born admitted, "but they talk well enough to make themselves understood." He smiled. "There are persons who talk less."

For some reason this caused both giants to launch into a long discussion between themselves, full of complex terms Born did not understand. This made him uncomfortable. Anyway, it was time they started Home, time he received the adulation and accolades due him.

"We must go now, but there is a condition."

That veiled threat was enough to cause the giants to break off their argument and stare at him. "What condition?" Logan asked apprehensively.

Born stared at Cohoma. "That he no longer calls

me short stuff. Otherwise I will call him clumsy-cub every time his foot slips on a pathway."

Cohoma managed a tight smile, but Logan guffawed openly. "He's got you there, Jan." The latter just grunted, muttered something about getting on their way, and started up the root after Born. "No time to waste," he added gruffly.

As they moved upward, Born considered Cohoma's last remark. The concept of "wasting time" was personally intriguing, since in the Home it usually had been applied only to him. Was it possible there were others who felt as he did about the way time was spent? If so, there was another reason for getting to know these giants better. He already knew of several others.

V

The forest had been burned back to leave a clear zone around the armored, domed station which sat in the largest open space—for that matter, the only open space—in the hylaea, a silver-gray bubble rising from an ocean of green, like the exhalation of a colossal diver swimming far below.

The circular, domed structure rested on the sheared-off trunks of three Pillar trees, whose neatly trimmed branches formed a system of braces and struts as strong as any artificial supports the builders could have provided. Eventually the cut-off giant trees would die and topple over, but by then the station would no longer be necessary, having been supplanted according to the master plan by much larger, more permanent structures built elsewhere.

The cleared zone around the station was designed to prevent any further deaths from the local saw-tooth, hook-clawed predators, who had killed three of the station's builders before its major defenses were installed and powered up. Discovering that no creature of the forest cared to cross an area open to the sky —and to the sky-borne killers—the construction engineers had burnt back the green ramparts many meters from the station, as well as several meters down below its bottom level.

Two occupants of the station had been carried off by aerial predators while walking along the peripheral strollway. Again the station's defenses were strengthened, until it resembled a small fortress. The lasers and explosive guns were hardly fitting to a structure dedicated primarily to research and exploration. The less lethal instrumentation was located within the gray building. It was that nexus of inner laboratories that the wall of weapons was erected to protect.

Scouting parties went out in armed skimmers to search the endless forest for useful products. They brought back one revelation after another—the forest proved to be an inexhaustible source of surprises— which were metamorphosed into commercial possibilities within the labs. These findings were relayed to other men who in turn relayed the information to a deep space beam operator, who by various devious means—since the presence of the station was illegal, as it had neither been registered nor inspected nor officially approved—passed it on to a distant world. There one man with a machine transcribed the myriad discoveries into figures, relayed them to a second, who took them to a third, who laundered them for a fourth, who laid them carefully on the desk of a person withered in body but not in mind. That person studied the figures. Every so often she would smile crookedly and nod, and then orders would go back along the carefully concealed chain of command until eventually they were disseminated within the dome on The World With No Name.

So closely guarded was the location of the world with no name that few of those who worked within the dome had any idea where it was, and no pilot was sent to it twice. Pilot relayed information to successor, for the coordinates could not even be trusted to mechanical safekeeping. This was chancy

51

since the coordinates could be lost forever, but the advantage of absolute secrecy made it worthwhile. Since no one knew its location, no one could divulge it voluntarily or otherwise to agents of Commonwealth or Church. Anyone questioned on the subject could admit freely to what he knew—which was nothing.

The whole operation was very professional.

In the largest of those inner laboratories, the most intelligent of the station's researchers studied the huge, ovoid chunk of dark wood that dominated the far end of the chamber. It had been cut open. This piece of wood had made all the expense and secrecy and effort worthwhile, and Wu Tsing-ahn had been working with it even before the construction of the station had been completed.

He was a small man, with delicate, tortured features and black hair turned prematurely white at odd places. The private agony which strained his face had not affected the clarity of his mind, or dulled his analytical abilities. Like everyone else in the station, he was aware that his activities on this planet were not in keeping with the Ordainments of the Church or Commonwealth law. Most were there for the money.

Tsing-ahn showed a certain fluttering of the hands, a twitch of both eyelids. Both were by-products of the drug which gave great pleasure at great expense. Tsing-ahn required it now, required it regularly in large doses. He had been forced to suspend his moral principles to satisfy the craving. But he didn't care any more. Besides, the work was not especially difficult and was intellectually pleasing. There was emotional refuge in that.

There was a knock on the door across the room. Tsing-ahn acknowledged the knock, and a large man entered, his slight limp noticeable and unavoidable, contact lenses reflecting the steady overhead light. The man was no giant, but each of his biceps was bigger around than the biochemist's thigh. He wore a holstered sidearm, prominently displayed.

"Hello, Nearchose."

"Hello, Doc," the big man responded. He crossed

52

the room, nodded toward the pierced and cut section of wood. "Found out what makes it tick yet?"

"I've been reluctant to risk chancing its drug-producing properties until just now, Nearchose," Wu replied softly. "Full dissection could destroy that." He reached out and touched the wood.

Nearchose studied it. "How much you think a burl that size is gonna be worth, Doc?"

Tsing-ahn shrugged. "How much is a doubled life-span worth to a man, Nearchose?" He gazed at the burl with something more than scientific detachment. "I'd guess a burl this size would yield enough extract to double the life-span of anywhere from two to three hundred people—not to mention what it will do for general health and well-being. No price has been put on the drug yet since it hasn't been exported except in small, experimental doses. The proteins have proven complex beyond belief. Synthetic production appears out of the question. Dissection may offer clues as to further lines of research." He looked up. "What would you pay for it, Nearchose?"

"Who, me?" The security guard smiled a crooked smile, showing metal teeth, which had replaced ones that had not been lost naturally. "I'll die when my natural time comes, Doc. A man like me . . . I couldn't ever afford the stuff. I'd give or do anything for it, of course, if I thought I could get away with it."

Tsing-ahn nodded. "Far wealthier men will do likewise." He winked. "Maybe I'll slip you a vial of the next batch. How would that appeal to you, Nearchose?"

The guard's genial manner faded. He looked solemnly down at his friend, whom he could break with one hand. "Don't tease me like that, Doc. It's not funny. To live a couple of hundred years in good health, instead of decomposing into pieces at seventy, maybe eighty . . . Don't tease me with stuff like that."

"Sorry, Nick. It's a defense mechanism with me. I've got my own hurts, you know. It's small and mean, but I fight back in these ways."

Nearchose nodded. He knew of the biochemist's addiction, of course. Everyone at the station did. The

53

brilliant researcher Tsing-ahn was deficient in body, though he was not crippled or broken. Nearchose was deficient in mind, though he was neither stupid nor ignorant. Each recognized his superiority over others of his own kind at the station, so the friendship that sprung up between them was one between equals.

"I've got outside patrol this shift," Nearchose announced, turning to leave. "I was just curious to see how everything's going, that's all."

"Surely, Nick. Come in anytime."

After the big man had left for his patrol duty, Tsing-ahn set up his instruments for the first full dissection of the invaluable burl. The operation could be put off no longer, despite the fact that this was the only burl of its kind found so far. Others would be located by the scout teams, he was certain. It was merely a question of time.

When extract from the burl's center was given casually to an experimental carew, the results were unexpected, astonishing, overwhelming. Instead of two days, the hyperactive mammal had lived for nearly a week. He had repeated the experiment twice, not believing his own results. When they were confirmed the third time, he had announced his discovery to Hansen, the station director. The reaction of those funding the project had been predictable: More burls *must* be found. But exploring by skimmer was erratic and difficult. Land parties had been sent out, but they had been discontinued by Hansen despite complaints from above. Too many parties, no matter how heavily armed, had failed to return.

Tsing-ahn was still fascinated by the fact that this unhealthy protrusion of the tree might prove more useful than the tree itself. He thought of ancient Terran whales and ambergris. He was extremely anxious to study the internal structure of the burl. It had a softish, center, according to long probes, quite unlike most burls, which were solid hardwood. And there was other evidence of a unique inner construction.

He worked at the dissection for several days, sawing and probing and cutting open. At the end of that time, a most unnatural and horrible scream shattered the peace of the station and sent people running from their posts to the laboratory of Wu Tsing-ahn.

Nearchose was the first one there. This time he didn't ask permission to enter, but wrenched the door open, breaking the bolt. To his enormous surprise, Tsing-ahn stood facing him and looked up at him calmly. One hand was trembling slightly and an eyelid flickered, but that was only normal.

A crowd had gathered behind Nearchose. He turned, shooed them away. "Nothing to see. Everything's okay. The Doc had a bigger bad-dream than he's used to, that's all."

"You sure, Nick?" someone asked hesitantly.

"Sure, Maria. I'll handle it." The crowd dribbled away muttering among themselves as Nearchose closed the broken door.

"What's the trouble, Nick? Why the indelicate entrance?"

The guard turned to him, studied the man whom he often did not understand, but whom he unfailingly respected. "That was you that screamed, Doc." It wasn't a question.

Tsing-ahn nodded. "That was me, yes, Nick." He looked away. "I'm flying on my morning dose and . . . I thought I saw something. I don't have your mental resilience, Nick, and I'm afriad I let it get a hold of me for a second. Sorry if it disturbed everyone."

"Sure, yeah," Nearchose finally replied. "Worried about you, that's all. Everyone does, you know."

"Sure, yeah," Tsing-ahn echoed bitterly.

Nearchose fidgeted uneasily in the silence, looked past the scientist toward the far end of the lab. "How's the work coming?"

Tsing-ahn answered absently, his mind obviously elsewhere. "Well. Better than one might expect. Yes, quite well. I should have some definite announcements to make in a couple of days."

"That's great, Doc." Nearchose turned to go, paused. "Listen, Wu, if you need anything, anything you'd rather not go through channels for . . ."

Tsing-ahn smiled faintly. "Of course, Nick. You'll be the first one I turn to."

The security guard grinned reassuringly and closed the door quietly behind him. Tsing-ahn returned to his work. He proceeded calmly once more and with his accustomed efficiency.

Nothing else disturbed the tranquility of the station until that evening, when a passerby thought he smelled something unusual in the corridor outside the lab. Following the odor led to visual confirmation—dark wisps of smoke issuing from the cracks around Wu's laboratory door. The man yelled *"Fire!"* and hit the nearest all-purpose station alarm.

This time others reached the lab well ahead of Nearchose. He had to work his way through the personnel who were putting out the last pockets of flame. Containment had been achieved before the blaze could spread beyond the confines of the lab, but the lab itself was a complete wreck. The fire had been brief, but intense. Not only was there plenty of flammable material within the lab, but Tsing-ahn had apparently utilized white phosphorous on stubborn materials and acids on anything that refused to ignite. The little biochemist had been as methodical in destruction as he had been in research.

Everyone clustered around the few charred scraps of wood that were scattered around the back of the lab. They were all that remained of the burl which had been worth untold millions. Nearchose's main concern lay elsewhere, so it was he who first found the body sprawled under a table across the room. At first he assumed the scientist had died of smoke inhalation, since there were no marks on his body. Then he rolled him over and the white cap slid off. Nearchose saw the needler still clutched convulsively in one hand, saw the tiny holes of equal diameter on both the front and back of the skull. He knew what a needler did, knew he could slip a pencil neatly through that hole.

The man's eyes were closed and his expression, for the first time that Nearchose could remember, was content.

Nearchose stood up. The pitiable, weak genius below him had run across something that had impelled him to his own death. Nearchose had no idea what that thing might be and was not sure he would care to know. No man is perfect. An old sergeant had first repeated that cliche to him. For all his brilliance, Tsing-ahn had been less perfect than most. A scrap of note here, a page of book there were all that had survived.

Employed at the station were a lesser biochemist named Celebes and a botanist named Chittagong. Together they did not quite make up one Tsing-ahn, but they were the best Hansen had. They were taken off their projects of the moment, and given the carefully gathered bits of paper and scraps of note-book, and ordered to undertake the reconstruction of Tsing-ahn's work. Eventually, a second burl of the type carbonized in the fire was located and brought back. It was presented to Chittagong and Celebes, who worked with it, while newly installed security monitors watched constantly, checking everything from the scientists' heartbeats to the growls in their stomachs. Both men were less than enthusiastic about the project, especially concerning the manner of their comrade's death. However, the orders came down from an enraged person at a large desk many parsecs away. They were not to be disputed.

Nearchose returned to his duties. He sat at his gimbal post and brooded on what there was in a simple hunk of wood that impelled someone as rational as Tsing-ahn to go off the deep end. Such things happened, and he need not concern himself with them. But he could not help it.

He sighed, and forced himself to turn his gaze and attention to the surrounding wall of forest.

God damn, but he was sick of green.

VI

"Ouch!"

Born stopped, looked back at his charges. Logan was hopping awkwardly on one foot on the cubble, holding a trailing liana for support. Born let go of the vine-root he was holding and dropped next to her. She sat down, holding her left leg. She seemed more angry than hurt. Cohoma was studying something Logan was concealing with a hand.

"What is it?"

She smiled up at him. Beads of sweat were beginning to form on her forehead. "I stepped on something." She looked around, gestured. "That flower there . . . went right through my boot."

Born saw the tiny collection of bright orange thorns sticking up from the middle of the miniature bouquet of six-petaled lavender blooms. His expression changed. A hand reached under his cloak and he brought out the bone blade.

"Hey!" Cohoma started to move between them. Born shoved the bigger man aside. Cohoma stumbled and nearly fell off the cubble.

"Lie down!" Born instructed Logan harshly, putting a hand on her chest and shoving. She went down, hard, then started to sit up slightly, bracing herself with her hands.

"Born what are you doing? It stings a little, but—"

He yanked the boot off and she fell backward again, hitting her head on the wood. Then he raised her leg and held the knife over it.

"Now wait a minute, Born!" Her voice turned panicky. Cohoma had recovered his footing, took a threatening step toward the hunter.

"Just a second, you misplaced pygmy. Explain—"

58

There was a warning growl just overhead and he looked up. Ruumahum was leaning over the cubble just above him, holding on with four legs, the front paws dangling and claws extended. The furcot smiled, showing more ivory than a concert grand. Cohoma looked into three eyes and clenched his fists, but kept them at his side.

"This will hurt a little," Born said quickly. He cut into the sole of her foot, directly over the three punctures.

Logan screamed violently, fell back and tried to twist free. Holding her foot tightly, Born put his mouth over the freely bleeding wound, sucked and spat, sucked and spat. When he finished, she was crying softly and trembling. After a cautious glance at Ruumahum, Cohoma moved to comfort her.

Born ignored the giant's tense questions while searching the surrounding foliage. He found what he needed, a cluster of herbaceous cylinders growing from a nearby limb. Finding an old one, he cut it off at the base. It was half the length of his arm. The knife took the top off, revealing a hollow tube filled with clear liquid. He drained it, sighed, and tried another one. This he offered to the injured woman. Logan finished rubbing at her eyes, stared at him.

"Drink it," he advised simply. She started to take it and recoiled at the feel of the mushy stem. Then she put her lips hesitantly to the rim and drained half of it, despite Cohoma's warnings. She passed the remainder to him.

Cohoma studied it warily. "How do we know he's not trying to poison us?"

"If he wanted to kill us," she sighed, "he could have left us for the flying meat-eater, Jan. Don't be a fool. There's nothing harmful in it." Cohoma sipped at it reluctantly, but finished what was left.

"Your foot . . . how does it feel?" Born inquired solicitously. Logan drew her knee up, pulled it in to where she could see the bottom. The wound was not as deep as she had feared, certainly not as deep as it had felt when Born was cutting it. It was already beginning to heal. Around the multiple punctures, though, the skin had turned a dull red.

59

"Like someone took a knife to it," she shot back. "How should it feel?"

"You feel nothing besides the cut?" Born pressed.

She considered. "A slight tingle, maybe, around where I stepped on the thorns . . . like when your foot goes to sleep. But that's all."

"Tingle," Born said thoughtfully. He started searching the brush again. Both giants watched him curiously. He paused before one plant, then plucked a pale yellow fruit from a branch far above, where it hung in neat clusters of three. "Eat this," he instructed Logan when he rejoined them again.

She examined it doubtfully. Of all the fruits and edible vegetation Born had introduced to them, this appeared the most formidable. It was shaped like a squat barrel, with brown riblike extrusions running around its circumference. "Skin and all?"

"Skin and all," Born said, nodding, "and quickly. It will be better for you."

She brought it to her mouth. So much of the foliage on this world was deceptive—maybe this tough-looking specimen would have a . . . then she bit into it. Her face screwed up in disgust. "It tastes," she told Cohoma, "like spoiled cheese seasoned with vinegar. What happens," she asked Born appealingly, "if I don't finish this thing?"

"I believe—I think, I got all of the poison out of your system. If not, you have a few moments left before the remaining poison spreads to your nervous system and kills you. Unless it is countered by the antitoxin in fruit."

Logan finished the yellow pulp with speed that belied her nausea. Still, she found time to wonder at how words like "antitoxin" and terms like "nervous system" had lasted in these people's vocabulary down through the years of their fall from knowledge. Undoubtedly, she reflected, these expressions were constantly used in this ever-threatening environment. As she reached this conclusion, her eyes widened, her cheeks bulged, and she turned and retched with such violence that Born and Cohoma had to move fast to keep her heaving body from falling off the cubble. Minutes later she was lying on her back gasping for air and running a forearm slowly across her mouth.

"Holy orders!" she wheezed. "I feel like I've been turned inside out." She put both hands to her abdomen and felt around gently. "Still there—you could have bet me it wasn't."

Born ignored her gasps and complaints. "How does your foot feel now?"

"Still tingles a little."

"Just your foot?" he persisted, staring intently at her. "Not your ankle, or your lower leg, here?" He touched her calf. She shook her head. Born grunted, got to his feet. "Good. If your leg tingled, the poison would have spread past my ability to halt it. Then it would have been too late. But you will be all right, now."

She nodded and started to get to her feet with Cohoma's help. Then she stared sharply at Born. "Hey—if it was so vital that I eat that fruit right away, Born, why did you hesitate before picking it and bringing it down? According to what you just said, I could have died in the interim."

The hunter stared back at her with the patient look one reserves for very young children. "I had to be sure the tesshanda would not object to my taking its fruit, since it was not yet quite ripe."

Both Logan and Cohoma appeared confused. "Are you saying," she went on, "that you had to ask that plant's permission? That you talked to it?"

"I did not say that," Born explained easily. "I emfoled it."

"Emfoled? Oh, you mean you felt the fruit to see if it was ripe—enfolded it."

Born shook his head. "No . . . emfoled. You do not *emfol* with your plants?"

"I guess not, since I've no idea what you're talking about, Born."

He looked satisfied without being pleased. "Ah, that explains much."

"Not to me, it doesn't," Cohoma replied. "Look, Born, are you saying you talked or conversed with that plant and that it gave you an okay to pick a fruit before it was ripe?"

"No, no, I *emfoled* it. If the fruit was ripe, I would not have had to, of course."

"Why of course?" Logan asked, feeling the conversation growing steadily more tenuous.

"Because then the tesshanda would have emfoled *me.*"

"Some kind of ritual superstition," she muttered. "The logic trappings are intriguing. Wonder where it sprang from? Give me a hand up, Jan." He did so and she immediately winced, bent over and held her stomach.

"Can you walk?" Born inquired, still patient.

"No, but I'm an accomplished stumbler." She forced a sickly grin. "Talk about the cure being worse than the disease . . . I don't think you'd make it as a Commonwealth physician, van Born, but this is the second time you've saved my life. Thanks."

"Third time," Born told her without explaining. "We are near to the Home, now. Another half-level up and two or three levels distant." Both giants groaned.

"I've never seen a tree like that, not on Survey or in any of the other reports," Cohoma announced when they had their first sight of the Home.

"You haven't been keeping up, Jan," his partner admonished. "The next to the last eastward skimmer brought back the details on it. It's called a weaver. The central trunk hardly narrows at all till it attains the five- or six-hundred-meter level. Then it splits and resplits into an interlocking maze of trunklets that form a . . . well . . . a kind of enormous central basket in the tree. Then the subtrunks recombine a few dozen meters higher to form a single bole again that reaches all the way to the forest top. According to the report the branches of the trunklet cage are lined with a red fruit, mostly sugar pulp around a nutlike center, that's about as rich in nourishment components as anything found locally so far —and rich in niacin, of all things." She pointed as they neared the first trunklets and walked along a thick tuntangcle. "See those pods growing from the pink blossoms? According to the report, if you brush against one, you get a face full of pollen. If you breathe that stuff, it's good-bye, according to the lab analysis. Fungal spores settle in the lungs and esophagus, spread instantly and choke you inside two minutes."

She was suddenly aware that Born showed no sign of swerving from the deadly flower-sprouting vines. "We're going around this tree, aren't we, Born? There can't be a poison here your people don't know about."

"Go around?" Born eyed her oddly. "This tree *is* the Home." He approached the tangle of flower-laden vines and branchlets.

"Born . . ." She followed him slowly, her eyes on the deadly pods. One touch would send a shower of suffocating pollen into the air.

Born stopped at the first vine, leaned over, and spat directly into one of the broad blooms, avoiding the swollen pod. A shiver appeared to pass through the vine as the glistening petals closed on themselves. The shiver continued. Then, like a twig curling back from flame, the vines tightened, retracted on themselves, revealing a clear path through the brambles.

"Quickly now," Born urged, starting between the passage.

A streak of emerald lightning shot past the two giants as they began to follow. Ruumahum had not waited for them to make up their minds. When they were through and safe, both turned to watch the tension slip out of the vines. They relaxed, once again barring the way as effectively as a duralloy wall.

"Remarkable," Cohoma murmured. He questioned Born as they strode deeper into the heart of the Home-tree. "What would happen, Born, if I were to spit in one of the flowers?"

"Nothing," the hunter told him. "You are not of the Home. The Home recognizes only its own."

"I don't see how—" he began, but Logan was already analyzing the possibilities.

"Tell me, Born," she asked, "do your people eat the fruit of the weaver—the Home?"

Born looked back at her, aghast. At times these giants seemed to possess knowledge beyond imagining; at other times, they could be incredibly stupid.

"Is there anything better to eat except perhaps fresh meat?" He had heard Logan's recital of the Survey report on the weaver, but had not understood. "Why would we not eat of what is so readily provided for us?"

"Interesting," Logan agreed. Then she again began using words of no meaning to Born and he willingly ignored their conversation. "You see the connection yet, Jan?"

Her companion nodded. "I think so. They eat the tree's fruit on a regular basis; it's their staple food. Chemicals from the fruit mass in their system. When they spit into one of the flowers, chemicals from the ingested fruit are included in the saliva. No wonder the Home recognizes its own!"

"I can see what's in it for the people," Logan confessed. "Food and shelter. What, if anything, does the tree get out of it?"

Their musings were interrupted by a shout, then another, and another. Soon they were surrounded by a group of goggling children—perfectly normal children in every way, if one discounted the predominance of deep brown skin, hair, and green eyes, plus their shortness. The youngsters eyed the two giants with the kind of awe they would have reserved for a pink furcot.

Din was there, too. He fell in step alongside Born. Puffing out his thin chest, he matched the hunter stride for stride, except for an occasional skip needed to keep up. Born muttered an indifferent greeting to the boy. Would the youth never cease pestering him?

Muf tagged along behind his person, his presence unusual for a furcot. Normally he would have been off with his brethren somewhere in the trunklets, sleeping. The cub nosed his way through the group of children and sniffed questioningly at Logan. She shied away at first, then reached out and hesitantly patted the cub on the head. A low rumble began to sound from somewhere deep within the six-legged ball of fur. The cub edged closer to Logan, nearly knocking her over.

A streamlined, rippling green shape was alongside

her in a second. "If cub troubles, slap," Ruumahum advised Logan in his rumbling bass.

She gazed down at the cub, who was staring up at her with worshipful multiple eyes. "Slap him—certainly not!" she objected. "He's only being affectionate."

Ruumahum snorted derisively, padded on ahead.

This unlikely parade—one person, two furcots, a gaggle of softly chattering children, and two giants—finally came to a halt by the side of the central leafleather pavilion.

Born's gaze swept over the surrounding homes. Somewhere an adult furcot yawned loudly. No crowd came running from the half-open doorways. No covey of adolescent girls hurried to feel his arms and torso and to make cooing sounds. No hunters arrived to study his giants with the awe the children had shown. There was no praise, no admiring compliments, no adulation or expressions of proper commendation for his courage and boldness—only the curious stares of a few oldsters peeping out from behind leafleather doorways.

Something hit Born at the back of his knees, and he fell forward, landing in a puddle of stagnant night-water. Muf scrambled and hid among the children. They laughed delightedly. Getting slowly to his feet, Born tried to regain his dignity while shaking the water free from the cloak. The laughter continued. He turned and yelled at them. They drew back slightly, but the smiles did not entirely vanish. He took a step toward the nearest child, his hand going threateningly to his knife. This time they scattered, naked brown bodies darting nimbly into the doorways of homes, or behind ridges and humps in the wooden paving of the square. Born found he was breathing hard. His capacity for making a fool of himself seemed limitless.

"Not quite the reception you hoped for, hmmm?" Cohoma ventured with surprising sympathy. "I know exactly how you feel. I've experienced the same lack of appreciation myself." He shot a significant glance at Logan that she missed.

All at once the anger flowed out of the hunter, and he relaxed somewhat, feeling at the same time an unexpected sense of kinship to this strange man who claimed to travel the Upper Hell in a boat made of axe metal.

"Where is everyone, anyway?" Logan wondered.

Born just shrugged and led them on toward his own vestibule, located high in the trunklets at the far end of the Home cage. "Gathering fruit, caring for the Home . . ."

"Parasite control," Cohoma murmured to Logan. "One point for the tree. Better the human parasite you know than the unreasonable animal or plant you don't."

"Symbiote, not parasite," Logan countered. "Both tree and man benefit. I wonder, though, what the weaver trees did for protection before Born's ancestors made them their home."

". . . or hunting, perhaps," Born concluded, ignoring their whispers. "All will return before the night comes." He smiled to himself. He could still count on Brightly Go's reaction when he introduced the giants to the council tonight.

Born's own living quarters elicited more peculiar words from the giants. "See," Logan went on, indicating the walls and ceiling, "the smaller branches and vines grow so close together here that it's a simple matter to close off the remaining space with woven material."

Cohoma murmured agreement, sat down and ran a finger along the smooth wood of the floor. An idea was forming that he needed additional proof to confirm. Born gave it to him when he explained the function of a circular crevice in the floor located near the back of the big room.

"I just wonder," he mumbled aloud, "who has adapted to whom, here—man to tree, or tree to man? Maybe nothing lived in the weavers before the colonists discovered them. But I don't understand how such detailed, specialized interdependence could have developed in a few generations."

Logan considered silently. Born eyed the two of them without understanding as they continued to talk between themselves. What did they mean, man adapt to tree or tree to man? The Home was the Home. It was only sensible that a man should take care of his

66

dwelling. What was it like, he wondered, on the world where these giants came from, that they found the natural order of things here so astonishing? He did not think he would care for it. Then a freak thought struck him—freak, because it seemed so impossible.

"Can it be," he said, the incredulity plain in his voice, "that on your world there is nothing that grows?"

"No," Logan corrected, "there's much that grows, but nothing we live in, as you do. But we use our growing things, as your people do."

"Use? I don't understand, Kimilogan."

She settled herself back against a branch. "Some plants we eat the fruit of, others we make into foods we can eat, some we still, but rarely, use in the building of our homes. Some we use for medicinal purposes, as you did the tesshanda. We use the forest world much as you do."

"I still do not understand," Born said. "We do not use the forest. We are a part of the forest, the world. We are part of a cycle that cannot be broken. We no more use the forest than the forest uses us." Cohoma murmured something unintelligible at that.

"Your people serve this tree," Logan explained slowly, "even if you don't realize it. You're its servants, in a sense."

"Servants." Born thought hard, spread his hands helplessly. "What is a servant?"

"Someone who performs a service at the bidding of another," she explained.

Madder and madder! Truly the giants had spells of idiocy, Born mused. "We do not serve the tree, the Home. The Home serves us."

Logan eyed him a little sadly, then she looked over at Cohoma. "They don't understand, all right. Probably wouldn't want to.

"And why not?" Cohoma added. "They seem perfectly happy with the arrangement."

"It ties them down mentally, though," she countered. "With shelter and basic food provided by nature, there's neither reason nor motivation to regain the knowledge they've lost. We'll have trouble trying to re-educate them. Tell me, Born," she asked gently, turning to him as he laid out a meal of fruit, nuts, and dried grazer meat, "would you ever consider leaving your tree?"

Born was so shocked he stood momentarily frozen. "Leave the Home? You mean, forever? Not to come back?" She nodded.

That confirmed the giants' madness. Why would anyone even think of leaving the Home? Here was shelter, food, companionship, security and protection from the unpredictable jungle outside. Away from the Home lay only uncertainty and eventual death.

Then he understood the reason, and it explained many of the giants' strange words. "I see," he told them as gently as possible. "I truly did not understand before. It is evident that you have no Home of your own."

"We have homes," Cohoma shot back. "Mine would overwhelm you, Born. It does what I tell it to, offers food when I wish it, and I come and go from it as I please."

"You do not have to care for it?"

"Well, yes, but—"

Logan's chuckle cut him off. "He's got you there, Jan."

Cohoma looked upset. "Not at all. I can leave anytime I want, for as long as I want, without worrying about it. But these people can't."

"That is not a Home, then," Born argued. "One cares for a Home, and one's Home cares for its own."

"Well, it's *my* home," Cohoma grumbled, sampling a spiral nut from the cluster spread before him. It offered a faint flavor of pepper and celery. He took a second.

"I see," Born replied. He was too polite to add what he knew. Though there had been no talk of material construction, of artificial abodes, Born knew that the giants' homes were not living, but were dead things, rotten with indifference. For all their wonders, Born would not live in a dead thing, dead like the axe. You could not emfol a dead thing.

Thoughts of axes and the waning daylight reminded him that the hunters and gatherers would soon return.

He would present the giants to them then and perhaps someone would finally venture to say that the hunter Born was a bit more daring and brave and worthy than the average hunter.

As he sat and ate and composed what he would say, he noticed toes below the leafleather doorway. He got to his feet, shoved the partition aside. Din jerked back, startled, but Born was too preoccupied with the anticipation of his own triumph to be angry. Instead, he invited the boy in to eat, putting a foot in the face of the cub Muf when it tried to follow. The cub whimpered, but stayed outside. Born found some food for the youth and the orphan consumed it eagerly.

So much for his audience: an orphan child and two giants afflicted with inherent insanities. He bit angrily into a tough slab of meat.

"A number of colony transports," Cohoma explained to the wary but politely attentive audience gathered around the evening Home fire, "were reported lost, sometimes in a natural disaster, sometimes through a careless shift in records by an incompetent clerk." He swallowed, aware he was treading on quasireligious grounds. "It seems likely," he continued, stressing the word likely, "that you people are descended from the survivors of one such ship and are trapped here. Though considering the inimical nature of this world I find it incredible that any of the misplaced colonists were able to survive after the initial supplies were exhausted." He sat down again. "That's our best guess, anyway."

No one seated around the evening blaze said anything. Cohoma and Logan eyed their shorter, better armed cousins a mite apprehensively.

"All this," Chief Sand finally responded slowly, "may be as you say." Both giants relaxed visibly. "But while we have not the benefit of your peculiar knowledge, we have explanations of our own for our existence."

He glanced over at Reader and nodded. The shaman rose. He was clad in his ceremonial raiment of spotted gildver fur, brilliant brown and red with orange stripes, and the feathered headdress wrought from moltings drifted down from the Upper Hell. And the axe, of course, which he brandished prominently as he rose. Swinging it like a conductor's baton, he told the story of how the world happened.

"In the beginning there was the seed," Reader intoned solemnly. The people listened reverently. They had heard the legend a thousand times, yet it still commanded their attention. "And not a very big seed at that," the shaman continued. "One day the thought of water descended, and the seed took root in the wood of emfol." That word again, Logan mused. "It grew. Its trunk became strong and tall. Whereupon it put out many branches. Some of these formed the Pillars which dominate the world. Others changed and became the two hells which envelop the world. Then buds appeared, buds uncounted, blooming. We are the offspring of one such bud, the furcots another, the peeper that lies still in the hyphae yet another. The seed prospers, the world prospers, we prosper."

Cohoma held his knees up and together. "If that's so, and if you believe we come from a planet different from this one, how does all that fit into your universe?"

"The branches of the seed tree spread far," Reader replied. There were appreciative murmurs from the circle.

"What if one of your branches was transplanted to another part of this tree?"

"It would die. Each blossom knows its place on its branch."

"Then you can understand our situation," Cohoma went on. "The same is true with us. If we don't return to our particular branch—or seed, or home, or station—we will surely die, too. Won't you help us? We would do as much for you."

Logan and Cohoma did their best to appear indifferent while the villagers discussed the situation among themselves. Someone threw another rotted section of log onto the fire. It blazed higher, tossing off angry sparks, slim smoke trails rising lazily to curl skyward around the edges of the leafleather canopy. Warm rain dripped down through the smoke.

Sand, Joyla, and Reader conferred in whispers. Finally, Sand raised a hand and the muttering subsided.

"We will help you return to your branch station, your Home," he announced in a strong voice that sounded as if it came from a distant loudspeaker and not that thin frame. "If it is possible."

Born held his place in the inner circle and stared groundward so his smile would not be visible to the chief or to Reader or to any of his fellows. He could hardly wait for their response when they found out how far away this precious station of the visitors actually was.

No one laughed when Logan told them.

"Such a journey is unthought of," Sand announced when Logan had concluded. "No, impossible, impossible. I cannot direct anyone to accompany you, cannot."

"But didn't I make it clear?" Logan said pleadingly, scrambling to her feet and gazing anxiously around at the silent brown faces. "If we don't get back to our station we'll . . . we'll wither, wither and die. We'll—"

The chief cut her off with a calming hand. "I said I could not direct anyone to accompany you. This is so. I would not order any hunter to undertake such a journey, but if one wished to go with you . . ."

"This is foolish talk," the gatherer Dandone commented from her place. "No one would return alive from such a trek. There are tales of places where the Lower and Upper Hells are joined and the world stops."

"You confuse bravery and foolishness," Joyla countered. "A foolish person is merely one who does brave things without thought. Would not any among us risk her life to return to the Home from a far place, no matter the distance or hazards? And would we not seek help from whomever we found ourselves among?" She looked over at the giants. "If these people are like us, they will go despite our entreaties and warnings. Perhaps we have some among us brave enough to go with them. I am no hunter, so I cannot."

"If I were a young man," Sand added, "I would go, despite the dangers."

71

But you are young no longer, Born thought to himself.

"But since I am young no longer," the chief continued, "I cannot. Let this not restrain others, those among you who may be eager to go."

He stared around at the assembly, as did Cohoma and Logan, as did the men and women, as did the wide-eyed children who peered inward from behind shoulders and heads and between calves. No one stepped forward. The only sounds were the brisk crackle of dead wood in the fire, the soft, indifferent murmur of falling rain. Before he had time to think it out, Born found himself saying, "I will go with the giants."

Innumerable stares of varying intent and intensity pinned him in his place. Now, at last, he hoped for some show of admiration and appreciation. Instead, those stares held sadness and pity. Even the two giants gazed on him with expressions of satisfaction and relief, but not of adulation. Bitterly he reflected how that might change in the many seven-days ahead.

"The hunter Born will accompany the giants," Sand noted. "Will any others?" Born looked around at his friends. There was stirring within the inner circle, but it came from men finding excuses to study the ground before them, to feel the warmth of the fire, to examine the seams in the leafleather canopy overhead—anything but meet his eyes.

Very well. He would go alone with the giants, and he alone would learn their secrets. "Possibly," he said coldly, getting to his feet, "it would not be too much to ask for some to see to the provisioning of our party." Then he turned and stalked out of the gathering, back toward his bower. As he did so, he thought he heard someone murmur, "Why waste good food on those already dead?" More likely, he had imagined it; nevertheless, he did not stop to find out.

Successful hunts, the killing of the grazer—all had brought him nothing. When he alone of all the hunters had been brave enough to descend to the giants' sky-boat he had gained only the accolades of children. Now he would do something so overawing, so

72

incredible, that none would be able to ignore him any longer. He would take the giants to their station-Home and return, or he would die. Maybe that would make them realize his worth, if this time he failed to return. They would be sorry then.

In his anger, he stumbled on a protruding rootlet and turned furiously to hurl imprecations at his thoughtless enemy. It made him feel a little better. The central fire was well behind him now, and the darkness snuggled close around him. He pulled his cloak down over his head to shield himself from the rain.

If the giants felt they could reach their mysterious station, then why should he not feel as confident? Why not indeed, unless . . .

What if there were no station? What if these two giants were imps of the Lower Hell sent here to tempt him to stray from the Home?

Bah, nonsense! They were as human as he, despite their great size and strange garb. How else could it be that they spoke the same language of man? Though what strange modulations and phrasings they used! And they did not emfol. Born could not conceive of a person who could not emfol, so he conveniently forgot about it.

He parted the leafleather dooring and entered his home, closed it carefully behind him. Untying his cloak, he slung it into a far corner. A muffled sound came from the darkness. Immediately he crouched, the bone knife jumping reflexively from belt to hand. A dim figure whimpered. Moving carefully in the blackness, he brought out the little packet of incendiary pollen, sprinkled it over the pile of deadwood in the center of the floor. A touch, and the wood coughed and blazed, revealing the huddled form of Brightly Go.

Relaxing, he replaced the knife in its sheath. After a curious glance at the girl, he sat down beside the fire and crossed his legs. Its yellow-bright depths were soothing, friendly, undemanding. They would leave tomorrow, the giants and he, and he would have liked a long, quiet sleep but . . .

73

"You come to laugh at me like the others," he muttered, without rancour.

"Oh, no!" She crawled timidly toward the fire. The light made olivine patterns deep in her eyes, and Born found the attraction of the fire waning steadily. "You know my feelings, Born."

He huffed, turned nervously away. "Losting you like, Losting you love—me, I amuse you!"

"No, Born," she protested, her voice rising. "I like Losting, yes, but . . . I like you as well. Losting is nice, but not nearly so nice as you. Not nearly." She looked at him imploringly. "I don't want you to do this thing, Born. If you go with the giants you'll never come back. I believe what everyone says about the dangers so far from Home and what is whispered about the places where the two hells come together."

"Stories, legends," Born grumbled. "Cub tales. The dangers far from the Home are no different than they are a spear's throw from this room. Nor do I believe there is a place where the two hells join. But if there is, we will go around it or through it."

She moved around the fire on hands and knees, to sidle close and put one hand on his shoulder. "For me, Born, don't go with the giants."

Looking at her, he started to lean close, started to agree, started to give in. Then the thing that drove him to lie in wait for grazers and to go down into the depths of wells reached out, interceded, crossed him up. Instead of saying, "I'll do whatever you desire, Brightly Go, for the love of you," he whispered huskily, "I've given my word and said before the whole tribe I will go. And even had I not, I will do this thing."

Her hand slid from his shoulder. She half-mumbled, "Born, I don't want you to," then bent over and kissed him before he could draw away. Then she was on her feet and out the door before he could react. The night-rain swallowed her up.

He was silent a long time, thinking, as the fire consumed itself and the tepid drops trickled off leaf-leather roof. Then he mumbled something there was no one to hear, rolled back onto his sleeping fur, and drifted off to a troubled, dream-filled slumber.

Ruumahum's left eye opened halfway, cocked sideways. A dark bulk stood on the branch by his resting crevice. He coughed, shook droplets from his muzzle, and snorted in the sibilant rumbling way of the furcot.

"Where is your person, cub?"

Muf jerked his head, in imitation of the human gesture, down toward the cluster of enclosed branches below. "Somewhere there, asleep."

"As you should be, nuisance." The eye closed, and Ruumahum rearranged his massive head on his forepaws.

Muf hesitated before blurting out, "Old one, please?"

Ruumahum let out a furcot sigh and lifted his head slightly to face the cub, all three eyes open this time. The cub dropped his head and eyed the village sleeping below.

"My person, the boy Din, is troubled."

"All persons are troubled," Ruumahum replied. "Go to sleep."

"He fears for his half-father, the person Born. Your person."

"There is no blood attachment," the big furcot mumbled, dropping his head down again. "The cub-person's emotional reaction is unreasonable."

"All cub-persons' reactions are unreasonable. I fear this time my person's reaction is reasonable."

Ruumahum's eyebrows rose. "Offspring of an accident, can it be that you enter into wisdom?"

"I fear," the cub continued, "the boy-cub-person will do something rash."

"His elders will restrain him, as I would restrain you. I will do worse if you don't leave me to my rest."

Muf turned to go, looked back over a shoulder, and grumbled defiantly, "Don't say I didn't tell you of it, old one."

Ruumahum shook his head, wondered why it was that cubs were so questing and inquiring, so disrespectful of an elder's rest. They rose with questions at all hours and times. The drive to dispel ignorance—a drive, he reminded himself, he also had been subject to—the drive was still there, but mellowed by ex-

perience. Mellowed also by the quiet assurance that
death explained everything.

He snugged his head back into his crossed paws,
ignored the steadily dripping rain, and was instantly
asleep again.

VII

Born angrily broke off another of the dead
branches from the trunk of a tertiary parasite, careful
despite his rage not to harm any of the healthy, living
shoots.

They were four days linear march out from the
Home, and his anger at the now distant group of
sullen hunters had not abated. But some of the anger
was directed inward at himself for locking himself into
this crazy expedition.

Ruumahum patrolled the hylaea off to Born's left.
He sensed his person's discomfort and kept his distance. A person made blind by anger was as unpredictable as any of the forest denizens, and one furious
at himself the most unpredictable of all.

Adding to Born's discomfort was the total incom-
petence of the giants. They seemed to know nothing
of normal walking or climbing. A child held better
footing than they. Had he not been close at hand, there
would already have been some serious falls. What
would they do if a brown many-legs or a Buna floater
charged them? Ruumahum moved below them when
they came to a more difficult place, but even the furcot's superfast reflexes might not be enough to stay a
fall of several levels. It would take only one such fall
to end the expedition.

He broke off the last branch, gathered up the wood
in his arms, and started back toward the wide section
of cubble he had chosen for this evening's camp.

Today it appeared the giants were doing a little better, moving a little less hesitantly through the trees. Cohoma no longer showed the same tendency to slip every time he jumped for the next vine, or to overextend his grasp for same.

Logan had finally been convinced it was dangerous to reach for each new bloom and plant they passed. Born did not smile as he recalled the incident two days past, when she had sought a drink from the gobletlike vermilliot. Only a quick step and a crisp blow on the forearm had kept her from touching it. She had glared angrily at him until he had shown her the minute differences in the vermilliot and the surrounding vermillion plants: the vermilliot had two extra petals, an unusual thickening of the base, a darker red color, and telltale spottings near the lip of the cylinder—all flaws in otherwise perfect mimicry.

Finally he had used the bone knife. Making sure both giants were well clear, he moved above the plant. With the point of the blade he had tipped the green cylinder so that the clear liquid inside spilled free. The vermilliot's water was clear, but rainwater it was not. The stream struck the meter-thick liana below, splashed, and sizzled, forming a dense cloud that rose into the air. When the mist finally faded, he beckoned them nearer. Cautioning them not to step on the lingering dampness, he showed them the hole the clear liquid had made through a meter of wood and into the depths beyond.

Lastly, he had carefully tapped the green wall of the false bromeliad. They heard the deep, almost metallic bong, utterly unlike the soft tap when he struck one of the true vermillions.

From that point on neither of the giants so much as brought a finger close to a new growth without first consulting Born. That made him only slightly happier, for innumerable questions slowed them down as effectively as a wound or a broken limb. They moved at perhaps a third of the speed he would have managed alone.

With a short jump he dropped down to the huge cubble selected for camp. From the first day, deciding on a camp had proved a problem. It seemed the giants could not tolerate many evenings without shelter from the night-rain. They insisted on protection despite the time and effort it cost, and Born had grudgingly complied. Their excuse was that constant exposure would engender a strange sickness in them, which they called a cold.

Born failed to understand. No person could be so fragile. Indigestion was the only illness he was familiar with, and that occurred only when he ate food other than the fruit of the Home tree. But the descriptions and assurances of sickness the giants gave him were so horrid he could hardly deny them their necessary protection.

"There he is," he heard Logan say to her companion as he approached. He wondered why they lowered their voices so often, speaking at a less than normal volume. The thought that they might be trying to keep something from him never occurred to him. Anyway, he could hear them clearly enough, even when they conversed in what was called a whisper. Who was he to question the peculiarities of those who could fly through the sky?

They might have spent more time, he mused as he dumped the load of wood on the main branch, improving and perfecting their own bodies instead of constructing new artificial ones to shield them from the world.

"We were getting a little nervous, Born," Logan explained with a broad smile. "You've been gone a long time."

He shrugged, set about constructing a crude lean-to from the accumulation of dead branches and extraneous leaves. "It is difficult to find adequate materials for a dry shelter," he told her. "Most deadwood and old leaves fall to Hell to be eaten, like all else that falls."

"Eaten's the word, I'll bet," Cohoma agreed, peeling the skin from a large purple spiral. "There should be bacteria down there big as your freckles, Kimi. The amount of dead vegetable matter that must fall to the ground here each day—"

There was a crash of leaves, and he jumped to his feet. Logan hurried to ready the bone spear she had been provided with. It was only Ruumahum. Born smiled as he studied the giants' expressions. Despite protestations to the contrary, it was clear they would never quite get used to the big furcot's presence.

"Person and furcot come," the emerald hexapod declared.

"Stranger or—?" Born stopped as a tall figure stepped into the light, and his hand moved instinctively for his knife. A second furcot, not quite as big as Ruumahum, was at the man's side.

Losting.

The big hunter did not smile as he met Born's gaze. Logan eyed Born questioningly. He ignored her. Nor did he move his hand from the hilt of his knife. The two furcots exchanged soft growls and moved off to converse on a nearby limb. Losting took a couple of steps forward.

"When two lone hunters meet on the trail," the bigger man said, taking his gaze from Born long enough to study the giants, "it is meet that the one who has made camp invite the latecomer to share with him."

"How come you here, now?" Born asked sharply, ignoring ritual courtesy for the moment. He looked groundward so Losting could not see the anger in his eyes. "I saw you last standing with Brightly Go as we left the Home."

"That is so," Losting admitted without gloating. "I think now, as I have these past days, that I should have stayed with her, as she will need someone to comfort her and make a life with her when you are dead."

"You did not follow alone for four days to taunt me," Born noted tensely. His anger was melting under the illogic of the situation. "Why then did you follow?"

Now it was Losting's turn to look away. Walking past the two giants, he squatted and rested chin on forearm as he examined the shelter being built. "I tried to forget what you said that night in council. I could not. Nor could I forget that you alone had gone down into the well in the world, to discover that the blue thing was not a demon, but a thing of axe metal. To discover them." He nodded at a curiously watching Logan and Cohoma. "I was ashamed I had been afraid, even though the others of our party who had returned are not. They excused themselves by saying you were mad. I could not so excuse myself." He looked back at Born. "Then when you said you would try to go with these giants to their Home, I too thought you mad, Born. And when you left, I was happy, for I had Brightly Go in my arms." Born tensed, but Losting put up a restraining hand. "I thought how good it would be now, with Brightly Go to myself. How good not to have you around, Born, always to come back with another, greater kill. How good not to have to compete for her with a madman. How good not to fumble with hard words while you always said the soft, proper ones."

The last of Born's anger vanished. An astonishing thought occurred to him. Could it be that Losting—massive, muscular Losting, mighty hunter and warrior Losting—could it be that he was jealous of Born?

"I stayed while you left," the other hunter continued, "but I stayed troubled. When Brightly Go left me, I went to the edge of the Home and sat there, staring into the world where you had disappeared. Thinking. Ashamed. For, I thought to myself, what if you should reach the giant's station-Home as you had reached their sky-boat? What if you should come back with this success on your shoulders? What then would Brightly Go think of me? And what, what would I think of myself?" Losting's face was twisted.

"You persecute me, Born, whether you are near or not. So I found myself thinking, maybe you are mad, but mad and skilled, even still you are no braver than Losting. None is braver than Losting! So I followed. I will follow to the giants' home or to the death. You will not have this triumph over me, you will not!"

"Born, what's this all about?" Cohoma asked.

Logan shushed him. "Can't you see it's personal, Jan? Something deep between these two. Let's not intrude."

"As long as it doesn't affect our return." Cohoma said.

"What of this, then?" Born queried, relaxing a little.

"Why do you not continue to follow as before? Clearly it was the better course of plan."

"And would keep me from your eyes," Losting finished, without anger. "And you from mine. But we cannot go on."

"You'll not discourage me with—"

"No, not I, Born." Losting's tone was conciliatory. "Not having to pause to construct shelters for the giants, I've traveled a little ahead of you each day, not behind. I've only just now come from," and he named a modest figure, "ahead. What I've seen prompts me to make contact."

"And what have you seen?"

"Akadi."

"I don't believe you."

"Then keep on this path, and be food for busy mouths. I've seen the column."

Born considered. Losting would not jest about something so serious—not even to embarrass Born before Brightly Go.

"What's going on?" Cohoma finally asked impatiently. "What's this talk about not going on? What's this acoti . . . whatever?"

"Akadi," Born corrected heavily. "We must go back."

"Now look—" Cohoma began, getting to his feet. Logan restrained him, but this time he shook her off. "No, I'm going to tell these regressives what I think of 'em. First they make a big show of helping us. Then they get a little ways away from the home fires, and they have second thoughts." He turned to Born. "Or maybe you're getting close to that five-day limit nobody's ever exceeded and—" Suddenly aware he was overdoing his frustration, Cohoma stopped.

"You do not know of the Akadi," Born murmured with quiet fury. "Or you would say only, when do we run."

"Born," Logan began, "I don't think that's—"

"You talk of delays, and bravery, and intentions. Do you think I'm risking my life out of the goodness of my heart? Do you think I'm doing it for either of you? I care nothing for the both of you, you great, cold people!" He calmed slightly and turned his attention to Cohoma. "You are different in size and color and mind. You come to us in a sky-boat of axe metal. I went down the well you made in the world not to save you, but to see what your boat was. To find out things. To please myself. I go to your station for the same reason—not to save your lives, but for me, *me!* And it is for me that we turn back, for myself and Losting and our people, not for you. You can go on and die, or hide and rot before the column catalogs your scent. It is nothing to me. But we cannot go on. We may never go on again. We must return to the Home."

"Born," Logan said after a long silence, "we are still ignorant of your ways and much of your world. You must pardon us. What are the Akadi, and why do they force us back?"

"We must warn the Home," said Losting. "The Akadi may pass it. If so, all will be well. If they do not . . ." He shrugged. "We must try to stop them."

"I believe you, Losting," Born confessed hesitantly. "But I would have final proof." He indicated Cohoma and Logan. "And I think it would speed our return if the giants were to see the sign of Akadi passing."

Losting nodded agreement and rose. "It is not far, not as far as I would wish. We can be near and return before the water falls."

Both hunters started off down the limb. Cohoma and Logan had to hurry to follow. Logan stumbled and twisted her way through the clutching thorns and branches and saw-edged leaves. Ruumahum paced below her as a precaution. The first two days had accustomed her to living the death of a thousand cuts every sunrise to sunset, and she was getting toughened. She marveled at how Born never seemed to get cut or scratched despite the thickness of the brambles he led them through. It was positively uncanny. No doubt, she reasoned, it was his smaller size, his lithe build, coupled with the innate knowledge of the hylaea's construction that enabled him to slip smoothly between the most closely packed webs of leaves and stems and twigs.

A bulky green shape appeared next to her. She didn't jump this time, just quivered a little inside. She was growing used to the furcot's size and silent approach.

"Ruumahum, what are the Akadi?"

The furcot sniffed. "A thing that eats."

"One thing, or many?"

"There are thousands of them, and there is one of them," Ruumahum replied.

"How can there be thousands and only one?"

Ruumahum growled irritably. "Ask Akadi." He plunged off the branch and downward.

Logan followed his path in her mind's eye, repeating to herself theatrically, "into the foliage below! . . . foliage below . . . foliage below . . . foliage. Fol—emfol—Empathetic foliation?" Precise terminology for an acquired superstition, she mused. That might explain the term, but not the rationale for the belief's intensity. She was missing something. It would have to wait. Losting had been right, they did not have far to go.

Now they were moving through a densely packed thicket of aerial greenery striped with bright yellow. It grew at right angles, forming a living checkerboard. Losting indicated they would have to pass around it, a detour of some dozens of meters.

Cohoma put out a hand and grasped the nearest of the interlocking, finger-thick stems. "Why go around?" he asked Born, with a gesture at the latter's broad-bladed knife. He squeezed the branch. "This stuff is herbaceous, soft, pulpy. If we're in a hurry, why not cut our way through?"

"You consider death with such indifference," Born told him, eyeing him in much the way Cohoma would study a bug under a microscope. "Can it be that on your own world you are a hunter of sorts, too?" There was a certain unidentifiable stress laid on the word sorts.

It was Cohoma's turn to stare at Born. "It's just some big succulent."

"It is alive," Born said patiently. "If we cut through it, it will become not-alive. Why? To save time?"

"Not only that. If there's some kind of multiple omnivore around here, I'd rather not be caught in tight quarters. The more space cleared around me, the better."

Born and Losting exchanged glances. The two fur-cots waited nearby. "He would kill for a few minutes of better light," Born observed wonderingly. "Your priorities are strange, Jancohoma. We will go around." Cohoma had additional questions, and Logan as well. However, neither Born nor Losting would answer them now.

Eventually they rounded the copse of the checker-board succulents. In another minute they were walking in dense jungle. A turn, cut, and suddenly they entered an unexpected open space, much as Cohoma had wished for, tunneled out of the forest. The tunnel was taller than a man, taller than Logan or Cohoma. It was a good five meters wide, stretching in a straight line to left and right until it merged into green.

"Akadi made this. They are mindless and of one purpose. They eat their way through the world, leaving—this." He indicated the clear space. Within that tunnel, life had ceased to exist. It had simply disappeared into . . . what?

"Is the line always so straight?" Logan asked.

"No. The column sends out scouts. If the food lies thicker in another direction, the Akadi swerve and eat in a new path. Once started, nothing turns them but their own hunger. See." He pointed down the tunnel. "They will eat through anything, consuming anything living in their path that cannot get out of their way. I have seen them eat through the heart of a Pillar tree and come out the other side. It is said that one can stand by the very edge of their tunnel and, though one could reach out and pull you in, they will not deviate from their chosen path. As those in front are sated, they drop back, letting new members eat themselves full. By the time the last has eaten, the first are hungry again. They stop only to rest and breed."

Cohoma looked relieved. "No problem, then, is there? Don't tell me you're concerned because they seem to be heading toward your village?" Born nodded.

The giant spread his hands. "What's the trouble?

All you have to do is pack up your kids and furcots and get out of the way until they've eaten their way through, then move back in, right?"

Born shook his head slowly. "No. The pods will kill some of them, but not very many. You do not understand. We could do what you say, but it is not ourselves we fear for. They are on the village level. They will reach the Home and eat their way through the trunk itself. Once the bark is pierced they will eat through to the heartwood. The Home will lie defenseless to parasites and disease. It will blacken and die, unless we can stop the column, or turn it."

There was nothing more to be said. They left the tunnel, Logan and Cohoma trailing.

"But Born," Logan persisted, "surely the presence of you two will not make any difference in the defense of the tree! Two men more. Take us on to our station. We have devices there which could halt this carnage before it reaches the Home, devices you can't imagine or conceive of."

"That may be so," Born conceded, "but we are uncountable days from your station-Home. At their normal rate of march the Akadi will reach the Home well before we could reach your station. We must warn the others and help prepare. You will help, too."

"If you think," Cohoma shot back, "that we're going to hang around while—"

"Of course we'll do what we can, Born," Logan said soothingly, after a sharp glance at her partner. "We'll be honored to help after what you've already done for us." She put a hand on Cohoma's shoulder and held him back. They dropped behind Born.

"What the hell's the matter with you, Kimi?" whispered Cohoma angrily. "If you'd just let me argue with them a little more I might have convinced them that we're of no use to them. They could leave us on the nearest branch and we'd—"

"You shortsighted idiot! We've no choice but to cooperate. We might as well. If this defense of the tree fails, we're as dead as if the Akadi had eaten us. Or do you think we can make it through this greenhouse Hades without help? You've seen what it's like. We'd be dead a dozen times over by now if it weren't for Born. Remember the false bromeliad I thought was full of water that turned out to be full of acid? We'll fight, sure. If it begins to look as hopeless as Born makes it sound, why, then we'll have plenty of time to skip clear." She stepped carefully over a magenta and blue fungus. "Until then, we'd better do our best to see that they survive. Unless you'd prefer to strike out on your own."

"Okay, I wasn't thinking," Cohoma admitted. "I'll go along as long as they're able. But I'm not dying for any damn tree. I'd rather take my chances in the hylaea."

Born would have wondered at this strange talk, but at the moment his mind was filled with thoughts that drowned out any other sound. The Akadi were marching toward the Home, marching toward Brightly Go. He suspected the giants would not fight to the death, if it came to that. He did not bother to tell them that once the Akadi had their scent, they would follow the smell of an enemy until it dropped. Once the conflict was joined and the Akadi senses heightened, all within range of their olfactory sense were doomed to death, unless the Akadi died first. If they somehow managed to stop the ravaging column and the giants discovered this information, they could berate Born all they wished.

Brightly Go had hurried back from gleaning the Home when word of Born's return reached her. She saw him talking excitedly with Sand and Joyla and started toward him, pleased and surprised at his sudden, unexpected safe return. Then she noticed that Losting was with them and talking easily with Born as well as with the elders. She slowed, stopped, stared for a long moment. Then she whirled and began walking slowly back toward the house of her parents. Now and then she would glance back over her shoulder, talk quietly to herself, and shake her head.

"How long?" asked Sand solemnly.

"Two days march for a man," Losting told them, gesturing back into the forest.

"No chance they will pass to one side or the other?"

Born shook his head. "I think not."

"They'll cut right through the middle of your village." Born turned as they were joined by the two giants and Reader. "You're all seeing this cockeyed," Cohoma continued. "You're going to sacrifice yourselves trying to save a *tree?* Listen, how long would it take for the tree to die when the Akadi have finished with it, eaten their way through?"

It was Reader's turn to respond. "By the old calendar, perhaps a hundred years."

Cohoma's face mirrored his feelings. "You could raise two or maybe three more generations here, be searching safely in small armed groups for a new tree. But if you stay and fight these Akadi, you'll all die, it seems. What's the point of that?"

"The Home will live," explained Joyla with dignity.

"Right," commented Cohoma bitterly. "Throw away your lives for a damned holy vegetable." He directed his words to Logan. "They're not human enough to be repatriated to the Commonwealth any more. They've regressed too far. The normal survival factor's been bred and cut out of them by this dunghill."

The chief shook his head sadly while both hunters simply studied the giants as they would a new variety of Chollakee.

"Giants who claim to come from another world, I do not understand you. It may be as you say, we are more different than we appear."

"And it's going to be left at that?"

Joyla and Sand nodded in unison.

"We don't pretend to understand you completely," Logan admitted in a conciliatory tone, while Cohoma cursed softly. "But some of our ways might be of some help to you."

"We certainly will consider any suggestions you would like to make," Sand replied politely.

"Okay," she said enthusiastically, "the way I understand it, the only thing these Akadi will turn for is to defend themselves against an attacker, right?"

"That is so," Born told her.

"Well then," she continued brightly, "why not hit this column from the side. Once they turn to defend themselves, won't they continue on the new pathway?"

Sand smiled, shook his head. "The Akadi remember. They would pursue and kill any creature foolish enough to assault them, then return to their original line of march."

"Oh," Logan murmured, crestfallen. "I'd wondered why nobody suggested a diversionary attack. All it would gain would be a little time."

"A very little time," Losting added.

"Swell, terrific," a frustrated Cohoma put in. These people were getting on his nerves. Here they had actually found someone to guide them back to the station and safety, and now this ridiculous bit of logic demanded they kill themselves off trying to save a tree for the fourth generation, instead of simply picking up and moving for a day or so. It went against reason!

But despite his earlier outburst, Cohoma had no illusions about their chances in the jungle by themselves. They would end up in the grip of some cyanide-spitting cabbage, or something equally bizarre.

He took a deep breath. It was essential, then, that these Akadi be destroyed. To that end, both he and Logan were vocal in volunteering their full cooperation. If the fight was won, they would get credit for great bravery and comradeship. If it were lost, well, they would take their chances in the forest. Neither knew of the Akadi's ability to follow the scent of their enemy down to the last straggler.

The two giants willingly helped raise the ramparts of sharpened ironwood stakes. These were wedged and then tied with woven vine into place on the side of the Home where the Akadi assault was expected to come. The bristling poisoned stakes and spines would blunt, not halt, the Akadi surge. The latter would overwhelm such pedestrian defenses by sheer weight of numbers, the living using their dead and impaled cousins as a bridge.

But the inhabitants of the great tree had other defenses, defenses which, despite their considerable experience in researching the vegetation of this world, Cohoma and Logan were unfamiliar with.

What, for example, was the purpose of the large nuts twice the size of a terran coconut that had been gingerly suspended over the cubbles the Akadi would use to enter the tree? Unlike the mountain of deadly jacari thorns and tank seed pods which had been gathered, there was nothing in the nuts to hint at concealed deviltry.

Cohoma came up with what he thought was an obvious, yet brilliant, solution. He overlooked something Logan did not—the fact that while Born's people were primitive, they were not stupid.

"Why not," he suggested to a small group of busy men, "just cut away all the vines and cubbles and lianas leading into the Home tree? Unless these Akadi can fly, too, they'll be forced to go around."

By way of reply, Jaipur, an elderly craftsman, handed Cohoma a finely honed bone axe and directed him to try it on the nearest big liana, which was about as big around as a man's thigh. Cohoma proceeded to do just that, hammering away at the incredible substance for a good ten minutes. The axe blade was finally dulled to the point where it would no longer cut. All he had achieved was a notch barely a couple of centimeters deep in the protective bark.

"You might have guessed, Jan," Logan reminded him, "that none of the natives would suggest deliberately hurting anything growing unless they knew you had no chance of success, even with a vine."

Jaipur made an expansive gesture, grinning a crooked grin out of one side of his face. The other had been paralyzed by an encounter in childhood with a certain spiny plant. "There are many thousands of such pathways, twining and entwining, leading to the Home from every direction. Many are far thicker than a furcot's body. There are not enough axes in the Home, or enough time in the world to cut them all, could they be so cut."

Before moving to sharpen yet another ironwood spear Jaipur also showed Cohoma how each cubble had six others supporting it. Cutting one or two without cutting its dozen or more supports would be a waste of time.

"You'd need a tripod rifle to make a start," Logan observed. "Hell, the undergrowth here is so entangled you'd have to cut down half the forest to make a decent gap between it and the tree."

Reader passed the group and regaled the two giants with tales of how the Akadi could cross considerable open spaces without any support by forming a living bridge of interlocked bodies. This story of rending alien limbs engendered a desire in both Cohoma and Logan for a little more instruction in the handling of available weaponry. Both had been presented with ironwood spears, plus bone axe and knife. Logan would have preferred a snuffler, but the bazookalike blowguns required time and skill to make. There weren't enough for all who knew how to use them.

They would have been abashed to know that one reason they had not been offered snufflers was that Born had convinced the chiefs that in a difficult spot, they were more likely to prick themselves on one of the toxic thorns than kill Akadi.

Requests for a more detailed description of the enemy resulted in Born's displaying an unexpected talent for illustration. Using a white chalklike substance, he drew on a plate of polished black wood. "You must try to strike here," he instructed them, "between the forelegs, or here between the eyes. Each Akadi," Born continued, "is about half the size of a man . . . myself."

"About the size of a German shepherd," Cohoma mused.

Born went on. An Akadi had a thick flexible body with no tail; it walked on six thin but very powerful legs, each leg terminating in a single long, curved claw that enabled the Akadi to scurry slothlike along any part of a branch or cubble. The front of the body tapered slightly, ending in double jaws with no neck, surrounded by muscle. The double jaw arrangement fascinated Logan. One set worked up and down in the usual fashion, while the opposing ones moved from left and right. Working in unison they created a biting phalanx which could cut through the toughest wood or bone as neatly as a laser could slice sheet metal.

The teeth set in the upper and lower jaws were triangular and razor-edged, while those on the side were square, serrated on top, and curved slightly backward to shove food into the ever-hungry gullet. Three eyes, spaced across the top of the head, lay just back of the jaws. There were three tentacles, one on either side of the head and another below that were equipped with jagged, tearing suckers on the tips for holding prey. In color the Akaki were a distinctive rusty orange, eyes and legs bright black. Despite the triple oculars their sight was rumored to be poor.

"This is countered somewhat by their sense of smell and of touch," Born concluded, "which is very good indeed."

"An eating maching in multiples," Logan declared quietly. "Very well designed, very efficient." She shook her head, murmured, "God on a seat, I wouldn't care to tangle with one of them. And we have to fight thousands." She looked evenly at Born. "You people really think you can stop something like this armed with a few glorified blowguns and spears?"

"No," said Born, wiping the polished wood clean with a forearm. "I have things to do now." He turned to leave.

"There's no hope for them, no hope at all," a disgusted Cohoma blurted when Born was out of earshot.

"I'm afraid there's not much left for us, either, Jan."

VIII

They heard the sound while they were resting just outside the first ring of the Home's pod-laden vines. Initially it was only a soft rustling in the distance, like wind moving through far-off branches. It grew steadily louder, became a hum, a buzzing like a billion bumblebees aswarm at a new nest.

It intensified, swelled, and resolved into a deafening crackling sound neither Cohoma nor Logan would ever be able to forget. The sound of hundreds of tons of organic matter vanishing down innumerable throats.

A familiar form bounded up from a liana below. "Be ready, giants. The Akadi near," Losting advised them.

Logan's grip tightened on the shaft of the ironwood spear and she checked to make certain bone axe and knife were still strapped securely to the belt of her rapidly disintegrating shorts, though she intended never to get close enough to one of the carnivores to use either. They would run before that.

Losting moved to go by them. Cohoma gestured at him to pause. "We haven't seen Born for a couple of days now, Losting. I know he's been busy. Is he manning another part of the line?"

"Born." Losting's face went through several changes of expression ranging from satisfaction to disgust. "You've not see Born for some days because he's been gone for some days." Losting clearly relished the shock on the faces of the two giants. "He left the Home one night and has neither been seen nor heard from since. It is certain he did not go toward the Akadi. We have had scouts out marking their progress toward the Home. His furcot has vanished with him." The implication was clear—the hunter had run.

"Born, a coward?" Logan sounded confused. "That doesn't make sense, Losting. When the rest of you were afraid, he was the only one who would come down to our skimmer."

"Those who are mad act for reasons of their own, which no man can comprehend," Losting countered. "Your sky-boat was an unknown quantity, unlike the Akadi, who are known too well. With them, one knows exactly what to expect. Death. Born is a hunter and a solitary person by habit. If the Home dies and the village dies with it, he could survive alone. There is no doubt he is the cleverest among us." His expression darkened. "But he has not been clever in this, for if there is any village to come back to, he will not be allowed to live among us. The chiefs and the shaman have ordained this already." He spun. Gripping the vine nearby, he pulled himself up to the branch

92

immediately above to check on the readiness of the defenders there.

"I still don't believe it," Logan whispered, turning back to face the forest. "I consider myself a better judge of human nature than that."

"I told you they'd abandoned their humanity in making concessions to this world," Cohoma grumbled.

"Oh, come on, Jan! How could they have regressed so much in so short a time? The earliest colony ships only go back a few hundred years." She quieted. "I could swear I had that Born figured."

"There's another possibility, you know, Kimi," Cohoma ventured after a pause. He eyed her appraisingly. "Even someone like Losting, who doesn't like him, admits he's a smart boy. Maybe . . . maybe he's figuring on us bailing him out."

Logan looked at her companion curiously. "How do you mean?"

"Well, think a minute," he said, warming to the subject. "He's out there somewhere"—he gestured back through the palisade of sharpened stakes toward the other end of the village—"waiting for us to join him if the battle goes as badly as everyone expects. We circle clear as soon as the end is in sight. He joins us, we make it to the station, he gets that burning curiosity of his satisfied plus he saves his life."

"That would imply," she countered vociferously, "that he cares nothing for his Home or his friends. I don't believe that. I think the tie is as strong, if not stronger, in Born than in any of these folk. I could understand such an attitude in some soldier-of-fortune, the kind of gun for hire you might meet in the back streets of Drallar or LaLa or Repler, but not in Born."

Cohoma grinned. "I think you see a little too much of the noble savage in our stunted cousins. Our friend Born is just resourceful enough to make the break, just iconoclastic enough to—"

The first line of Akadi broke through the dense wall of green and all conversation died. The column measured seven or eight Akadi across and extended into the forest until it disappeared in verdure. They were packed body to body, so close that the front resembled a single monstrous snake, all woolly orange fur, clawed legs, weaving tentacles. Filtered green light shone on orbs like ebony cabochons, dark wells of unsapient malignance.

Tiny explosive pops sounded as the ring of carefully positioned hunters let loose with a dozen tank seeds. at once. The Akadi crumpled, tentacles and clawed legs digging in blind fury at the pricking thorns, chewing at themselves. Even before the frantic flailings of legs and tentacles ceased, the first row had been shoved aside and tumbled and bounced off branches and epiphytes into the depths below.

A metropolis of scavengers was going to form beneath this place, Cohoma reflected.

While the first dozen hunters reloaded, the second group fired and more Akadi died. Then the first fired, and the second reloaded. Such elementary tactics were only temporarily effective. It was like fighting the sea, wave upon wave, a living red-orange ocean of suckers and teeth moving forward as though squeezed from a tube.

As the lesser hunters slowed, the firing of the snufflers grew more erratic, less deadly. Now men and women armed with long lances of ironwood moved forward to stab and cut at the furry bodies. Others holding axes and clubs stood ready around the spearmen, prepared to fend off any Akadi that tried to escape the spears on either side, above or below.

The blood of the Akadi, Logan noted with the eye of a trained observer, was a dark dirty green, like thick pea soup with streaks of brown in it. The spears were more effective than she would have thought. Each time one of them moved, an Akadi died, clutching briefly with tentacles and claws until the lance was drawn free.

Logan had to admire the efforts of the tribe, primitive or not. While the hunters high in the branches used their snufflers to pick off as many of the attackers as possible, the forward rank of the Akadi army, reduced in strength, ran into the wall of spears, were punctured and cut, and plunged in a steady rain of corpses to a green grave.

The spirited defense would have worked but for one

overriding factor. There was an endless number of Akadi. The furry killers perished by the dozens, the hundreds. But the river of death never stopped, never slowed or rested, but bored steadily onward.

Eventually there would be a pause while a couple of the hunters waited for a fresh supply of thorns and tank seeds to be brought up to them. Now and then one of the spearmen would grow too tired to strike any longer and would have to be replaced by a reserve.

Then the Akadi would gain another few centimeters, would press the line of ironwood back a little further. Nor were casualties absent among the defending people. A man or woman might tire and slip on the never-too-certain footing of cubble and branch and would have to be helped back by companions. Another few centimeters lost, if not the defender.

Given an endless supply of jacari thorns and tank seeds, and inhuman reserves of strength, Cohoma estimated the tribe could continue to fight the Akadi with minimal losses. But they couldn't prevent the omnivores from gaining ground. Once a centimeter of footing was lost to the invaders, it could not be regained. That living torrent would not be forced back.

But the line held, held with the determination of churchmen. Those in the front rank who finally collapsed from exhaustion continued to be replaced. Yet, there were only so many fighters in the village, and now the replacements were growing fatigued as well. Occasionally an Akadi would slip under a faltering spear to grab a leg or arm with steely tentacles. Then an axeman would have to hurry to cut the monster away, for once having a grip they would let go only in death.

Steadily the little knot of humans was forced backward, back toward the tree-vines themselves which formed the natural and last line of defense for the Home-tree. Once through the pods, the Akadi would begin devouring the body of the tree itself. Then it would be only a matter of minutes before irreparable damage was done.

Logan knew what would happen. The villagers would throw everything into a final futile effort to push the Akadi back. For a moment, heads, and arms would rise above the writhing tentacles. Then all—men, women, children—would be engulfed by the unthinking mass, leaving the tree to perish despite their sacrifice.

The fighting raged continuously. It was not as noisy as a war between men would have been, but neither was it silent. Along the line of spearmen, men and women shouted encouragement to each other, defiance at their dog-sized tormentors, while the Akadi pressed blindly forward, chattering like a million castanets.

Slowly, grudgingly, the people gave way to the pressure of the untiring Akadi. The army was three or four meters from the first winding pod-vine when shouts traveled up and down the line of defenders. Logan recognized the voices of the shaman and the chiefs Sand and Joyla, that of Losting, and several other hunters. A sudden flurry of thorns from the snufflers held the Akadi for a moment while the line parted and fell to the sides. But the army did not pursue, so the living stream moved on, eating as it went. They began to gnaw at the nourishing bark of the tree, eager for the living wood beneath, as others rushed on to the first vines.

Cohoma felt a hand at his arm, saw one of the hunters pulling at him. The man's tone was urgent. He followed him into higher branches, Logan with them. Even as they ran, she turned to gaze over her shoulder as a shout rose behind them. She saw the big nuts dropping, to land and burst among the slithering line of Akadi. As they burst, a fine powder gushed forth. It shone iridescent in the light of the receding sun. The Akadi slowed, stopped, began to paw among themselves with legs and thrashing tentacles. They tumbled over and over on each other, fell and rolled on their backs, beating against one another, against the wood of the Home, in a sudden, inexplicable frenzy.

Cohoma found himself racing down toward the Akadi with others, stabbing with his spear, only to withdraw it and stab again. He was amazed at the ease with which it punctured the surprisingly soft bodies. Green blood covered his lance. Nearby he saw Logan stabbing and hacking with her own spear.

A violent pain stabbed through his ankle. Looking down he saw that one of the Akadi had somehow slipped clear of the re-formed line of spearmen and had locked three tentacles firmly around his leg. Multiple teeth were chewing at his lower calf. He tried to get his spear around, couldn't and found himself falling as his damaged leg gave way under him. Then something cut the creature between the second and third eye, pierced completely through the nightmare shape.

"Thanks, Kimi. Jesus, get it off me!" She stabbed again and green ichor squirted all over them, but the triangular teeth refused to relinquish their grip. Eventually she had to use an axe to cut the tentacles clear and then pry the jaws apart. Bright red circles covered his calf where the suckers had held. He had a steadily bleeding square wound in the back of the ankle. Using Logan as support, he limped clear of the fight. A small bottle of spray from their one survival kit stopped the bleeding. Coagulation set in immediately. A simple self-adhesive bandage was slapped into place.

"Didn't see where the bugger came from," he told her through clenched teeth. Sweat was standing out on his forehead and he wiped it off.

Logan studied the wound beneath the transparent bandage. "You're going to have a square scar. Going to be fun explaining that."

"I hope I have someone to explain it to . . ."

His words were drowned out by a roar that shook the Home-tree itself. The band of humans redoubled their efforts as they were joined by dozens of powerful green shapes.

A massive paw would rise and descend. Every time it did so, an Akadi would die, spine or skull crushed. For once the furcots roused themselves en masse from their daily sleep. For once their services were offered without consideration or discussion. The muscular hexapods wreaked havoc along the line of Akadi. Logan recognized Geeliwan, Losting's furcot, among them; but there was no sign of Ruumahum.

One enormous furcot rose up from the midst of the fray with several Akadi hanging from him, their tentacles seeking vainly for a vulnerable place in that thick fur, teeth snapping and biting futilely. A second furcot appeared alongside the first, began picking the furious Akadi off his companion's body, methodically crushing them.

Occasionally a furcot would be submerged by the stream, only to rise and dip like a breaching whale. However, thick fur, tough hide, and tremendous strength could not prevail forever against the untiring army. Every so often a furcot would disappear in the orange-red river of death and not rise again.

Then when it happened, it was unmistakable.

"Look!" Cohoma gasped at Logan for support and pointed. "They're turning back, retreating. They've been beaten!"

Indeed, the Akadi had ceased moving forward, were in fact moving backward, back into the tunnel they had eaten through the world. They took nothing with them, leaving their dead and dying behind and trampling the injured and maimed in their retreat.

Now the people of the Home, some too exhausted to move, watched as their more energetic comrades moved about with axes and clubs—carefully, lest they slip on the blood-soaked cubbles and branches—dispatching those of the killers too crippled to flee.

The furcots gathered to themselves, idly killing a still biting Akadi, licking and grooming each other's wounds. Some hunted through the branches and vines for those of the brethren who would no longer gather with them.

The exhilaration was temporary. Logan and Cohoma watched as the human survivors went among the legion of corpses, carefully searching among the mutilated and bleeding for any who still lived. Some were missing arms and legs, others heads or parts of same, while still others lay with their insides strewn over bright green leaves and blossoms, still beautiful in the last rays of the distant setting sun.

"By the Ordainments, they're a courageous bunch. It's almost enough to make me regret—"

"Shussh," Logan cautioned him, nodding at the big hunter walking toward them.

A series of square-edged gashes decorated one side

of his chest. Some had been crudely bandaged with long thin strips of a certain leaf. A snuffler rested loosely on his right arm and he carried a club in the other. There was hardly a centimeter of his body that was not covered with the tiny crimson circlets left by the probing suckers of the Akadi.

"You beat them . . . in spite of everything," Logan said, when it appeared the hunter was about to walk past them.

"Beat them?" Losting turned to stare wildly at them, and they recoiled at the naked blood-fury in his eyes. "Beat them—no. Do you think they stopped because of our efforts?" He hesitated. "We slowed them, true. It was a good fight. One I'd be proud to tell to my children. We slowed them enough to win the day . . . the day only. But stopped them, no. They stopped themselves."

"Stopped themselves!" Logan blurted in spite of herself.

"Look about you," Losting advised. "What do you see?"

Both giants turned their attention back to the battle-field. "Very little," Logan told him. "It's getting too dark."

"Yes, it is getting too dark. For the Akadi as well as us. They have stopped because the day is at its end. While the night-rain falls they will sleep, to rise again tomorrow and come on with as much determination as they did today. We have only so many jacari for the snufflers, only so much blood. I do not see us holding them for another night. But we will try. We would not have stopped them today but for the fur-cots—and for this."

He bent and reached down with the tip of the club, apparently slipping its flatter side under something. Logan and Cohoma leaned forward. At first they saw nothing. Then a last bit of daylight reflected off something tiny and bright as a jewel.

"That little thing?" she wondered, reaching forward with a thumb. "I can squash it like an ant."

Losting moved the club aside before she did just that. "I'm not fond of you giants, though you fought well enough this day. But I would not allow my worst enemy to touch the seed of the adderut." Rising, he looked around until he found a severed tentacle of a dead Akadi. He brought it back and laid it before them.

"Watch." He tilted the club, shook it gently. The tiny metallic-hued, multilegged thing slid onto the tentacle. As soon as it made contact it seemed to disappear.

Cohoma stared harder in the fast fading light. "Where'd it go?"

"Look hard."

Nothing happened. Then Cohoma thought he detected a slight swelling under the skin of the tentacle. Several minutes passed, during which the swelling became a bulge as big as a pebble, then a toe. Losting took out his knife and used it to touch the top of the bulge. The taut skin burst and a tiny purple ball popped out. It began rolling, rolling, toward the edge of the branch. He put out the club and stopped it, rolled it back. Cohoma and Logan could just see a tiny, many-legged spot near the base of the bloated globe—the original gemlike creature.

"That is the dust of the adderut," Losting explained. "When it bursts, it scatters millions of these," and he indicated the tiny bug. "If they touch wood or plant, nothing happens. But should they touch flesh, whether of man or furcot or Akadi, they burrow into it and . . . eat. Ah, how they eat!" This last was uttered with enough relish to make Logan slightly ill.

Cohoma was feeling none too well himself. This revelation was enough to make even an experienced, detached observer a little queasy.

"See," Losting suggested, nudging the purple ball with the edge of the club, "how it moves, tries to run. The flesh under the skin where it burrows is quickly softened and consumed by the dust-bug. When one of these scrambles clear of its host and falls to a soft plant, the legs bury in and become roots. The pulp contained in this gross obscene body turns green as it is converted into food. Eventually the sac bursts and a new adderut plant grows on a new host."

"Fascinating," admitted Logan, who was turning slightly green herself. She was enough of a scientist to hold on to her last meal. But someh̃ow this botanical marvel nauseated her in a way the day-long carnage had not. She could imagine several of them landing on her own body, digging in, eating. "Are they mobile little plants," she asked hurriedly, "or insects, or what?"

"Maybe a little of both," Cohoma suggested. "You've noticed the preponderance of green in animal life here—the furcots, the blood of the Akadi. I'm beginning to think, Kimi, that the usual clear-cut dividing line between plant and animal may not exist on this world."

"Even so," she replied, "this is one line of research I'll be glad to let somebody else pursue when we get back to the station."

Losting was not sure of the meaning of all their words. "True, they are dangerous things to fight with. One must work hard to emfol an adderut. If one should burst while being cut clear . . ." He didn't need to finish the thought.

"No wonder the Akadi column halted," Logan observed. "That whole forward section must have been literally eaten inside out in a couple of minutes." She looked nervously at the wooden ground they were standing on. "What happens to the millions of those things that didn't get anything to eat? Are we going to find them in bed tonight?"

Losting shook his head. "Their furious speed and energy is necessary, for those that fail to find sustenance immediately upon release die quickly. All will be dead before the sun is down. You need not fear them. Nor," he added regretfully, "need the Akadi. We have no more adderuts. They grow far apart and infrequently. Though I wish for a thousand now, I cannot honestly say this makes me sorry."

Logan stepped on the pulsating monstrosity. It burst, purple-green dye staining the wood of the branch.

They followed the hunter back into the village. "What happens tomorrow, then?" Logan asked. "Is it completely hopeless?"

"There is always hope till the last is dead," Losting reminded them. That did not seem encouraging to the giants. "We have our snufflers," he said as he hefted

101

the green wood weapon meaningfully, "and our spears and axes and our furcots. Then there are still the pollen-pods of the Home itself. After they are gone . . ." He shrugged. "I have my hands and my teeth."

He left them. Logan looked after him while Cohoma muttered, "That's great . . . commendable. I think we'll do better taking our chances—poor as they may be—in the forest. I don't feel quite so indebted to this noble tree." He looked around at the sheltering trunklets. "At least we'll die on the way home, not in defense of some stinking vegetable!"

Exhaustion had a single advantage. Sleep was no problem for even the most worried of the humans in the Home.

The last drops were still making their way down from the upper levels of the canopy as the tired tribe of humans once more prepared for the Akadi assault. Once again the hunters took up their positions high in the branches, snufflers ready, making quiet promises that each precious jacari would take an Akadi with it. When the toxic thorns were gone, they would lay snufflers aside and move down with axes and clubs to fight alongside their families. And once more the thin line of spearmen set themselves in defiant silence across the path along which the Akadi army would soon crawl—set themselves there knowing that those who should back them up now lay supine in the village, unmoving, asleep.

Cohoma and Logan took places well up in the curve of one of the major Home-tree branches. They would have an excellent view of the coming fight, be a little less anxious to throw themselves into battle. If Losting's pessimism was born out, they would work their way back into the village, gather what was available in the way of provisions, and circle around the Akadi column. Then they would strike off southwest by compass, toward the distant station. Maybe they would reach it, maybe not, but at least they would have their chance.

Logan thought she heard a distant, feathery rustling far back in the undergrowth. The Akadi were rising, shaking off the lethargy of night, getting ready to ravage and destroy and kill again.

The giants readied themselves, as did the snuffler-armed hunters. So did the line of spearmen and their covering axe-wielders. They had no scouts out to warn of the Akadi's approach. They were not needed. A few moments of advance warning meant nothing now. It was known where they would come from. Every man, woman, and child hefted a weapon and stared at the green hole in the forest.

Logan whispered to her partner, her knuckles around the shaft of the spear turning white. "Remember, if the tribe starts going under, we get out fast."

"What makes you think the vine barrier will open for us?"

"There'll be some last-ditch fighters going through. Remember, the vines are the tree's last line of defense. We can always grab a kid from the line and use him. Besides," she added coolly, "we've been eating the fruit from this tree for several days. We might have accumulated enough of the appropriate chemicals for the tree to recognize us, too."

The rustling increased, but it seemed at once louder and more distant. The noise was chilling. Could the Akadi experience anything as complex as anger, she wondered? Where they preparing themselves with some furious war cries and speeches? What kind of brains did those orange horrors possess? Did all thoughts fuse in a single mindless evil, or were they capable of emotions beyond desire for killing, eating, and sleep? She had no way of telling.

Long moments came and went, and the volume of distant castanetlike sounds neither diminished nor increased, was loud enough to drown out all other forest sounds. Those manning the line of spears before the green tunnel were showing signs of edginess now. The hunters in the branches shifted constantly, nervously into new positions. All the while the sun climbed higher in the green sky. And still that orifice of hell declined to reveal its multiple horror.

Then there was a definite, if slight, motion detected at the far end of the tunnel, and shouts sounded up

103

and down the line of defenders—shouts almost of relief. For it was the steady, nerve-breaking waiting that eroded the determination and broke the concentration of the hunters and spearmen and was worse by far than actual battle. However, there was no mass trembling in the herbaceous fronds fringing the tunnel's mouth, no swaying of branches under massed weight. A few leaves rustled lightly as the first shape became visible. But it was not the Akadi. A human shout came from the tunnel, rising above the maddening, distant din. A second shape appeared alongside the first, thick green fur matted with rain, triple eyes half-closed in sleep.

The hunters slid their snufflers off their shoulders and stared, their eyes widening in shock as Born and Ruumahum walked slowly out of the tunnel. Born's cautionary cry proved unnecessary. Everyone was too paralyzed to think of prematurely letting loose with a thorn. If the Akadi had rushed from the tunnel then, no one could have raised a hand against them.

Then there was a noisy, mass rush, and Born was surrounded by men and women, cursing and questioning him at once. Ruumahum loped off unnoticed. While the humans, including an excited and puzzled pair of giants clustered around Born, the furcot joined his silent brethren and commenced an explanation in his steady, grumbling tones.

"What happened . . . We thought you'd run . . . Where did you go . . . What of the Akadi . . . What of . . . ?" the persons asked Born.

"Please, could I have a drink?"

A container of water was passed up to him. Ignoring the continuous babble of questions, he put the wooden cylinder to his lips and drank long and deep. Then he turned it upside down and let the rest of the tepid liquid cascade over him.

A deep, commanding voice finally rose above the noise—that of shaman Reader. "Hunters, to your posts. Re-form your spear line, people of the Home! The Akadi—"

Born shook his head tiredly. "I don't think the Akadi will bother us again. Not for a long while, anyway." He smiled softly as a fresh wave of astonishment passed over the crowd. "The idea was mine, the stimulation came from Ruumahum's information." He gestured over to where the furcots were gathered. "He'd been out hunting, ranging far to the north. I don't know why, he isn't sure why, but he brought back word of what he'd found, and that prompted a thought in my mind. I thought it might work."

"What might work?" several people asked at once. "Why didn't you tell—"

"Why didn't you tell someone you were going, Born?" came the voice of Brightly Go. She pushed into the circle of people.

"Would it have mattered? There would have been loud objections, arguing, demands that I remain to lend my snuffler to the fighting. I would rather have you think me a coward and mad, and laugh at me. I'm used to being laughed at. If my scheme had not worked, nothing else would have mattered, would it?"

There was some uneasy shuffling among the assembled folk. Born had been respected in the village as the cleverest of hunters, and simultaneously derided as the maddest of thinkers. Now it seemed he might have produced a miracle, so there were some embarrassed stares.

"It was not far away, down on the mid-Fifth Level."

"What was?" Joyla boomed, her penetrating voice not to be ignored.

"A way of stopping the Akadi."

"Miracle or no miracle, this truly is madness," Reader thought aloud. "Nothing stops the Akadi—nothing!" His voice was adamant. "In my youth I saw a column rip apart a herd of grazers. The furcot cannot stand before them. It is said even the demons of the Lower Hell respect a wandering column." There were murmurs of respect from the crowd.

"What could you find, Born, on the Fifth Level, or any level, that could stop the Akadi?"

"Come, and I'll show you," he said, and he turned and started back down the tunnel. He had taken but a few steps when he realized no one was following. For the first time now, the exhaustion and effort of the past days was forgotten, and his face spread in a wide grin of satisfaction.

105

"Are you all afraid?"

Go into the tunnel? The tunnel from which the children of hell had poured only the evening before? On the word of a madman? It would take more than a little courage.

Losting was the first to step forward. He was as fearful as the rest, but he had no choice—Brightly Go stood there, watching. Then the crippled Jhelum followed, limping on his injured leg. Almost to the step, Reader and Sand and Joyla joined him. The little knot of humanity moved down the winding tunnel.

They walked down the green tube, its floor and walls and ceiling formed as if by a colossal drill. As they did so the noise of angry Akadi grew louder, loud to the point where one had to lean close to his neighbor and shout to be heard. There was a sharp bend in the tunnel, an unexpected bend unlike the usual paths of the Akadi. Born stopped and gave directions. A few chops with axes broke through the roof of saliva-cemented growth, and they emerged into the open forest again. Born beckoned them first upward, and then on again. Finally he went on ahead, alone, then returned with an admonition to the others to be silent and to follow.

After carefully and silently crawling among a thick twisted limb, they were staring down at an eldritch carnival, an orgiastic celebration of death unrivaled except in legend.

A second roofed-over tunnel, its faintly translucent ceiling snaking back many meters into distant forest, intersected the tunnel they had just come through. Where the two tunnels joined, Akadi precision and order had become chaos.

The Akadi column from the north and lower level was composed of slightly smaller, redder horrors. They had dark stripes encircling their abdomen. Where they met the first column the tunnels were shattered, spilling the combat into surrounding foliage. The battle raged over a great circle dozens of meters in diameter. Within that circle, nothing existed save stripped wood and dead, dying, fighting Akadi. Green blood drenched everything.

106

"Ruumahum found the column," Born told them softly. "And I had the thought. What could stop the Akadi, but the Akadi? We attacked before morning when they were sluggish and slow. We stayed within strong scent range and they followed. Now they will continue to fight till only a few of each column are left. These few will be too weak and disorganized to offer any threat to the Home. We can easily kill any who attack, and we have finished with not one, but two threats."

"But how did you get them here so fast?" Reader wondered.

"I was afraid I would not have enough powder, but Ruumahum continued to fetch more and more dry wood to keep the torches going. I stayed close enough to the lead Akadi to keep them awake. They followed and the others blindly followed them even in the dark. I have neither slept nor rested for two days and nights. I think," he finished, sitting down on the branch, "I had better rest now."

Joyla and Reader grabbed him as his completely drained body fell from the branch.

IX

Born opened his eyes, saw a monster Akadi staring down at him. He sat up like a bursting pod and blinked, rubbing at his eyes.

"About time you came around," Logan commented, stepping back from his mat. "You don't even recover slowly, do you?"

Born looked around. He was in one of the rooms in the chief's multi-chambered quarters. "You've been out," she added, "for about eighteen hours."

"Hours?" He eyed her questioningly, his mind still fuzzy with sleep.

"A day and a half, and I don't wonder, with what they tell me you went through."

Born had only one thought. "Have I missed the Longago—the burying time?"

Logan looked confused, stared back to where Cohoma was sitting and sharpening a knife. "You know anything about a burying time, Jan?" Her companion shook his head.

Born sat up and grabbed her by the shoulder of her blouse and nearly fell. The tough material didn't tear, supported him.

"No, Born," a strong voice replied. "You have preserved too many lives for us to proceed with the Longago without you. Now that you are returned to us, it can be done tonight."

"What's this Longago—some kind of ceremony?" Logan asked, glancing behind her toward Joyla, who stood in the portal.

"It is a returning. Those who were killed by the Akadi must be given back to the world." She looked over at Born. "There are many who must be returned. It has taken this long to find enough of They-Who-Keep to take so many. The boy Din is among them." Seeing the sudden change of expression that passed cloudlike over his visage, she suddenly became solicitous. "How do you feel now? You have slept long, and sometimes—"

"All right . . . I'm all right," Born mumbled, letting go his grip on Logan. He tried to stand, staggered slightly, then sat down hard on the woven mat and held his head in both hands. This did not keep it from spinning, but it helped.

"I'm hungry," he said abruptly. Since his head was proving uncooperative, he would concentrate on less intractable portions of his anatomy.

"There's food," Joyla said simply, beckoning him into the next room. "Do you need help to—"

"For half a Home fruit I would crawl on my belly, dragged by my nails," he answered. Moving slowly, he rose from the bed. Logan got out of his way. Still weaving, he walked unaided into the room from which a host of smells issued. Joyla held him steady on the other side.

"Mind you do not overload your roots with too much nourishment too soon," she advised him, and then she grinned. "Or I will have this room to clean yet again. And you will have to start afresh."

Born nodded without really hearing her. He stumbled into the room, where fruit, fresh meat, and preserved pulp was laid out in abundance on the eating mat. Joyla beckoned to Cohoma and Logan, indicating they might as well eat too.

"Thanks," Logan replied.

"You can watch him as he eats and restrain him."

"Why don't you?" Logan asked, as she sat down at the edge of the mat and selected a bright yellow gourd-shaped fruit with blue striping.

Joyla shook her head, studied Born, who was shoving food into his mouth at an appalling rate. "I have already eaten, and there is much to be done now that the Longago can proceed." Her smile became sad. "Tonight I will return many old friends to the forest, and a daughter as well." She started to say something else, reconsidered, and left through the leaf-leather curtain behind her.

Logan continued thinking on this Longago that now seemed of paramount importance to these people. She bit into the gourd, found it had a taste like sugared persimmon. How did Born's people dispose of their dead, anyway, with no earth to bury them in? Cremation, maybe, in the firepit at the village's center.

She said as much to Born. He mouthed contradictions through mouthfuls of food. "The earth? Would you offer up the souls of your own friends to hell? They will be returned to the world."

"Yes, Joyla mentioned that," she replied impatiently, "but what exactly does that mean?"

But Born had returned to his food. She continued to prod him, arguing that the rest between eating would do him good. Born still showed no inclination to talk, but the giant's constant pestering compelled him to satisfy her. "It is plain," he finally mumbled, "that you know nothing of what happens to people after they die. I cannot describe the Longago to you. You will see it tonight."

Born had demonstrated a remarkable ability to recover from a totally debilitating experience, Cohoma mused. He avoided a hump in the tuntangcle, hard to see by torchlight.

The tribe was leading them through one turn after another in the black forest. Well, this was the kind of strength you could expect from people who lived in as harsh an environment as Born's did. Only, such regression seemed impossible. He told Logan as much.

"These people," he said, with a nod at the marching column ahead and behind, "aren't that primitive. They're the descendants of some long-lost colony ship. Physically, except for those prehensile toes, they're as advanced as we are, but I don't see how their proportions could change so much in a few centuries." He stepped over a tiny dark flower growing in the tuntangcle. It held an explosive, poisonous spine. "In less than, oh, at the maximum, ten generations, they've lost a sixth of their size, developed those toes, undergone tremendous expansion of the latissimus dorsi and the pectoral muscles, acquired uniform coloration of skin, eyes, and hair. Evolution just doesn't work that fast!"

Logan merely smiled softly, gestured ahead. "That's fine, Jan. I agree. So, how do we explain this?"

"I refuse to believe it's parallel development. The differences are too minor."

"How about rapid mutation," Logan finally hypothesized, "induced by consumption of local chemicals in their foodstuffs?" She eyed an exquisite grouping of globular chartreuse fruit surrounded by lavender blooms.

"Possible," Cohoma finally conceded. "But the scale, and the speed—"

"Yes, that," Logan interrupted, "coupled with the need to adapt rapidly or die, could force some extraordinary physiological accommodations. The body is capable of some remarkable changes when survival is at stake. Though I admit this would be the most radical case ever discovered. Still"—she waved a hand leisurely at the forest—"if you'd seen some of the reports coming out of Tsing-ahn's or Celebes' labs . . ." She shook her head wonderingly.

110

"This planet is a googaplex of new forms, unusual molecular combinations, combination proteins. There are structures of local nucleic acids that defy conventional classification. And we've only scratched the surface of this forest, barely probed at the upper levels. We've no idea what the surface itself is like. But as we dig deeper, I'm sure we'll find—"

Cohoma silenced her. "I think something's going to happen."

They were approaching a brown wall, a monolithic trunk so vast as to belie its organic origin. Surely nothing so enormous could grow—it had to have been built.

The party was beginning to fan out along one of the big emergent's major branches, torches flashing umber off the meters-thick bark.

"The trunk must be thirty meters thick at this point," Logan whispered, impressed. "Wonder what it's like at the base." She raised her voice. "Born!"

The hunter turned from his place in the line of march and waited politely for them to catch up.

"What do you call this one?" She indicated the grandfather growth whose central bole was now behind them.

"It's true name is lost to the ages, Kimilogan. We call them They-Who-Keep, because they hold safe the souls of the people who die."

"Now I see," she declared. "I was wondering how you disposed of your dead, since you never descend to the surface, to the First Level. And I didn't think you'd hold to cremation."

Born looked confused. "Cremation?"

"Burning the bodies."

Any of Born's older associates, Reader, for example, or Sand, would have been openly shocked at this thought. But Born's mind did not work like those of his friends. He merely regarded the question thoughtfully. "I had not imagined such a possibility. Is that how you dispose of those among you who change?"

"If by change, you mean die," Cohoma responded, "yes, it is, sometimes."

"How strange," Born murmured, more to himself than to the giants. "We come of the world and believe

111

we should return to it. I guess there are those among you who are not of the world and therefore have nothing to return to."

"Couldn't have put it better myself, Born," Cohoma admitted.

They walked on in silence several minutes more, until the column began to spread out onto a slightly wider section of branch.

"We've come to the place?" Logan asked softly.

"One of the places," Born corrected. "Each has his place. A proper one must be found for every man." He looked upward, considered the black branches in the sky. "Come. You will see better from above."

After several moments of ascending the ever-present stairway of vines and lianas, they found themselves looking down on the wide section of branch below. Everyone was bunched tightly around a deep crack in the branch. It was several meters across and not many more long. The feeble light from the torches shielded against the rain made it impossible to tell how deep it went into the wood.

The shaman was murmuring words too fast and soft for either Logan or Cohoma to interpret. The assembled people listened in respectful silence. One of the men who had died fighting the Akadi and a dead furcot were brought forward from the heavily laden litters.

"They're buried together, then," Logan whispered.

Born studied her sadly, a great pity welling up in him. Poor giants! Sky-boats and other miraculous machines they might possess, but they were without the comfort of a furcot. Every man, every woman had a furcot who joined them soon after birth and went with them through life unto death. He could not imagine living without Ruumahum.

"What happens to those furcots whose masters die before they do?" Cohoma asked.

Born looked at him quizzically. "Ruumahum could not live without me, nor I without him," he explained to the attentive giants. "When half of one dies, the other half cannot long survive."

"I never heard of such a severe case of emotional

interdependence between man and animal," Logan muttered. "If we hadn't observed any sign of it, I'd probably suspect some kind of physical symbosis had developed here as well."

Their attention was diverted from this new discovery by the actions below. Sand and Reader were now pouring various smelly liquids over the two bodies, which had been lowered into the split in the branch.

"Some kind of sacred oil, or something," Cohoma ventured. But Logan hardly heard him. Emfol . . . mutual burial . . . half of oneself . . . Thoughts were spinning around and around in her head without forming any pattern, refusing to mesh, to reveal . . . what?

The furcots pining away for their dead masters she could understand. But for a man to die of loneliness for his animal, probably Cohoma was right. Born's people had been forced backward along the path of development by the sheer necessity to concentrate on surviving. This emotional entwining was a symptom of that sickness. One of the pounding thoughts swamping her brain suddenly demanded clarification.

"You said men and women," she whispered, staring downward. "Do furcots and people match up by sex?" Born looked puzzled. "You know, female furcots to women, male to male? Is Ruumahum a male?"

"I do not know," Born replied absently, involved in the ceremony playing to its conclusion below. "I never asked." As far as he was concerned, that was the end of the question. But it only stimulated Logan's curiosity further.

"And Losting's furcot, Geeliwan. Is it a she?"

"I do not know. Sometimes we say 'he,' sometimes 'she.' It matters not to a furcot. A furcot is of the brethren of furcots. That is sufficient for them and for us."

"Born, how do you tell whether a furcot is male or female?"

"Who knows, who cares?" This woman's persistence was irritating him.

"Has anyone ever seen furcots mating?"

"I have not. I cannot vouch for what others may have seen. I have never heard it discussed, nor have

I desire to discuss it. It is not meet, or seemly, some-how."

The thought suddenly went out of focus again. It was something to be pursued later. Her attention was directed downward once again. "What are they doing now, Born?" Leaves, humus, dead twigs, and succulents were heaped on the bodies, filling the crevice.

"The Keep must be sealed, of course, against predators."

"Naturally," Cohoma agreed approvingly. "The oils and mulch speed biological degradation as well as masking the odor of decomposition."

They studied the burial procedure while a steady chant rose from the assembly, oddly soaring and unlike a dirge. Reader made several passes with his hands over the tightly packed, filled crack, bowed once, then turned and walked toward the trunk, heading for an-other, slightly higher, branch. The rest of the tribe followed. They had many, many such interments to perform this night.

The subsequent burials grew repetitious, and the drenched Cohoma and Logan used the opportunity to study the design of seemingly crude torches, which burned steadily despite the unceasing rain.

Torches of slow-burning deadwood were cut and then treated with the ever-present incendiary pollen. The globular leaf of a certain plant was then punctured through, and the pulp inside cleaned out with a knife. This left a stiff-sided sphere about thirty centimeters in diameter. The sphere was then slid over the top of the torch and a small hole cut in the side. Contact with a finger through this hole served to ignite the powder and then the wood, while providing an exit for smoke and soot, although the wood appeared to burn almost smokeless. The tough fiber of the leaf was highly resistant to heat and flame.

The procession wound through the damp darkness like a chanting, glowing snake spotted with flickering dots of yellow-green iridescence. Everyone who could walk, from small children to some older than Sand, joined in that twisting, spiraling column. None com-plained, none argued when the column turned upward, none wished for a rest or return.

Something came out of the forest piercing the normal night-chitters and the lullaby of falling rain. Born came back to them. "Stay here with the column. Whatever happens, do not leave the light."

"Why not, what's—?" Logan began, but Born was already gone. The chlorophyllous sea swallowed him and the six-legged bulk that shadowed him.

They waited with the others in the rain. Then a great crashing and moaning sounded above the column and to the right, echoed by the sound of many voices. The moan rose in pitch, became a screeching, deep-throated laugh. It rose and fell in a succession of thunderous whoops.

It ended with a gurgling, choking sound. Something massive and distant fell to their right with the sound of shattering branches and torn vines. The light from the torches penetrated the forest only faintly.

Though given only the briefest glimpse of whatever had stumbled on the column in the dark, neither explorer had any desire for a closer look at that monstrous outline.

The crashing faded, dimmed, as the gigantic bulk vanished into the dark depths like a pebble down a dry well. There was no definite final crash. The breaking and tearing merely faded to a whisper, then a memory of a whisper, until the rain replaced it. Born returned to their side as the column started forward and up once more.

"What was it?" Cohoma asked softly. "We had only the faintest sight as it fell past." He was startled to notice that his hands were shaking. "Another species new to us." It made him feel better to see that not all of the moisture on Logan's brow had fallen from the sky.

"One of the big night-eaters," Born informed him, his eyes never straying from the coal-black walls on all sides of them. "A diverdaunt. They will not come near the Home because of the pods, but a man or two who meet one in the forest will not come Home. It was crossing our line, and hungry. Otherwise it would never have attacked. They are very powerful, but slow—no match for a band of hunters and furcots

115

this large." This last was uttered with an unmistakable hint of satisfaction.

"Couldn't we have waited till it went past?" Logan wondered.

Born was shocked. "This is a burial march. Nothing can be allowed to interrupt a burial march."

"Not even a nest of Akadi?" Cohoma murmured.

Born looked at him sharply, eyes flashing in the torchlight. "Why say that?"

"I'm evaluating your parameters," the research scout explained, knowing full well Born would have no idea what that meant, and reminding him that there were things not even a great hunter could understand.

Logan cursed silently at her partner's lack of tact, hurriedly asked, "I was just wondering how all these creatures came by their names, if they were originally classified by your ancestors?"

Born smiled, back on familiar ground. "When one is young, one asks. An adult points and says, that is a diverdaunt, or that an ohkeefer, or that the fruit of the malpase flower which is not good to eat."

"According to the reports of the first colonists trapped here," Cohoma muttered to Logan, "who were in no mood to engage in standard scientific classification. So the names that stuck were colloquial rather than generic."

Born heard this clearly; he heard everything when the giants engaged in their odd, secretive soft-speak. But as usual, he gave no indication that he had heard. It would have been impolite. Though there were many times when he wished he could *understand* more of what he heard.

The column continued onward. Once a series of spits and squeals sounded from directly above. Another time something that thrummed like an unmuffled navigational computer approached from below and to their left. Hunters were sent to ferret out the sources of these threatening sounds, but found nothing. The people were not attacked again.

Eventually the last who had fallen to the Akadi were returned to the world. The final words were chanted, the penultimate song sung.

They returned to the Home. By what method or

signs Born's folk found their way through the forest neither Logan or Cohoma could determine. And they were more relieved than they cared to admit when the first flowering vines with their multitude of pink blooms and leathery spore sacs came into view.

It was only later, when the entire troop had re-entered the comforting trunklets of the Home, when the last slow-burning torches had been extinguished, when the last leafleather curtain had been drawn tight, only then did muffled sobs and the lonely sounds of weeping become audible, held in check throughout the Longago. Night closed around the village, a moist black blanket, and brought the mindlessness and comfort of sleep.

So there were none to see the movement at the fringe of the trees, none to see the long shapes stir from apparent sleep to gather by the topmost curve of webbed branches.

A lazy cuff to the side of the head brought a sleeping cub awake and squalling. Triple pupils blinked in the near-absolute darkness. Ruumahum stood before Suv. On Muf's passing, this new cub had been assigned to his care. There was no twinge of regret, no lingering sadness at the death of the other. He was with his person, and that was the Law.

"Old one, what have I done?" Suv pleaded.

"Nothing, as you will doubtless continue to do." Ruumahum snorted and started to pad up toward the gathering place. The cub started to follow, stumbled over his middle legs, then got all six working together and shuffled along behind.

"Then what is it?"

"You will see. Be quiet for now, and learn."

Suv detected an unusual solemnity in his new old one's voice and decided that this truly was a time for cubs to keep tongue close to palate until otherwise instructed. Already he was used to this new elder, though not knowing the Law as well, he still felt an ache for Toocibel, who had died in the great fight.

When Ruumahum and Suv arrived, all were gathered. In a column of twos they filed out from the Home, moving through the hylaea with a stealth and silence that belied their bulk. Sensitive nocturnal carnivores on the hunt detected the mass movement and slinked near, till they smelled or saw what was pacing purposefully through the treepaths. Then they froze motionless, or crept away, or tried to become one with the forestscape until the column had passed.

Other meat-eaters in their lairs stirred at the noise of many feet moving and prepared to defend their territories and dens against whatever dared approach. A chance gust of nightwind rustled leaves and petals and brought the scent of furcot to flaring nostrils. Whatever their size or number or species, no matter how terrible, those who caught that pungent scent gave up their territories, their dens, and took themselves elsewhere. Occasionally a living cloud of luminescent flitters, all growing crimson and green and azure, would float down between the branches and cubbles to hover curiously over the column.

The furcots looked neither left nor right, nor up at the dancing motes performing their chromatic choreography. Now and then a flitter would dip close, brilliant wings flashing gemlike in the night. Colors would dance in triple cat-eyes.

A certain tree was reached, monarchical in size, a veritable goliath among local growths. But it was not its bulk which made it significant to the furcots, who arranged themselves according to age around a broad series of interlocking lianas.

Leehadoon, who was furcot to the person Sand, took the place in the center of the semicircle. He paused to meet eyes with each of the assembled brethren in turn. Then he threw back his head. From between machete-sharp canines and upthrust tusks came an unearthly sound that was part cry, part mewling, and part something undefinable in human terms. The rest of the group joined in without instruction—just as Suv and the other cubs were able to participate without knowing how or why, or the meaning of what they howled in the dark.

Most animals within range of that nerve-tingling caterwaul fled. But some crept near, curiosity overpowering fear, to stare and wonder animal thoughts at the rite that was at once old and new. It was different this time, more complex than Ruumahum or

Leehadoon or any could remember. It would be different the next time and the next, the chorus always building, growing toward some inexplicable, unimaginable end.

It was two days before sufficient supplies could be readied for the second attempt to reach the giants' station-Home. Two days to prepare for a death the Akadi had not achieved, most of Born's fellows believed.

He had proved himself thrice now in a span of time no longer than a child's dream. This did not alter the belief among his fellows of his madness. They thought, as Losting did, that there is a peculiar bravery that is part of insanity. Therefore they exhibited respect toward Born now—but not admiration. There is no recompense in admiring madness.

Born felt only their indifference, without sensing the attitude that provoked it, since none would admit their belief in his madness to his face. This made him madder, but in a different sense. So he sharpened axe and knife till it seemed there would be little left of either, and he thought private angry thoughts.

He had come back from the fight with the grazer. He had come back from the giants' sky-boat demon. He had come back from the Akadi. And he would come back from the giants' station and bring all the wonders they promised him! Maybe, maybe then, at last, Brightly Go would see daring and courage and intelligence whereas everyone else saw only madness; see that they were worth much more than bulk and strength.

Of all the hunters, only Losting, for his own peculiar reasons, would come with him still. Had Born not saved the lives of the others? True, they admitted, but all the more reason not to carelessly throw them away. Losting, then, whom Born could go without seeing for the necessary weeks or months of travel and be blissfully content, would accompany him. He was secretly glad of the aid the big hunter would provide, but publicly taunting.

"You think I go to my death. Then why come with me?" he sneered, knowing the reason full well.

"Some say the forest protects the mad. If so, it surely will save you. And I am as mad as you, for is not love a kind of madness?"

"If so, then we are surely both mad," Born agreed, tightening the clasp on his cloak. "And they have been right all along, and I am the maddest of the lot."

"Remember, Born, you'll not convince me to stay. I'll see you die or come back with you." He turned his attention to the two waiting giants, who were talking with the chief.

Both had consented to accept a present of water-repellent cloaks, though they still insisted unreasonably on wearing their own tattered clothing underneath. When Born argued the absurdity of retaining such fragments, they countered with their old argument of catching cold. That stopped Born, for who was to say what strange maladies might exist among the giants?

"They have learned much in the days they have lived among us," he observed, "though each is still as clumsy as a child. At least now they ask before touching, look before stepping."

"What do you think of them, Born?" Losting asked.

"We must watch constantly to see that they do not kill themselves before we reach their station-Home."

"Not that," Losting corrected. "I meant, do you like them as persons?"

Born shrugged. "They are very different. If all they claim is true, they can do us good. If not"—he made a noncommittal face—"it will be a tale to tell our grandchildren."

That simultaneously brought the picture of a certain young female to both minds. The conversation ended by mutual agreement. It would not do to begin a journey longer than any had ever made with fighting. There would be fighting enough in the world before they reached their goal. On that one thing, both were agreed.

Many in the village had come to see them off with good wishes and gifts of food, though none would meet Born's eyes. They had long since returned to the daily business of gathering food and caring for the Home.

So they took their leave of the Home, the chief

and one lone child watching them go. A fat ball of fur rocked near the child, the cub Suv. The sight reminded Born of another child, another cub, now returned to the world.

He turned his gaze outward.

The sky-boat had been equipped with a good Mark V ranger, new beacon tracker, tridee broadcast unit, and automatic beam-homing device. Now all this equipment was so much scrap, broken and twisted by gravity and by the sky-demon.

Logan took out the tiny black disk with the clear face and once more blessed whoever among their outfitters had seen fit to include the compass in their tiny boot survival packs. She hoped this planet possessed nothing in the way of magnetic abnormalities. At least, they had not been told of any. But then, skimmers were supposed to be foolproof, too.

Different variations on the same thought had occurred to Born. In that respect this journey was suicidal, for they had only the giants' word on where they were going. The possibility that they did not have a good idea of where their station lay was something he preferred not to think on. It did his spirits no good. Besides, he reasoned, if they did not have a fairly accurate idea, surely they would not have forsaken the safety and comfort of the Home on the wild chance that they would stumble across the station by searching at random. As to what might await Losting and himself on their arrival at the mysterious station, he did not know. Handling himself among new people was not a major concern at the moment.

Many days had passed since they had left the Home. Though it now lay many rests behind them, the emotion uppermost in Born's mind was neither homesickness nor apprehension of what might lie a-head. Rather, he felt a peculiar combination of tedium and tension—tedium arising from the day-to-day discovery that each new section of the world was identical to that which lay within throwing distance of the Home and tension from the inescapable feeling that tomorrow it might not be.

After the first seven-day the giants kept to them-

121

selves as much as possible, save for an occasional question whenever they encountered a plant or forest dweller new to them. That left Born with no one to talk to but Losting. Not surprisingly, the expedition proceeded with a dearth of jovial patter.

The hunters continued to regard each other with a mixture of hatred and respect. These cancelled each other out and kept the party operating on an even emotional keel. Both men knew that this was neither the time nor the place for a violent settlement of their differences. Mutual slaughter would have to wait until their glorious return.

As Born had predicted, the specially designed jungle-resistant fabric of the giants' clothing began to rot away under the steady assault of a forest which had failed to read the manufacturer's label. Cohoma and Logan were more grateful each day for the green cloaks they had been given. A good cloak offered its wearer concealment from enemies, and protection from the night-rain, served as bedding, and had a dozen and one other uses.

The giants grew more assured, more confident of their surroundings, as each new day came and went without incident. Considering their still incredible awkwardness in negotiating the treepaths, Born felt the little knot of humans had been exceptionally fortunate so far. The only serious encounter they had had could hardly have been predicted. It nearly cost them Logan.

"I'll be damned," she had remarked to her companion, pointing up and to their right. "Is that a patch of clear sky over there, or am I hallucinating?" Born and Losting were moving just ahead of them, and neither hunter was paying much attention to the giants' conversation.

Cohoma looked in the indicated direction. He saw what certainly looked like an oval section of blue sky streaked with fluffy white clouds. "Not unless we're both seeing things. Must be another hole in the forest, like the one our boat made coming down." They angled toward it.

At that moment Losting turned to make sure their charges were safe behind them. "Stop—this way!"

122

Born was slightly ahead of Losting. At the other's shout, he turned and immediately saw the cause of the hunter's concern.

"It's all right," Logan answered confidently. "I know about the sky-demons from first-hand experience." She shook her head, smiled. "We're too far down in the forest, and this hole's too narrow to let even the smallest flier descend. We're safe." She took another couple of steps along the broad cubble toward the ellipse of clear blue.

Losting yelled again and hurriedly tried to explain, even as both giants continued walking. Knowing the ineffectiveness of trying to argue with Cohoma and Logan, Born was already running toward them. As he jumped from branch to cubble, his snuffler clattering and banging against his back, he was fighting to untangle his axe from its belt loop. The two blind giants were almost to it now. He could see the slight rippling around the edges of the blue. The axe would be too late.

Fortunately, others had also detected the danger. Ruumahum and Geeliwan were there. Powerful jaws closed gently but firmly on tough cloak material. Another function of the multipurpose cape was abruptly demonstrated as the two furcots yanked backward in unison. Logan yelped. Cohoma's exclamation was more detailed.

Born had the axe out and ready just in case, as the two giants were dragged clear of the blue patch. The fluttering around the fringe of that broad blue circle matched the stuttering of his heart. Both quieted simultaneously. Thank the Home! An axe would not have been much good against a clouder, and he would have hated to depend on Losting's speed with a snuffler. Either way, the clouder would certainly have killed one if not both of the giants before the jacari poison could take effect.

Losting came up alongside him. The big hunter had his own axe out. Together they examined the oval section of sky and clouds, ignoring the two giants who were now struggling angrily to their feet. Ruumahum and Geeliwan had let loose their cloaks, but rested close by, watching. Born nodded to Ruuma-hum, once. The old furcot snorted and disappeared with Geeliwan into the brush.

The hunter studied Logan as she fought to remove her tangled cloak from between her legs. Her face was flushed.

"What's the harm in letting us have a look at the sky again, Born? Still afraid of sky-demons? Maybe it doesn't mean much to you, but we've had nothing over our heads but green for two weeks now. Just a glimpse of normal sky—even if it's a bit green-tinged—is a visual treat for us. To panic like this just because—"

"I would risk leaving you a look at your Upper Hell were we high enough for it," Born replied calmly.

"Well, this'll do since we're not. What's wrong with it? It's just another well in your world, a natural one, unlike the one we made when our skimmer fell."

Born shook his head. One must force oneself to be patient with these giants, he reminded himself. They could not emfol. "You see no sky and no clouds. That which you see is a clouder resting in killing mode. It was about to make a meal of both of you."

If the situation had not been so deadly serious, Born might have found Logan's expression amusing. She turned a confused gaze on the circle of "sky," examined the clouds drifting within it. She eyed Cohoma, who shrugged and looked blank. "Born, I don't understand. Is there some kind of animal that sits around such openings and waits for something to enter the open space? I don't see anything like that."

"There is no open space," Born elaborated carefully. "Watch."

They withdrew to a position behind some thick succulents and waited. Ten, twenty minutes of silence, at the end of which both giants were growing nervous and fidgety. At about the twenty-fifth minute a small brya—a four-footed, four-clawed herbivore about the size of a pig—wandered toward the patch of blue while rooting in the dense growth beneath it for edible aerial tubers.

Again Born detected the fluttering around the fringe of the sky, but didn't point it out to Cohoma and

Logan. He didn't have to—they saw it for themselves.

The brya wandered into the space beneath the sky. When it was in the exact center, the sky fell, clouds and all. The quivering clouder resembled a thick mattress lined on its edges with hundreds of cilia. It literally enveloped the brya, which squealed only once. The clouder moved jerkily for a minute or two, then relaxed.

Five minutes later the fringe of tentacles or cilia extended. The clouder climbed back up to its nesting place, stripping the surrounding vegetation in the process to keep plenty of clear space beneath it. It settled into place once more, four meters above the nearest growth. It was pebbled and green on top. Its underside was shaded so much like a section of sky speckled with clouds that Logan had to blink to make sure it had really moved. A few bones, too tough for even the clouder's supremely efficient digestive juices, were carefully thrown clear once excreted.

"Camouflage, yes. Protective mimicry, yes," Logan whispered. "But a carnivore that imitates the sky—"

Cohoma was equally awed, especially when he considered he might easily have gone the way of the brya had not the furcots intervened.

Born sighed and turned to lead on. "I am not sure what that means, but the sky is the sky and a clouder is a clouder. Walk under the last and soon see nothing." He started back down the cubble. A suitably chastized Logan and Cohoma followed, looking uneasily to their right as they passed the innocent-seeming circle of blue and white.

"Just when you think you've got this ecosystem figured," Cohoma mumbled, "got the predators and the prey identified and cataloged, something like that nearly snaps your head off. Carnivores that imitate the sky! Next thing you know, Born'll be warning us about something that imitates nothing!"

Three days later they encountered the palinglass and again barely escaped being consumed.

Weeks had passed. Many nights later they secured an especially good camp in the hollow of a Pillar branch. The wood-walled cave was more than large enough to accommodate all six of them comfortably, if it was unoccupied.

Born and Losting motioned for the two giants to stay behind when they first saw the orifice. They then approached the cavernous scar cautiously, loaded snufflers held ready. It seemed unlikely that such a fine, solid shelter, so spacious, would be devoid of life.

Such was the case, however. Neither Ruumahum or Geeliwan had detected any scent. When the hunters entered the hollow, they found only very old droppings, and more deadwood than they could use in a hundred fires.

That night a lavish blaze illumined the interior of the branch, reflecting off dark nodules and twisted stalactites of cracked wood and bark. Born studied the giants. Under the soothing effect of the fire and the excellent shelter, he felt more inclined to talk than he had for many days.

"I have almost come to believe that you truly come from a world other than this, Kimilogan." Cohoma's expression didn't change, but Logan appeared pleased.

"That's a big step, Born, and an important one. I'm not surprised, though, that you made it. You're obviously the most perceptive of your people, and the most receptive to change, to new ideas. That's going to be very important." She stirred the coals nearest her with a twisted stick, listened to the ever-steady trickle of night-water outside. "You know, Born, when you and your people and the other tribes here rejoin the family of man they're going to need someone to speak for them with our company." She glanced up at him evenly. "I can't think of a better candidate than yourself. With what you've already done for the company in rescuing Jan and myself, I don't see how you can help but be chosen. Such a position would be very advantageous for you."

Losting listened to this and said nothing. His respect for Born's cleverness was as great as his dislike for his person. He snuggled back against Geeliwan and listened to what Born, not the giants, had to say.

"The world you say you come from does not sound

126

very inviting," Born replied, and then held up a quieting hand as Cohoma seemed ready to object, "but that is a matter of personal choice. Clearly you feel much the same way toward this world. That is of no matter." He paused thoughtfully, leaned forward to lend emphasis to his next words. "What I wish to know is—if you are so satisfied with your own world and the others you say exist, why come with much trouble and difficulty to this one?" Suddenly, his face shadowed by the firelight, the hunter did not look quite so primitive.

Cohoma and Logan exchanged glances. "Two reasons, Born," she finally replied. "One is simple to understand; the other . . . well, I think you will, in time. I don't know if chief Sand or Reader the shaman would." She toyed with the stick, flicked a glowing coal outward into the rain-drenched edge of the cave. It hissed as the tepid drops struck it. "It has to do with the acquisition of something called money, which in turn has to do with commerce. All will be made clear to you at the station. Once you understand your own special position regarding it, you'll see why I'm reluctant to go into details just yet. All I will say is that you—and your people—will benefit considerably, just as Jan and I and our friends will.

"The other thing is lesser for some men, more important for others—curiosity. The same thing that drove you to descend to find out what our skimmer really was. The same thing that's driving you, against your better judgment, against the advice of all your friends, to try and return us safely to our station. It's the same thing that's carried mankind and the thranx from star to star—curiosity, and the other thing."

"What are thranx?" Born asked.

"Some folk I think you'd like, Born." She stared out at the darkness. "And who'd like this world very much, more so than my people."

"Are there any of these thranx at your station?" Losting suddenly asked.

"No. None are a part of our"—she hesitated—"company, or group, organization, tribe, if you will." She smiled brightly. "Everything will become much clearer when we reach the station."

"I'm certain it will," Born mused agreeably, staring into the dancing flames.

Later, as he rolled himself up in his cloak and over into the softly snoring bulk of Ruumahum, he wondered if he would. He also wondered if he wanted to.

X

No one knows how silently a big animal can move until an adult furcot has unexpectedly padded up close to him. Ruumahum moved that way when the odor woke him, rising so muffled-ear quiet even Born, lightest of sleepers, failed to awake. The aroma came from outside and above, so heavy with its distinctive musk it penetrated down through two levels and the still falling rain. Geeliwan stirred in sleep as Ruumahum padded to the front of the cavern. He stuck his head outside, stared upward with triple piercing eyes, which blinked frequently against the stinging rain.

The smell was unmistakable, but there was no harm in making sure. He gripped the wood with forelegs, followed with the middle pair and then the hind, and swung out onto the side of the trunk. Close-bunched leg muscles worked in unison as he clawed his way up the trunk. It was harder than finding a spiraling path in the thick vegetation, but time was important if his suspicion was correct. The hair behind his ears bristled as the threatening miasma grew stronger and stronger. Few sensory impressions can raise the hackles of a furcot. Ruumahum was absorbing one of them now.

The long vertical climb was tiring, even for him. Then he saw it, still far above, but moving steadily downward, and he knew why their excellent shelter had been empty: This was a silverslith's tree.

It had their scent, that was certain. They were already dead, unless the persons could devise a new thing. Turning, he rushed back down through branches and vines, eating up the meters with prodigious plunges and leaps. He was making enough noise to rouse every night prowler nearby, which was the idea. Perhaps one would be foolish enough to investigate. The temporary snack might divert the silverslith for a few precious minutes.

They had little time. The silverslith was moving slowly, deliberately, playing with its intended prey. And the giants would slow them further. He burst into the cave noisily enough to wake Born and Losting instantly. Geeliwan gave a warning growl, relaxed at the familiar smell.

Ruumahum stood panting before them, wet fur glistening in the glow from the coals. "Wake others," he puffed. While Losting moved to rouse the giants, Ruumahum whispered something in the talk of furcots, which prompted Geeliwan to hurry to the cave entrance. He stationed himself there, staring upward.

"What's going on? What is it now?" Cohoma grumbled sleepily as Losting shook him. Logan had already moved to a sitting position and waited to be told.

"We must leave here immediately," Born told them. He fastened his cloak more tightly at his neck, moved to gather his few things. Losting was doing likewise. "This is a silverslith's tree. It explains why we did not have to fight for this shelter. It is shunned, as we should have shunned it. There was no reason to suspect, none. I feel no better for it, though."

"All right," Logan asked tiredly, "another pesty beast. What's a silverslith, Born, and what can we do about it?"

"Leave," he replied tightly, using a thick fragment of wood to push the glowing embers from the fire toward the cave mouth. The rain would put them safely out.

"In the middle of the night?"

"The silverslith dictates this, not I, Kimilogan. We can only run and weave, weave and run. There is a chance it will tire and leave us."

"Something that will follow us, like the Akadi?" Co-

129

homa wondered. The seriousness of the situation had finally penetrated his sleep-numbed brain.

"No, not like the Akadi. Compared to the silver-slith, the mind of the Akadi is as changeable as . . . as"—he fumbled for a suitable analogy—"the desires of a woman. Once having the scent of one who has invaded its tree, the silverslith will follow till the invader is eaten. Nor can it be outrun like the Akadi. And unlike the Akadi, it does not sleep."

"Now that's got to be legend," Cohoma insisted, fumbling with his cloak. "There's no such thing as a warm-blooded creature that doesn't sleep, and only a few cold-blooded ones can go without rest."

"I do not know the temperature of its blood," Born commented, moving toward the cave mouth, "nor even if it has blood. No one has ever seen a silver-slith bleed. I will not banter with you now." Oddly enough, he grinned. "When you are tired from running, I suggest you stop for a nap and see what wakes you in the night."

"Okay, we believe you," Logan confessed, trying to arrange her clothes. "We've got to, after what we've seen. A creature whose living cycle runs in weeks instead of days. So many weeks of wakefulness, so many weeks of sleep."

"The silverslith does not sleep," Born reiterated forcefully. Deciding it was useless to argue with those who refused to accept the truth, he finally made a curt gesture to them to follow.

Losting had prepared torches, bundles of torches. But they still had to locate the globular leaves that would shield the flame from the rain, and there was no time to look. They had to get away from the tree. Hopefully they would encounter some of the fairly common growths along the way. Until then they would be forced to make their way in darkness.

"Quickly," Ruumahum growled with furcot impatience. "It senses us."

"Geeliwan!" Losting whispered. The furcot moved to the nearest liana, jumped from it to a lower branch growing from another tree, down to another and another. Then it looked back up, eyes gleaming in

130

the night. They would be the only beacons they had in the forest.

Losting went next, followed by Cohoma. Logan looked back up at Born as she was about to move to the liana. "I thought it was too dangerous to travel at night?"

"It is," he admitted, "but it is death to stay here."

She nodded. "Just wanted to make sure this wasn't some kind of test," she replied cryptically, turning and moving from liana to branch.

Born hesitated long enough to murmur to Ruumahum as the furcot stared upward into the rain. "How much time?"

"It will search every niche of cave. Then follow."

"Any chance we could fight it, old friend?" Ruumahum snorted.

"Born dreams. Fight silverslith? Not even silverslith-young." His gaze went upward again. "Not young. Old one, big. Very big."

Born grunted noncommittally, glanced upward. He had another new thought. It was a frightening thought, but nothing else offered itself in substitution, and there was no time for detailed speculation. They could probably stay ahead of the silverslith. But they could not run away and leave it, nor could they shake it from their trail, or fight it. Eventually fatigue would slow them, stop them, and the untiring killer would finish them at its leisure. Still reluctant to propose the thought, he moved rapidly with the others away from the tree.

They had been traveling for some time when faint thunder boomed across the forest from somewhere behind them. It was caused by an abrupt displacement of air, but its source was not electrical in nature.

"It has discovered our absence," Born explained to Logan, in response to the unvoiced question. "It will spend a few minutes voicing its rage and then come after."

"Tell me, Born," she asked, struggling to stay behind the vague shape of Losting working his way through the dense growth, "if a silverslith never gives up till its quarry is killed, how do you know so much

131

about its habits, and what it looks like? You do know what it looks like?"

The giant was wasting too much energy on talk. Ever polite, he responded, "There are tales of a party of twenty or thirty being attacked by one. They scattered in as many directions. Not even a silverslith could follow every scent to its source before some had faded. A few survived to tell of the monster."

"You're saying not even twenty or thirty of you . . ."

"And as many furcots."

". . . and their furcots could fight one of these things?"

"Too big, too strong," Born told her.

"I thought your jacari poison would kill anything."

"Silverslith skin is too thick," he explained. "Also, jacari poison works on . . . on"—he searched his memory for the ancient term—"the nervous system."

"Then why wouldn't it affect a silverslith?" Cohoma asked. "It's got to have some vulnerable points."

"When it comes, you show me," Born muttered. "Anyway, silverslith has no nervous system, the tale says."

Logan's willingness to credit the creature with the ability to go long periods without rest or sleep did not extend this far. "Oh, come on, Born," she said with the confidence of superior knowledge, "every animal has a nervous system."

"Has it?"

"An animal couldn't live without a nervous system, Born."

"Couldn't it?"

"At the very least," she added, "it must have some kind of rudimentary brain and central locomotor system."

"Must it?"

She gave up. Cohoma hadn't paid much attention. He was still musing on the fact that this thing pursuing them could put thirty furcots to flight.

"Look, how much of this is true and how much of it has been embroidered by the survivors of that attacked party? Naturally they'd want to make out the invulnerability of anything that forced them to run."

Born was about to reply, but Ruumahum interrupted him. It was unusual for a furcot to break into a conversation between persons. Ruumahum did so to keep Born's adrenalin level low until more energy was needed later. "Silverslith tree," he growled softly, "only thing in world Akadi change march-path for. Big persons shut up now and watch own path."

That information was enough to cause Logan and Cohoma to overlook the fact that they had been given an order by an overgrown pet. They pondered it as they hurried on in silence.

Meanwhile Born continued to turn his earlier thought over and over in his head. He tried to argue his way out of it; it held him tight as a grazer's arm. He tried to avoid it; it stood firmly in the way of his thoughts like the silverslith's Pillar-tree. Temporarily he managed to forget it by cursing himself for failing to recognize the tree for what it was. That huge, dry, inviting shelter, so empty, so shunned. Fool! "Fool's fool!" he muttered aloud.

"And I with you," Losting muttered nearby, but Born hardly heard him.

"Don't berate yourself, Born. You said there was no way of telling what it was," Logan told him.

"No. If it had been lower, Ruumahum would have scented it. But it was far, far up the trunk, near the very top probably, hell-hunting."

"Hell-hunting?"

"Fishing the night sky for air-demons," he explained. "Reaching up to pull down fliers at the treetops, like the one that attacked your skimmer when it fell."

"Oh," she murmured. Another sobering thought.

"It did not sense us till it started downward. That's when Ruumahum smelled it."

They finally found the globular leaves growing to one side of their treepath. Geeliwan saw them, moved with Ruumahum to stand watch while Born and Losting cut and prepared several. Though if the silverslith attacked, they could give the humans only a couple of extra minutes.

A little of the fire pollen and they had real light again. It cheered Cohoma and Logan. At least they

133

could see where they were stepping now. At the same time, Logan expressed a new worry to Born. "Won't these make us easier to see for any other local predators?"

"It does not matter now. The silverslith is too close. No other creature of the night will come near, having scented it. They will run, too. Have you noticed the silence?"

Logan listened and knew what Born meant. The usual night sounds, the normal whistles and clicks, beepings and hums interspersed with an occasional deep-throated roar, were missing. Only the constant drip, drip of the rain remained, punctuated by a wandering wisp of lost wind. They hurried on in eerie silence.

"It nears," Ruumahum soon rasped. "Slowly, but it nears."

"I'm sorry, I'm sorry, Born," Logan said at the same time, gasping, fighting for breath. "I can't keep this up. I don't know which'll go first, my eyes or my legs."

"Then," Born said, sighing heavily, making the decision he had been putting off for hours, "it is better to start now."

"Start where?" The query came from Losting.

"Down . . . to the other levels."

Neither Losting nor the giants cared if the monstrous apparition now close on their trail heard their shouts and yells.

"What's the good of descending to another level?"

"We'll only lose the daylight when it comes."

"The silverslith will follow us easily," Losting added. "Follow us forever. You know that, Born."

Born looked at his ally and rival. "Even to Hell?"

That was the first and last time either Cohoma or Logan ever heard a furcot produce anything like a startled grunt. Losting was too stunned to reply as Born continued.

"I will not stay to argue with you, Losting, or with any of you. I am going down to the Seventh Level, if the silverslith still follows. Down to whatever is there."

"Death is there," Geeliwan sighed.

134

"Death to wait here, sleek friend," Born reminded. He looked ahead to Losting again. "We know what the silverslith will do when it catches us. At the very least, we may find a new way to die."

"Born, you said yourself that to go to the Lower Hell, the surface, was certain death," Logan said softly.

"Less certain than to stay here. Maybe the silverslith will not follow, for it lives here near the top of the world. It may live equally well among its relations at its bottom, but we do not know that. I think it is a chance, at least. I will not try to force any of you to come with me."

He would do what he thought best, assuming the others would see the wisdom of his ways and follow him. That was what he had always done. It worked now as he began the slow descent to depths unseen, plunging into even blacker, more ominous darkness.

They followed, all of them, but not out of respect for his greater wisdom, as he thought. They followed because in a crisis, uncertain people will follow whatever leader declares himself. In that respect Losting proved himself as human as Logan or Cohoma.

Cubbles and lianas came and went. Downward-sloping tree branches, parasitic growths the size of sequoias and greater passed and were left behind. One such tree sprouted a thousand thick air-roots all entwined. They used them to drop with greater speed for many meters. They left the Fifth Level behind and entered the Sixth, moving into a region of brown and white and purple growths that started crowding out the green.

Then they were through the center of the Sixth, then through its bottom, to emerge into a ghost world. A world feebly lit by torchlight that seemed to huddle close to its parent wood in fear. A world of Pillar-tree bases with boles as big around as starships. Buttresses, multibladed and massive, rose on all sides. There were glowing fungi the size of storerooms, which thrived and grew in a riotous profusion of obscene, grotesque shapes. Small glowing things crawled in and among them and hid from their torchlight.

135

Here there was no morning and no evening, no day and no night—only a perpetual darkness that belonged neither to the sun or the moon. Even though the phosphorescent fungi and their twisted relatives gave enough light to see by, the torches were kept lit. It was a cleaner, purer radiance than what shone here. Yellow and red and white light issued from around them, a ghostly, ethereal evanescence, which suggested outlines rather than whole forms, hinted rather than described.

At last they came to a stop at the base of one ridge-backed buttress, the final stairway to the surface. A cluster of orange saplinglike growths grew here—things that would never know the internal logic-magic of photosynthesis. They had surely reached the ground, the Seventh Level, Lower Hell itself. Yet, there seemed even here to be another level below, for nearby the ground turned soft, sticky and wet, thicker than water, thinner than mud.

Logan turned, breathing painfully, and stared back up the way they had come. The buttress behind her was like a dark brown-black cliff. Above it she could detect only darkness and the faint glow of distant fungi. There was nothing to indicate that a couple of hundred meters above them was a world of light and green life that pulsed and rustled with wind and rain.

It was humid here to the point of suffocation, though only an occasional persistent droplet from the still falling night-rain penetrated this far. The rest had been absorbed or caught high above by a thousand million bromeliads or other water-holding plants. The rare drop was a reminder that they had not died, that a living green world still existed above this dark place.

Born also turned his gaze upward along the face of the wood, solid as granite. "Ruumahum?"

"It comes still," the furcot muttered after testing the air. "But slower, much slower, even cautiously."

"We have no time for caution." He turned to Logan and Cohoma, indicated the swampy morass which spread around their tiny, dry peninsula. "I know nothing of footing like this. Yet we must leave this spot before the silverslith's fury overcomes its care."

Long moments, precious moments, came and went while all four humans considered the problem. Logan found herself running a hand up and down the side of one of the orange trunks that flared from where the buttress of the great tree entered the water. More than anything else they resembled bright red-orange reeds, though they surely were no member of the reed family.

She took out her bone knife and tried the material. It cut, but not easily. The fiber was dense, not pulpy or water-filled, but they had axes. "Born, see if you can locate something that would serve as cord. Some kind of vine or something. I think these will make a decent raft—a machine for traveling on the water— if we stack them crossways two deep."

They worked so fast it was a wonder no one lost an arm or leg in the building. As each orange bole was felled, it exuded a thick odor redolent of stale onion. Construction proceeded apace when Born and Ruumahum returned with loops and loops of some sticky, gray waterplant coiled around themselves.

Logan and Cohoma laid and held the "logs" and instructed Born and Losting on how and where to set the ties. All the while, Ruumahum and Geeliwan kept watch on a ridge above.

Their periodic guttural warnings, shouted down from high up on the buttress, indicated that the silverslith was still moving and with that same unnatural slowness. It did not occur to anyone to wonder at the monster's caution.

It did, however, occur to Logan suddenly to ask, "Born, we didn't ask permission, emfol, whatever, of these, did we? Isn't that against your religion, or moral stance, or something?" She indicated the felled logs.

"They are not of the forest, of my world." He looked disgusted. "They are a kind of life I feel only distantly akin too. I cannot emfol with them. There is nothing to emfol with."

"It's finished," Cohoma announced loudly, forcing Logan to stifle further questions. Fascinating as this still unresolved thing called emfoling was, survival was more important.

A shout drifted down to them. "Quickly, Born!" Ruumahum again. "It sees us. It comes fast now."

Seconds later, it seemed, both furcots had rejoined them at the base of the buttress. The hair was erect on their necks, and they glanced continually upward. Logan stared up also, as did Cohoma, but as yet there was nothing to be seen. Their meager equipment thrown aboard, the two furcots climbed on. At least there was no space problem. The raft was big enough to hold twice as many men and furcots. Cohoma, Born, Logan, and Losting all shoved, lifted and shoved. The raft refused to budge.

"Ruumahum, Geeliwan," Cohoma directed, "move to the far end of the raft a little!" The furcots did so, and this time when the humans shoved, the raft slid cleanly into the brown sludge.

The first thing Cohoma did was test the depth of the muck. The split section of tapering reed disappeared until his fist was immersed. They would not be wading through this.

The thick liquid made for slow paddling, but by the same token, it also helped support the makeshift raft. Everyone pushed furiously, their progress hampered initially by Losting and Born's ignorance of paddle mechanics. But they learned quickly. With increasing speed they made their way out a considerable distance from the shore.

Above them the black sky arched high overhead. It was like rowing silently through some unimaginably vast, dark cathedral. The vegetation growing on the little patches of dry earth and on the trunks of dead or living trees was dense, but there was no furious desire to reach for open space here, since there was no need to compete for the sun.

"Where's the tree we came down?" Logan asked. She squinted back the way she thought they had come. Everything beyond a certain distance looked the same, since the light from the glowing fungi did not reach very far. Then she saw the thing and knew which bole it was they had come down, and what a silverslith was, and she screamed.

It stopped when it reached the base of the buttress —at least the front part of it stopped there. The rest of it extended back up the tree, up and up into the blackness beyond for an unknown distance. Its body was a fifth as big around as the Pillar-tree itself. It looked like an animated forest, its cylindrical body bristling with thousands of independently writhing cilia the color of polished antimony. They reached and clutched at the air. The head was a bloated horror, a creation of an aberrant nature. Numerous pulsating mouths dotted the globular head, gray teeth sprouting in every direction. Tentacles grew around the mouths seemingly at random, and the whole nauseating visage was liberally pockmarked with featureless black blots that may have been eyes.

It uttered low mewling sounds, incongruously soft. These rose and shifted to a high, piping titter that sent icy chills through Cohoma and Logan. The head alone stretched out many meters over the water. It swung slowly from side to side as if it were smelling the surface. Then the head lifted. Though those black orbs went in all directions, it felt to Cohoma as if it were staring directly at them.

"Oh, my god, my god," Logan croaked. "It's seen us."

"Not like this . . . not this way," Cohoma was moaning.

"Be quiet and—what do you call it—paddle!" Born growled through clenched teeth, though he was as frightened as the giants, and fresh sweat dropped from his forehead.

They had gained real distance on the raft and were well out on the water. But the silverslith had pursued them into Hell itself. Born sensed that it was not about to be deprived of its prey.

It reached out for them, mewling loudly. More of that seemingly endless body flowed in humping motions down the Pillar trunk and along the buttress, and still the tail was not visible. It was not yet trying to swim. Instead it was stretching to the left, reaching for the buttress of the next major growth.

Born saw with despair that by moving in this fashion, it would soon be able to pluck them from the false safety of the raft without ever having to touch water. Losting saw it too, and together the hunters began a frantic search for a crevice, a crack in the base of one of the enormous boles where they might hide, though such was the strength of the silverslith that it would rip even those huge boles apart to get at them.

A faint rushing noise sounded behind them, like a child stepping into a vat of grazer lard. Then the water erupted, vomiting forth a colossal, soulless shape so vast it could not be believed. The thing occupied the whole broad basin of open water they had just crossed.

The behemoth ignored them just as Born would ignore a leaf falling on his head in the forest. They were not worth bothering with. Long multijointed legs with claws the size of small trees shot out and hooked around the stretching form of the silverslith. A single eye bigger than the giants' skimmer flashed for a merciful instant between those taloned legs. What they could see of its body, where it emerged from the water, was a mad hybrid of the sacred and the profane. For it was encrusted with jewels—emeralds and sapphires, topaz and tormaline, set in weaving patterns of natural luminescence. It was overpoweringly beautiful, awesome, terrifying.

Everyone fell and held tightly to the orange logs and gray lashings as the raft began to rock, caught in the turbulence spawned by that titanic battle. Born knew nothing of swimming and tried to conceive of breathing water. He decided he would rather be eaten.

Hours later, it seemed, the rocking finally subsided. When Born was able to raise his head, the first thing he saw was Ruumahum and Geeliwan standing side by side at the rear of the raft. The furcots were staring at the water behind them. Born struggled to his knees. There was nothing behind them now but silence —silence and the far-off shining shapes of distorted fungi and lichens lit by their own cold, internal light. And distantly, a soft bubbling sound, which a child might have made by blowing into water. Of the silverslith and the hell-born that had come to meet it, there was no sign.

Logan sat up, emotionally and physically exhausted. She wiped the hair out of her eyes and tried to get her heartbeat under control, with little success. Born watched her for a moment, found his paddle where he had shoved it between two logs, and then resumed paddling.

"Which way, Jancohoma?" he asked. There was no reply. "Jancohoma, which way?" he repeated, more loudly.

Cohoma pulled out the compass, found his hand was shaking too badly to take a reading. He grabbed his right wrist with his left hand and stared at the luminous face. "Better . . . better turn us a little to the right here, Born. A little more . . . more . . . Losting, don't you paddle yet. There, now paddle together."

They forced themselves not to think of what they might be paddling over, of what a touch of the paddle might stir to wakefulness. They were almost too tired to care.

Logan leaned back, lay down on the smelly logs and stared up at a tiny universe formed by glowing mushroomlike things growing upside down from the bottom of a major branch high above. "You wouldn't think hell could be so beautiful." Her expression twisted, and she suddenly looked over her shoulder at Cohoma. He sat behind her, his head between his arms, and he was shaking. "Jan, if we meet another raft, let's ask its pilot directions, even if he's got a three-headed dog with him."

"I don't like dogs," Cohoma replied flatly. From his tone, one might almost believe he took the suggestion seriously.

There was no sunrise to bring peace to the tiny knot of humans and furcots who rode the orange speck between wooden towers, beneath a black sky speckled with pseudostars. On what should have been the morning of the following day they were attacked twice in the space of fifteen minutes. They saw nothing till they were set upon. Fortunately, neither of the creatures was bigger than a man. They encountered nothing which approached the size of the armored colossus which had attacked the silverslith.

The first assault came from the air, in the form of a four-winged flier equipped with a long mouth full

141

of needlelike teeth. It dove silently at them from between the soaring roots of a great tree. Enormous goggling eyes gave Losting time to sound a warning. Its first dive missed completely and it hooked around, wheezing like an old man. Both hunters were readying their snufflers for the second swoop. They never had a chance to use them.

Rearing up on hind legs, Ruumahum brought powerful forepaws together. They closed on one wing, and the flier screeched, crumpling to the raft. The long jaws snapped frantically till Geeliwan shattered its skull with a single swipe of a clawed paw.

No sooner had the carcass been disposed of than something that resembled a pineapple with sixteen long thin legs tried to crawl onto the deck. Axes rose and fell on articulated limbs until the crippled carnivore slipped back into the slime.

"Internal lights can attract others of the same species for purposes of mating," Logan mused, "as with certain deep-sea fish on Terra and Repler. They can also draw predators. Born, Losting, put out your torches."

The hunters looked doubtful. A man caught at night in the hylaea without light had no chance to see his enemy, but Logan and Cohoma managed to persuade them to try it. Reluctantly they removed the protective globes and dipped the torches in the water, but not before two fresh ones were readied just in case.

They were not used. With the torches out, their eyes adjusted to the lesser light emanating from the glowing life around them. There was still enough to make out their course between the tree boles which supported the world above. And they were not attacked again.

They had been traveling on the raft for several hours when Born discovered he was thirsty. He dropped to his knees and bent his head to the murky water.

"Wait, Born!" Logan yelled. "It might not—"

She need not have bothered. Born's nose wrinkled as the noxious smell struck him. He had no advanced degrees, no knowledge of biochemistry to draw on. His nose was sufficient to tell him that the substance they were gliding on was not fit to drink. He told the others as much.

"Hardly surprising," Cohoma commented. He turned his gaze upward. "The bacterial count in this swamp must be nothing short of astronomical. When you consider how many tons . . . *tons* of already decomposing animal and vegetable matter fall on every square kilometer of the surface every day . . . Then consider the stifling heat down here." He mopped his forehead. "And the daily rainfall. You can figure this world is built on a sea of liquefied peat and compost the Church only knows how deep!"

"Obviously these trees, despite their enormous requirements, can't handle all the rainfall," Logan ventured thoughtfully. She leaned back on the drifting raft and stared at the bole of the growth passing on their right. It was not quite as big around as an interstellar cargo carrier. "I'd like to know how some of these half-kilometer-high emergents draw water from the surface and pump it to that height."

"I'd hate like hell to paddle this thing past the station before we climb again," Cohoma suddenly mused. "We know our direction, but we've no way of estimating our daily progress."

"Born and Losting know how to judge distance."

Cohoma smiled. "Sure, through the treepaths. Not on this." He indicated the raft, then turned to face Born. "What do you think?" he asked the hunter. "Don't we stand a better chance in the canopy than down here, as long as we don't chose the wrong hidey-hole the next time we feel like a nap!"

"I have been watching for a good way up ever since we left the dwelling place of the surface demon," he replied. "We must begin our return to the world soon anyway. See?" He pointed ahead and downward while Losting paddled on grimly, scanning the mammoth roots and buttresses for one the giants could climb.

As Cohoma and Logan stared, Born dug down into the orange log with his heel. A shallow groove appeared. Then he drew his leg up and brought his heel down on the log. It disappeared, his foot vanishing up to the ankle in the orange punk. When he tugged it free, a yellowish-brown suppuration oozed from the break. The hole did not fill in.

"What was it you said about bacterial action and decomposition here, Jan?" Logan muttered sardonically. She turned to survey the slowly passing, glowing dreamscape. "Born's right; if we don't find a place to land soon, this raft's going to dissolve right under us."

The murky, thick soup of the surface was lapping their ankles when Losting finally located a possible stairway leading them upward. A wooden peninsula was formed by the twisting bulk of a great root, which extended horizontally into the water before disappearing. Instead of shooting a hundred meters skyward in precipitous vertical assault, the root curved gently into the central trunk.

Some hard paddling grounded the shaky craft on the hardwood beach. None too soon, for instead of resisting or splintering, the front fifth of the raft collapsed on contact. A quick study showed that it could not have carried them more than a kilometer or so further. Nearly all the logs were rotted at least half through. More damaging was the fact that most of the gray lashings Born had found were completely gone. Had they remained on the raft much longer, they would have come to an abrupt, not gradual, end, as the lashings gave out and the logs came apart beneath them.

Once up the easy ramp provided by the great curved root there were knobs and protrusions which would make climbing manageable. Even so, going up was going to be quite a different proposition from their rapid descent.

Cohoma voiced Logan's sentiments as well as his own. "We're going to climb *that?*"

"All men can fly," Born mused, "but sadly, only in one direction—down. I'm afraid we must. Losting and I will go first and search out the easiest way, so that even a child might ascend in confidence. You will follow." He turned to the furcots. Geeliwan yawned noisily as he spoke. "Follow the friends closely. Do not let them fall," he ordered.

"Understand," Ruumahum snorted. "Follow close. Will care for." The massive skull swung around for a last thoughtful look, white tusks gleaming in the

144

misty phosphorescence that surrounded them. "Go now. Something comes."

If either Logan or Cohoma had entertained thoughts of arguing for another avenue of ascent, perhaps one still less perpendicular, Ruumahum's curt warning was enough to send them hurriedly up the chosen route.

"We've been left alone since extinguishing our torches," Logan puffed. "Why would anything suddenly attack us now? I thought we had made ourselves pretty inconspicuous."

"'Your eyes have grown used to the light here," Born shouted back to her. "Look down at yourselves."

Logan stared down at her protesting legs, and her breath drew in sharply. She was flickering like a thousand tiny lasers. Legs, feet, torso—all glittered crimson and yellow with light of their own. Life of their own. She held her hands out in front of her and even as she watched, the photonic effluence spread to her arms. Then she could feel a faint, feathery tickling spread across her face, and she brushed frantically at eyes, nostrils, and mouth.

She fought down the panic when the feathery touch remained no more than that. Born was shining now, too, and Losting. She saw Jan staring at her, his electrified face a mirror of her own. Behind them, Ruumahum and Geeliwan were rippling streaks of light.

A spine-quaking moan reverberated in the distance behind them. They redoubled their efforts.

Actually the climb was not that difficult from a technical standpoint, merely nerve-wracking and arduous. It seemed to Logan that they had been climbing for days instead of hours.

Once it grew darker for long moments as the luminescent fungi and lichen and mosses grew fewer and fewer. Another dozen meters and the first light from above reached them, feeble, tenuous probing of a far distant sun. Their acquired illumination left them at the same time. Logan slowed long enough to examine her glistening palms. The infinitesimal lights shifted and flowed, then began fading in a cloud from the skin. Tiny, incredibly tiny fliers, living light specks. That single soul-freezing moan had now faded behind them, but it was no wonder they had suddenly

145

become quarry for a while. For the billion glowmites that had slowly gathered to them must have turned the moving forms of man and furcot into fiery silhouettes in the darkness, flickering, brilliant beacons beckoning to photosensitive predators. Another symbiotic marriage, she mused. This world offered hundreds and hundreds of such, in places unexpected and unique.

They rose into thicker and thicker growth, not fungi now, but the stygian precursors of real plants. The first pale shadows formed by sunlight were like answers to prayers.

First they climbed the air-roots that dangled from the larger parasitic trees and vines, then those of the lesser epiphytes and bushes. Eventually they emerged into the first leaves—enormous disks barely kissed with green. Some were more than five and six meters wide, designed to catch even the slightest hint of sun from above.

Fungi still flourished here, but reduced to a friendly, unthreatening size—not the nightmare colossi of the Seventh Level. Gigantic ferns, ivies, and unclassifiable bryophytes still crowded out flowering plants.

"Please, let's stop here," pleaded an exhausted Cohoma, settling down on a wide vine overgrown with a diamond-patterned ivy. "For a minute, just a minute, please." Logan collapsed alongside him.

Born cast a questioning glance back at Ruumahum. The furcot was looking back along their precipitous path, long ears cocked forward and down, listening intently. Then he turned. "Not climber, not follow. Danger gone."

What seemed to Cohoma only seconds later, Born tested a dangling root. A gratifying tug and he was pulling himself up the helical formation. Losting followed behind, his snuffler clattering against his cape. Cohoma looked at his partner, muttered something else Born would not have understood, and started to follow. Logan sighed, stood up and tried to stretch the kink from her neck. She found it led only to strains in other muscles. She grabbed the root and began climbing. Ruumahum and Geeliwan chose their own path.

Additional hours of hard climbing carried them into something approaching a foggy twilight, where one finally could see without squinting. This time it was Logan's turn to announce she could not move a step farther. Born and Losting consulted as the two giants collapsed in a bed of rectangular leaves so thick they looked like little boxes.

"Very well," Born told them, "we will stay the night here."

"The night?" Cohoma wondered aloud. "But when the silverslith chased us out of that tree, it was already night."

"You must learn to read the light," Born told him. "The sun is dying, not budding. We have traveled the rest of that night and run the following day. There is little enough time left for preparing a fire and shelter."

"Wait a minute. How do you know the sun's going down and not rising?"

Born waved at the surrounding forest. "One has only to emfol."

"Never mind," Cohoma grunted. "I'll take your word for it, Born." His expression changed. "Are you and Losting going to hunt, or are we going to have to masticate that boot material you call dried meat again?"

Born was unpacking his axe. "No time left to hunt, unless you would prefer fresh meat to shelter?"

"No thanks," Logan cut in. "I'd rather be dry—you have enough time?"

"There are many dead branches and dying leaves here," Born told them. "And as low as we are in the world, drip water will not penetrate till late at night. Besides, this is still a region unfamiliar to us, this Sixth Level. Some of the forest growth is familiar, but some is not. The same is true of the sounds, and probably of the sound-makers. Not a good time to go exploring, the evening."

"We will eat what we brought with us," Losting said. "Tomorrow we can climb to the Third Level and hunt for fresh game, find fruit and nutmeats. For now, be glad of what you have."

"Look," Cohoma explained, "don't get the idea I was complaining or anything." He remembered that

147

they were here due to Born's recklessness and curiosity, not Losting's. "The steady change in our diet these past weeks has been kind of a shock to my innards."

"Do you think this is a feast for us?" Born reminded him, and he and Losting moved off to search for any of the platterlike green disks they had passed that showed signs of blight or disease.

Cohoma leaned back in the foliage until the two hunters had disappeared into the green wall. Then he rolled over and watched Logan, who was busy with the compass. "Still on course?"

She shrugged. "As near as I can tell, Jan. You know, what you said before is true. We have to hit the station dead on. We've got three chances to miss it—by going under it, too far right, or too far left."

He picked at the leaf they were sitting on. "I wish we hadn't had to make that surface detour, damnit."

"Could hardly be helped. What's the matter, Jan, didn't you find it interesting?"

"Interesting?" He let out a sinister chuckle. "It's one thing to study alien aberrations from the skimmer in back of a laser cannon. Being eaten alive by an entry in the catalog is the kind of experience I can do without."

"We're going to have a problem soon, you know."

"Oh, you're full of surprises, Kimi, you are."

"Seriously. If we're not going to risk missing the station, we're going to have to convince our friends of the need of traveling near the treetops. With their sense of distance thrown off by our little raft ride, the sooner we move up in the world, the better."

"The station's built only a little ways into the canopy, true."

"And Born and his people," she continued, "are deathly afraid of the sky. Not as much as they are of the surface, though." She looked thoughtful. "With that successfully survived now, maybe he'll be a little less reluctant to move upward. Remember, he doesn't know the station is located at the top of the First Level. He may have come to half believe we do come from a world other than this one. I think that's more likely to find place in his imagination than the possi-

148

bility we might chose to live here in his Upper Hell."

Cohoma shook his head. "I still wish I understood what this emfol business is all about. It would seem to be some kind of adaptive worship of the undergrowth."

Logan nodded. "Is it surprising they'd look underfoot for succor and supernatural aid? The bottom of their world is hell, and so is the upper. That leaves them neatly sandwiched in between, with no way out. Naturally their development would proceed along restricted, unorthodox lines. It's too bad, in a way. Born, the chiefs Sand and Joyla, and several others have a kind of nobility about them."

Cohoma snorted, rolled over. "The biggest mistake an objective observer on a world like this can make is to romanticize the primitive. And in the case of these people, even that's not valid. They're not true primitives, only regressed survivors of people like ourselves."

"Tell me, Jan," she murmured, "is it really regression, or is it progression along an alien path?"

"Huh? What's that you said?"

"Nothing . . . nothing. I'm tired, that's all."

IX

The meal of tough dried fruit and tougher meat was long concluded when the sleepless Logan finally edged over to where Born was sitting. The hunter was resting close to the fire, his back pushed up against the bulk of the snoring Ruumahum. Losting was already asleep at the far end of the large, crude lean-to. Wrapped awkwardly in her brown cloak, her partner dozed fitfully.

There was one important question she wanted to resolve now. "Tell me, Born, do you and your people believe in a god?"

149

"A god or gods?" he replied interestedly, at least not offended by the question.

"No, a single god. One all-powerful, all-seeing intelligence that directs the affairs of the universe, that accounts for and plans everything."

"That implies the absence of free will," Born responded, surprising her as he sometimes did with a very unprimitive reply.

"Some accept that, too," she admitted.

"I accept nothing of it, nor do any I know," he told her. "There is far too much in this world for any one being to keep account of it all. And you say there are other worlds as complex as this, too?" He smiled. "No, we do not believe such."

At least she could go to Hansen with that much, now. It was too bad. Belief in the existence of a single god would imply a fixed set of ethical and moral precepts on which to base certain proposals and regulations. Spiritual anarchy made dealings with primitive people more difficult. One couldn't call on a higher authority to serve as a binding agency. Well, that was a problem for Hansen and whatever xenosociologists the company chose to send in to deal with Born's people. She started to turn away, then hesitated. If she could at least plant that seed in Born's mind . . .

"Born, has it occurred to you that we've had incredible luck on this journey?"

"I do not call sleeping in a silverslith's tree good luck."

"But we escaped it, Born. And there've been any one of a dozen . . . no, several dozen times we could all have been killed. Yet we haven't even suffered a minor injury, beyond the usual nicks and scrapes."

That caused him to think a minute, as she had intended. Finally he murmured, "I am a great hunter. Losting is a good hunter, and Ruumahum and Geeliwan are wise and experienced. Why should we not have been as successful as we have?"

"You don't think it strange, despite the fact that five days' journey is the longest any of your people have ever traveled from the Home before and returned?"

"We have not yet reached our destination, or returned," he countered quietly.

150

"That's so," she admitted, edging back toward her own sleeping place. "So you don't think this implies the intervention of a guiding, watchful presence, like a god? One who always knows what's good for you and watches over you?"

Born looked solemn. "It did not watch over us when the Akadi came, but I will think on it." And he turned away from her.

She had planted the seed. Satisfied with that and with what Hansen would have to say about it, she rolled up in her cloak and closed her eyes. Not that there were any missionaries at the station who would thank her. The station was hardly a Church-blessed enterprise. The steady drip of rain trickling down to this level through a million leaves and petals and stems formed a lulling rhythm on the lean-to roof, allowing her finally to fall asleep.

"We've got to go up to the top of the First Level, Born," Logan insisted the next day.

Born shook his head. "Too dangerous to travel so much in the sky."

"No, no," she went on in exasperation. "We don't have to stick our heads out into open air. We can stay a good twenty-five meters," and she translated that into percentage of level for him, "below the top-most leaves. No sky-demon is going to dive through that much brush to get at you."

"The First Level has dangers of its own," Born countered defensively. "They are smaller than those of the Home level, but faster, harder to find and kill before they strike."

"Look, Born," Cohoma tried to explain, "we could miss the station completely if we travel below that point. It's constructed—like our skimmer—out of materials set down into the forest top, but not far into it. If we miss it and have to try and backtrack, we could get so confused as to direction that we'd never be able to find it. We could wander around in this jungle for years." For emphasis, he grabbed the compass, showed it again to Bo and Losting as though they could comprehend its principle. "See this direction finder of ours? It works best the first time you hunt with it for a place. It grows less useful with each successive failure."

Eventually Born gave in, as Logan suspected he would. Their iconoclastic hunter had only two choices —take their advice now, or abort the journey. After all they had been through, she did not think he would suggest the latter.

So they continued upward. Gradually this time, not in a muscle-killing vertical climb, but on a slant. In this manner they moved forward as well as higher, through the Fifth Level, the Fourth, and Third. She could sense their reluctance to leave those comforting, familiar surroundings for the danger and uncertainty of the upper canopy. Both she and Cohoma had grown so hylaea-wise by now, however, that neither hunter attempted to fool them into believing they had reached a higher level.

Up they mounted, through the Second Level, where the sunlight was brilliant yellow-green, where it struck most vegetation directly and not with the aid of mirror vines. Where the day was bright enough to resemble the floor of a north temperate evergreen forest on Moth or Terra. Logan and Cohoma expanded, while Born and Losting grew steadily more cautious.

Then they were in the First Level itself, climbing amid a profusion of riotously colored flowers, etched and engraved and painted by a nature delirious with her own beauty. Logan knew that any of the botanists restricted to the station and to studying specimens recovered by the skimmer teams would give an arm to be here with them now. Company policy forbade it, given the inimical nature of this world. Botanists were expensive.

All the basic shadings and hues merged together with more exotic coloration. Logan passed a maroon bloom half a meter across, its pigment so intense it was nearly purple in places. The petals were striped with aquamarine blue, and it rested on a bed of metallic gold leaves.

Nor was drunken variation limited only to color. One blossom boasted petals which grew in interlocking, multiple spirals of pink and turquoise and almond. Cohoma promptly dubbed it the clown plant. There were flowers that grew like a phalanx of pikes, green flowers springing from green stems, and green branches that sprouted green grapes. There were flowers inside flowers, flowers the color of smoky quartz, flowers with transparent petals that tasted of caramel.

And these were matched in glitter and evolutionary exhuberance by a swarming multitude of nonvegetable life, which crawled, hopped, glided, buzzed, and swung about like animated dreams before the spellbound gaze of the two skimmer pilots. Born was right—they were smaller and they moved faster, some darting across their pathway too rapidly to be seen as other then a blur.

Hunters and gatherers here would have to work four times as hard to gather the same amount of food. There was greater natural competition here and, according to the hunters, greater danger as well. Which explained why the survivors of the trapped colony ship had chosen to forego this aerial paradise for the less competitive regions of the Third and Fourth Levels. Having observed the thunderous nightly storms from the comparative safety of the station, Logan assumed the protection the depths offered from violent weather was another factor in the decision to descend.

The noise might have been still another factor. It was deafening here. Much of it seemed to emanate from huge colonies of little six-legged creatures about the size of a man's thigh. About half-a-meter long, they were slimly built and moved rapidly through the thinner branches with six-clawed legs. Hard-shelled limbs joined to a furry cylindrical body, one end of which tapered into a long, whiplike tail, the other ending in a snout like an aardvark's. The familiar triple oculars were set back of this, and behind them rose a single, flexible ridge of flesh, which appeared to be a sound sensor.

They were the mockingbirds of this world, the hexapodal kookaburras, uttering everything from a high-pitched whistle to a tenor cackle. Tribes of them accompanied the party as it made its way through the vinepaths, offering unintelligible insults and suggestions. Occasionally one of the furcots would snarl menacingly at them and they would scatter, only to reappear when communal courage grew strong enough, to berate and admonish once again. Only boredom drove them off.

Yet another reason for living lower down offered itself. Even here, many dozens of meters below the crowns of the trees, the branches and cubbles were thinner, less roadlike. Vines and lianas and creepers thinned in proportion. More often than they liked, Logan and Cohoma found themselves using their arms instead of their legs to move from one place to the next. When Born asked if they were tiring and wished to drop to more easily negotiable paths, both gritted their teeth, wiped the sweat clear from eyes and forehead, and shook their heads. Better to expend all one's reserves here than risk passing below the station.

They continued on that way, now and then dipping downward when the forest top thinned too much for Born's comfort, rising again where the hylaea bulged into the sky.

It rained early that night. For the first time since their skimmer had crashed, both giants were subjected to a thorough drenching before the two hunters could erect suitable shelter. Without hundreds of meters of intervening foliage to protect them, they caught the full force of the nightly downpour. The volume and fury they had anticipated from having observed similar storms from inside the station. It was the noise that was surprising—the station was effectively soundproofed against it. They had descended a good thirty meters more in hopes of securing a little protection. Even here the forest shook and rattled. Real, steady wind up here, not the lost, dallying zephyr they had encountered at the Home's level.

There was no soundproofing to shut out the lightning and thunder, which rattled their brains in counterpoint to the flogging rain. Logan sneezed, reflected miserably that the first colonists here could have perished from pneumonia had they not chosen to live at more sheltered depths. It was only a momentary chill—the humidity and constant warmth made it hard to catch the serious cold she feared. But when the sun rose

154

steamily bright the following morning, both pilots remained soaked to the skin.

Under the concerned directions of Born—and Losting's more taciturn comments—they underwent a re-education in the following days. This world nearer the sky was as deadly as Born had indicated; only here the methodology of murder was matched in deadliness by the subtlety of execution. Without the advice and protection of Born, Losting, and the furcots, both giants would have been dead within a day.

The danger which remained sharpest in Logan's mind was a brilliant yellow fruit. Hourglass-shaped and about the size of a pear, its blossoms exuded a fragrance redolent of spring honeysuckle. The epiphytic bush was top-heavy with this fruit. Born pointed out how tokkers and other fruit-eaters assiduously avoided it.

"Bitter taste?" Cohoma asked.

Born shook his head. "No, the taste is wondrous, and the pulp nourishing and rejuvenating to a tired wanderer. The danger is in separating the fruit from the seeds within."

"That's a problem with most fruit," the pilot observed.

"It is a particular problem with the greeter fruit," Born told him, as he reached up and casually plucked one free. After staring silently at the plant for a long minute, Logan noted—emfoling again. "No animal of the world has been able to solve the problem," the hunter continued, turning the attractive, harmless-looking fruit over and over in his hand. "Only the people."

He hunted around until he found a long, thin, dead branch growing from a nearby bush. Breaking it off cleanly, he sharpened one end with his knife. Then he slid the point into the fruit, taking care not to pierce the center. Laying the impaled fruit on a branch, he used the knife to make a multiple incision on the side away from the stick. Then he lifted the branch high overhead and began tapping the incised area firmly against the protruding knob of a small cubble.

On the sixth tap there was a bang of such unexpected volume that Logan and Cohoma ducked. There was a violent snarl from their left. Ruumahum stuck his head out from a clump of wire bushes. Seeing that no one was injured, he uttered a snort of derision at such foolish goings-on and vanished once more.

Born drew the stick downward, showed it to the giants. The whole left side of the fruit, where the incisions had been made, had been blown away as though there had been a small bomb within it, which was exactly the case.

"This is how the greeter spreads its seed," Born explained needlessly. Peeling off sections of the remaining undamaged fruit, he extended them to Cohoma and Logan. Logan slipped it hesitantly between her lips, the recent demonstration having dampened her appetite somewhat. As soon as her taste buds made contact with it, she sucked in the whole piece and rolled it around in her mouth, squeezing the juices free. It was exquisite, sugary, yet tart, like grenadine and lemon.

"What finally happens to the seeds?" she asked, when the last drop was drained, the final scrap of pulp swallowed.

By way of reply Born directed them upward and to the left of the parasitic bush. Born studied the trunk of the tree nearby, finally pointed. The pilots stared close. Arranged in a tiny, neat spray pattern on the trunk were a dozen small holes, penetrating the solid wood for several centimeters. At the bottom of each hole they could barely make out a tiny, dark seed. Six spines protruded from each. Each seed was perhaps a half-centimeter in diameter, including spines.

With his knife, Born dug one of them out. Logan reached to touch it, and Born had to block her hand—had she learned nothing of the world these past many seven-days? She and Cohoma studied the minute seed with interest. Closer inspection revealed that the edges of the six spines were razor-sharp and lined with microscopic, backward-facing barbs.

"I see," Cohoma murmured. "The seeds germinate in the trees. But how do they get spread? Does the fruit dry up to the point where internal pressure sends them flying?"

"Can't be, Jan," Logan objected. "If the fruit dries

156

out, where's the source of this kind of pressure? No, it has to be—"

Born shook his head. "The greeter does not root in a plant. When an animal which is old or ill has lost its judgment, hunger may drive it to eat a greeter." He resumed the march.

Logan paused long enough for another glance at the little spray pattern where the seeds had bored holes in the thick hardwood, then followed the hunter.

"An animal tries to eat one of the fruits, bites through the pulp until it punctures the inner sac and gets the whole barrage right in its face," Cohoma theorized grimly. "If it's lucky the seeds kill it outright. Otherwise it probably bleeds to death. Meanwhile the corpse serves as a ready-made reservoir of nutrients."

"Jan, the plants have struck an even balance on this world. No, I take that back. They have the upper edge. The animals are outnumbered, outsized, and outgunned. I wondered how Born's ancestors could have lost so much technology so fast. I don't wonder any more. How can you fight a forest?"

The discovery came days later, announced in the usual phlegmatic fashion of the furcots. "Panta," Ruumahum called back to them. Both furcots were sitting at the end of a long, relatively clear cubble.

Born's spirits rose. "A Panta is a large open space, a depression in the world. Of course," he added hurriedly, seeing the look on the giants' faces, "it might be a natural Panta. There are half a dozen within two days' walk of the Home." He turned back to Ruumahum.

"How big?"

"*Big*," the furcot replied softly. "And in the middle, thing of axe metal like sky-boat." Triple eyes stared suddenly at Logan.

Without knowing why, she looked away, concentrating instead on Born. "The station! It's got to be!"

"It is done, then. Quickly." He turned to jog down the cubble.

This time it was Logan who put out the restraining hand. "Not too quickly, Born. There are mechanisms—like our compass—which protect the station

157

from marauding forest-dwellers and sky-demons. No creature of the hylaea world can reach it."

"Silverslith?" asked Losting with uncertainty.

"No, Losting, not even a silverslith."

The hunter persisted. "Has your station-Home ever been attacked by a silverslith?"

Logan had to admit it had not, but she was adamant in insisting that even that gigantic animal could not stand up to a gimbaled laser or explosive shell. Both hunters were forced to confess they had no idea what these magical weapons were. Cohoma assured them with a barely supressed smile that they were more toxic than jacari thorns.

"Then the demons of your own worlds must be far, far greater than even those of Hell," Born surmised, "for you to need such weapons."

"They are," she admitted, without bothering to explain that the demons in question were two-legged. Besides, now that they were within hailing distance of the station, there was an experiment she had been waiting all this time to try. She looked straight at Ruumahum. "All right," she said in a commanding tone, "take us to the Panta, Ruumahum."

The furcot eyed her strangely for a moment, then turned and trotted into the greenery ahead. Born said nothing. Perhaps in his mind the event held no significance. But it indicated to Logan and Cohoma that the furcots would respond to the commands of humans other than those of Born's tribe. That could be most important in smoothing certain things over.

A few more lianas, some two-meter-tall leaves, and a couple of branches eased aside—and they were standing on the fringe of what looked like a vast green circle paved with green, beige, and brown.

The floor of the Panta was composed of the tops of hundreds, thousands of trees, cubbles, and epiphytes which had been sheared off to provide the station with a protective "moat" of open space devoid of concealment. In the center of the green-walled amphitheater the station itself rose on the cut-off crowns of three Pillar trees grown close together. They supported the whole weight of the station. The structure itself consisted of a single vast metal building with a sloping, domed top. A large blister of transparent acrylics emerged from the apex. A wide porch, protected by a waist-high mesh fence, encircled the entire structure. At each point of the compass, a covered catwalk extended from the central edifice, terminating in a bubble of duralloy and plastic. The narrow, blunt end of a laser cannon projected from each of these turrets.

The independently mounted cannons could swivel so that three could be brought to bear on any one point as near as twenty meters to the station. Any impartial observer surveying this awesome array of firepower might have calculated that the modest exploratory outpost was expecting an invasion in force from the surrounding forest. Actually, they were also there to protect against assaults from other than local predators.

The "sky-demons" the founders of the station were really worried about would attack at high speed, backed by intelligence, and armed with writs, ordainments, ordinances, and regulations. These last-named were more to be feared than the teeth of roving carnivores.

Halfway between the bottom of the station and the top of the cut-off forest, a series of interlocking struts laced with thick cable mesh surrounded each Pillartree trunk. A steady electric current flowed through those cables, sufficient to discourage any curious meateater, which might somehow have evaded starlit eyes and electronic surveillance systems.

That explained, Born inquired as to the purpose of the flat disk of metal set off to their right. A fifth catwalk, slightly larger than the others, extended from it to the station. A smaller-topped tree was sufficient to support this lesser weight.

Born did not recognize the oblong shape resting on the platform as a larger cousin of the giants' skimmer. The shuttlecraft differed sufficiently in shape to remain unidentifiable to both hunters, as did the web of grids and antennae which projected from the station's sides and from the observation dome at its top.

Behind the gimbaled gun placements and metal catwalks, behind the encircling double-meshed fence and walkway, lay living quarters, laboratories, administrative offices, quartermaster's stockrooms, a communications center that would be the envy of any operator on a planet with a million-plus population, skimmer hangar and service bays, solar energy concentrator and power plant, plus a host of peripheral chambers, alcoves, and rooms. Even a casual traveler, with minimal outplanet experience, instantly would have recognized the extraordinary expense that had gone into the construction of this first station.

"Here goes," said Logan.

In theory everything had been thoroughly pretested, and nothing in the way of automatic weaponry would vaporize her before a thorough check on body and type was run. In theory. She had never had the chance to verify it personally. She had it now.

There was a half-cut cubble leading in the general direction of the station. She stepped out of the green wall and into the open. Two stubby nozzles immediately swung around to cover her. She hoped whoever was on shift at the computer board was not sleepy, doped up, or just itchy for a little target practice. Nothing happened for long moments. She waved, made flapping motions. Cohoma waited expectantly, while Born and Losting kept wary eyes on the open sky and fingered their snufflers.

Other thoughts fought for attention in Born's mind. The half-dream of the giants station-Home was real. It existed, sat solidly before him. Whether it held all the wonders promised remained to be seen. For now, while exposed to all manner of sky-demons, they would put their trust in the efficacy of jacari poison and not promises.

Figures could be seen moving rapidly and carefully toward them. As they neared, Logan looked down at her feet, then up, and saw that a path—doubtlessly one of many—had been traced out across the forest top. She had been briefed about the existence of such pathways but had not committed them to memory, since she never expected to have to use one.

The figures carried handguns and were clad in the same kind of gray jumpsuits Born had first seen on Cohoma and Logan. As they drew nearer their eyes grew wide. There were three of them. The one in the lead pulled up before Logan, looked her slowly up and down. His expression was half hysteria, half astonishment.

"Kimi Logan! I'll be damned!" He shook his head slowly. "We lost all contact with your skimmer weeks ago. Sent out scouts and didn't find a thing. You missed a nice burial ceremony."

"Sorry, Sal."

"Where the hell did you come from?"

"I couldn't have put it better myself, Sal." She turned and called back into the brush. "All clear, come on out, everybody."

Cohoma stepped clear of the treetops. At the appearance of Born and Losting, the man with the gray sideburns and cleft chin temporarily ran out of expletives. "I'll be double-damned," he muttered finally.

After a glance from Logan he holstered the handgun. His gaze went back to the two hunters. Born fought down the urge to fidget nervously under the evaluating stare. Besides, he was occupied studying the three new giants. The biggest one, the one Kimilogan called Sal, was no different from Cohoma, though slightly taller and heavier. The other two giants were Logan's size, though only one was female.

"Pygmies, no less!" He eyed Logan inquisitively.

"Natives." She smiled back at him. "Too many similarities for parallel evolution. We can't be positive, of course, until they've been given a thorough run-through in Medical, but except for a few minor differences I'll bet they test out as human as you or I. Jan and I figure they're the remnants of a century's-lost colony ship. Maybe even pre-Commonwealth. Incidentally, they speak excellent, if sibilant, Terranglo."

Sal continued to stare in wonderment at Born and Losting. "Sounds right. There were enough of those first colonizers who ended up in the wrong place. Might not have met the thranx for another millennium if it hadn't been for a lost ship." He grunted. "Minor differences . . . you mean those toes and their size?"

Logan nodded. "That and their acquired protective coloration. Look, Jan and I have been going through that theoretical hell you just mentioned. I've spent

161

weeks programming the kitchen in my head to turn out everything from steak to afterdinner mints. And I haven't had a real bath since we left."

"And some decent clothes,", Cohoma added fervently. "Oh Lord, for clean underwear!"

"Hansen will be glad to see you both back," Sal smiled. "I wish I could see the old man's expression when you walk in with your two friends, though. Priceless!"

"You ought to see him when we tell him some of the discoveries we've made. You ought to get out and walk around, Sal. It's the only way to learn about a world."

"Yeah? If you don't mind, I'll leave the hiking and grubbing to you two enthusiasts." Cohoma took a playful swing at him. "Tell me about 'em?"

"Sorry, Sal." Cohoma grinned. "Province of the discoverers, you know."

"Oh Churchfire, Jan, I wouldn't try to mad any of your bonus money. How could I prove any of it, anyway? But it's good to hear you had a profitable little walk. The old man's been under some heavy pressure from the home office, story has it, ever since Tsing-ahn killed himself."

Cohoma and Logan weren't too tired to be shocked. "Popi killed himself?" Logan whispered, using the biochemist's nickname.

"That's the chat they're handing out. Nearchose—you know, the security whale who was a friend of the prof's—was the last one to see him alive. Report from Nick was that the guy was depressed about something, but hardly suicidal. Went vibrato and blew up everything in his lab. 'Course, when a guy gets as dependent on the silly stuff as Tsing-ahn was, you can't tell what he's liable to do. Company assumes a calculated risk hiring guys like that. This time it didn't pay out."

"Too bad, I liked the little joe," Cohoma muttered.

"Everybody did."

An awkward silence followed, each absorbed in his own thoughts and fully aware that he or she was on this world because of some serious weakness of their own—money, drugs, or something best not mentioned.

Whenever the subject surfaced, it was quickly dropped. Discussion of such things was avoided by mutual consent.

They walked in silence halfway to the station when the something that seemed to be missing finally surfaced in Logan's mind. She looked behind them, then over at Born. "Where are Ruumahum and Geeliwan?"

"Both said they would feel uncomfortable away from the forest," Born replied truthfully. "They do not like open space. You didn't say you wanted them to come with us."

"Well, it's not important." She stared longingly back toward the emerald, flower-speckled rampart. To parade the pair of omnivorous hexapods like a couple of lap dogs before the excitable Hansen was a pleasure she had been looking forward to. But she was halfway to that bath and steak, and she was not going back into the jungle now. That could wait.

Omnivorous—she had assumed the furcots were omnivorous. Come to think of it, she had never seen either of them eat anything. Oh well, as Born said, they felt uncomfortable in certain situations. Probably they liked to eat in private as well as make love away from prying eyes. Still, it seemed odd she had never seen either of them take a bite out of anything.

Further speculation was interrupted by a cry from Born. He spotted the demon first. "Losting! 'Ware zenith!" Again she felt that shock at words which didn't seem to fit Born's way of life.

Losting looked overhead, reaching simultaneously for his snuffler. Then she saw the tiny brown spot circling far above. There were many such spots, always clear of the station. Apparently, Born had somehow detected belligerent motion in this one. He was right. The spot became a recognizable shape, one she had hoped never to see at close range again. Broad wings, clawed feet, long jaw armed with razor-sharp teeth.

She could not entirely repress a faint smile of superiority as she noticed them hurriedly going for their primitive airguns. "Don't worry, Born, Losting. Relax and watch." Born eyed her questioningly, but managed to force down his natural inclination to load and set.

Logan studied the diving demon. It drew nearer in a tightening spiral, mouth agape.

She could not see which of the weapons on the perimeter had turned to cover that particular section of sky until the red beam lanced out and up from one of the gimbaled turrets. The sky-demon disintegrated in a brief flare of carbonized flesh and powdered bone.

Born and Losting stared quietly at the sky where the demon had been plummeting toward them only seconds before. Equally silent, Logan watched them. So did Cohoma and Sal and the other two.

"It's something like a very advanced kind of snuffler, Born," she explained finally. "How to make you see . . . Well, it uses a kind of light to kill with."

Born turned and pointed to the spherical turret which housed the cannon. "In there?"

"That's right," said Cohoma. "There are others placed around the station. With them and the electrical shielding on the supporting trunks, we're quite safe here."

"Remember, Born," Logan told him excitedly, as they resumed the walk to the station, "how your people arrayed themselves to meet the Akadi? A system of weapons like that one," and she indicated the motionless turret, "could be set up around your village to protect the Home. You'd never have to worry about the Akadi or silversliths or anything else again."

"Have to fire very fast, and move it quickly at such close distance," Losting commented.

"Oh, that's no problem," a self-assured Cohoma explained. "Once you've cleared a space around the Home like we have here and set up a decent detector system, a predator couldn't even get close without being spotted."

"Clear space?"

"Yes, you know, cut away the close-in vegetation like I originally proposed to stop the Akadi. Just leave a few cubbles or vines to serve as a kind of drawbridge. It would be easy. We can give you tools similar to these light weapons, which would make the cutting a simple job. You could obtain them for the asking, and for helping us find our way around your world and locate certain substances, you'd earn the goodwill credits in no time."

"Cut away," Born murmured. "Clear space."

"Yes, Born." Logan looked puzzled. "Is something the matter? Can't you just emfol first and then—?"

"Nothing's the matter." The hunter's expression brightened. "So many wonders all at once. I'm a little overwhelmed. I would like very much to learn more about such things as light weapons and defensive systems and what we must do to get them."

"The details of the last part aren't for us to decide, Born. We're only minor employees of a great concern, of the people who established this station here. A man named Hansen will decide those particulars. You'll meet him soon. But I don't see any trouble working out an arrangement that will be advantageous to both our peoples. Especially after what you've already done for Jan and me."

There was a lift waiting for them. It took them through a gate in the underside of the charged grid and up into the lower floor of the station. As they passed the grid, the ever curious Born asked again about the principle behind it. Cohoma had a hard time making him understand, but references to lightning seemed to satisfy both hunters.

The lift pulled Born and Losting into a world of new wonders. First among them was the sudden, almost physical shock of color change. The all-pervasive green, flecked with bright colors and every shade of brown, was abruptly replaced by a stiff, straight-angled world of silver and gray, white and blue. The only touch of green in this section of corridor was provided by a row of parasitic bushes growing in a long deep planter, which served as a divider between sections of corridor.

Born saw that the chaga was not well. The flowers were big and colorful, but the leaves were not straight and were not reaching for the sun the way they should be. He had time for only a quick glance. There were too many new things here to see and try to understand. More giants, engaged in various inexplicable tasks, hurrying on alien errands, filled the corridor.

Some were clad in garb even stranger than the gray suits worn by Logan, Cohoma, and Sal.

A man saw them, came over to speak in a whisper to the one called Sal. Born heard him clearly. "Hansen wants to see the two natives immediately. He's up in his office." He looked over at Logan and Cohoma. "You two also."

Logan groaned. "Can't we at least get cleaned up a little first? Andre, what we've been through, these past months—!"

"I know. You also know Hansen. Orders." He shrugged helplessly.

"Hell, let's get it over with," Cohoma grunted.

"This Hansen person," Born asked as they walked toward an interior lift, "he is chief of your tribe?"

"Not chief, Born, and not tribe," Logan explained with a hint of irritation, which was caused by the order, not Born's question. "This station houses people who are engaged in similar hunts. But it's not the same kind of organization as you have in the Home. You might regard the people in this station as a hunting party, with Mr. Hansen the leader. That's the best I can do. I'm not sure I could explain what a corporation is if I had a month."

"It is enough," Born replied as they turned a corner and started down a white, brightly decorated tunnel. "He is the one we must ask for light guns and other wonders for our people."

"You understand, Born. I knew you would," she declared cheerfully. "Help us in exploring your world and finding a few things you don't use yourselves, and wonders will be granted gladly in return. It's an old principle among my people. Among your own ancestors." And just a touch illegal in this one instance, that's all, she thought, but did not say to him.

"What sort of man is your hunting party leader?"

"That depends on where you're coming from," Logan told him enigmatically. She seemed ready to explain further, but they had reached a door, and Sal beckoned them to be silent. He held it open for them and then remained behind while the other four entered.

Hansen sat behind a narrow, curved desk which he

166

managed to give the appearance of wearing, like an enormous plastic belt. The desk was piled high with tape spools, cassettes, reams of paper, and dozens of separate reports bound in simulated leather binders. The walls were given over to shelves lined with books and tape holders. The rear of the room was filled by a floor-to-ceiling window which offered a panorama of the Panta and the suffocating forest beyond.

As they entered, Hansen was staring at the screen of a tape viewer mounted on a flexible arm. "Just a moment, please. Jan, Kimi, good to find you alive." He spoke without turning, his voice mellow, reassuring.

His stature enhanced his middle-aged pudginess. He was not much taller than Born. Hair started halfway back on a forehead that seemed to be made from dark putty and fell to his shoulders in long waves. Save for the thick brush mustache which clung to his upper lip like a hibernating insect, his hair had turned completely gray.

He was sweating despite the air-conditioning. Indeed, that was the first thing Born had noticed upon entering the station—an apparently deliberate, abnormal chill. Even on cool nights in the world, it rarely got this cold.

Neither hunter minded the extended wait. They were fully occupied with studying the room and its contents. Born did not miss, however, the respectful silence with which the tired, impatient Logan and Cohoma waited.

Hansen touched a switch on the side of the viewer, then pushed it back and away on its arm. It locked into place out of his way as he turned to eye his visitors. His right arm rested on an arm of the chair and he rubbed at his perspiring forehead with the other. He looked tired, and he was. Running this station had prematurely aged as experienced and toughened an old hand as Hansen. If it was not something breaking down that he could not get replacements for because of the risk of a supply ship running afoul of a Church or Commonwealth warship, it was some nonmechanical crisis. It seemed like every time one of his people put a foot on this world they were promptly stung, bitten, punctured, nibbled at, or otherwise set upon by the local flora and fauna.

Nor had he recovered from the loss of the life-prolonging burl extracts, the burl itself, and Tsing-ahn, the man who knew most about them. If only that poor madman had not been so thorough in the destruction of his notes and records! The news of the biochemist's suicide and concurrent destruction of everything relating to what had come to be called the immortality extract had not gone over well with Hansen's superiors—not gone over well at all.

He did manage a slight grin as he examined the two returned members of the skimmer team. The mental lift provided by their miraculous survival had come at a badly needed time.

"We'd given you up for sure, for sure," he told them. "Couldn't believe my ears when Security reported four people standing at the edge of the forest." A corner of his mouth twitched at the remembrance. "You two've caused me no end of trouble, you know. Now I've got to re-call all the paperwork detailing your deaths, the requests for replacements, everything. Somebody in Budgeting's not going to like you two."

"Sorry, Chief," Logan said, smiling back.

"Now," Hansen puffed expansively, leaning back slightly in the chair and folding his hands over his slight paunch, "tell me about your aboriginal acquaintances, here."

"They saved our lives," she replied, matter-of-factly, "and I doubt they're aborigines, sir. Near as we can figure, they're the descendants of the populace of a colony ship that lost its way and wound up here. They've lost the memory of that origin, all Common-wealth and pre-Commonwealth knowledge, and nearly all their technology. They have developed a rudimentary tribal social structure. As a result, our friends Born and Losting are convinced that they are in truth natives of this world."

"And you're pretty certain they're not."

"That's right, sir," Cohoma chipped in. "Too many similarities, an axe made of ship alloy, other things.

168

Same language, although they've developed a dialect all their own, family structure is—"

"Yes, yes," Hansen cut him off with a casual wave. "Saved your lives too, did they? And brought you all the way back through that rooted Hades out there—how far did you say you'd come?" He cocked a querulous eye at Logan. She named a figure and the chief of station whistled. "Just the four of you then, that many kilometers through that?" He gestured over his shoulder toward the window.

"Yes, sir—and a couple of very domesticated animals."

"It was a very gutsy thing for them to try, sir," Cohoma added. "Up until this trek none of their tribe had been more than a couple of kilometers from their home village."

"All of which is most gratifying—and utterly implausible. How the Churchwarden did you survive?"

"Sometimes I wonder myself," Logan responded. "Chief, could I sit down, please. I'm a little worn."

Hansen shook his head dolefully. "I forget priorities. Excuse me, Kimi." He called and Sal appeared at the door. "Salomon, bring in some chairs for everyone."

The chairs were brought. Born and Losting imitated, rather hesitantly, the sitting motions of their two giant companions.

"We pulled it off with a combination of good luck and the skill of these two." She indicated the hunters. "Born and his folk know their forest world. They live with it in the truest sense. Their village is set in a single tree. The adaptations on both sides exceed anything I've ever heard of. Frankly," she said casting a speculative glance at Born, "I think the tree gets the best of the setup. Born's people would disagree, of course."

Born felt no anger at her words. There was no shame in being considered inferior to one's Home. Even after many seven-days in the forest, many long hours of patient explanation, it seemed that the giants still did not understand. From what he had overheard in this station-Home thus far, he doubted they ever would. The casualness with which "cutting" and making "clear space" were mentioned had left him with a lingering numbness. He returned his attention to the graybeard.

"It seems that some kind of reward is in order. Something beyond our deeply felt thanks, Mr. . . . uh, Born." He smiled in a fatherly way. "Tell me, Born, Losting, what would you like?"

Born looked across at his companion. The bigger hunter squirmed uncomfortably in his chair and mumbled, "The sooner we leave this cold, hard place for the Home, the better I will like it."

Born nodded and turned back to Hansen. "I too would like to leave. But first I would like to know more about the light weapons and electrical vines and such things."

Hansen leaned forward, studied the unblinking hunter. "An aborigine you're not, Born. Oh, it's just as well. The less primitive you've become, the simpler it will make negotiations. As to advanced weapons systems, well, we'll have to think about that a little, I believe. You'll get them when we've worked out some mutual assistance agreements even a priest couldn't break in Commonwealth court."

"They can be very helpful, sir," Cohoma put in. "We've lost so many people in the forest that—"

"I'm aware of that, Jan." Hansen dismissed the others from his mind to concentrate fully on Born. "What this is called, Born, is an initial survey outpost. It's the first home for my people on this world. It's been established at great expense and with much secrecy because there's so much at stake here. Do you retain knowledge of what a mine is, Born, a mill, a processing plant?" Born remained blank-faced, his expression unchanged.

"No, I can see you don't. Let me try to explain. There are many things we can make, like the material for this station and the acrylic of this desk. There are many we cannot. This world, insofar as we've been able to determine, appears to be a storehouse of such valuable things. Obtaining these substances can make—let's see—can make a better life for all, my people as well as yours. Your help in developing all this would make things much simpler for us." He took a deep breath. "In particular, there is one sub-stance we've discovered which can—"

"Excuse me, sir." The interruption came from the man named Sal, who had remained with them. "Do you think it's—?"

Hansen made a quieting gesture. "Our friend Born isn't going to return to his tree and get on the deep space tridee to report to the nearest Commonwealth peaceforcer. Besides," he continued, looking back at Born, "I believe in being straightforward. I want our new friends to understand the importance of all this.

"There is a drug, Born, which can be derived from the heart of a certain burl." Born looked blank. "A burl is a woody growth that forms on a tree to con-tain the spread of a foreign infection or parasitic in-festation. The burl forms around this foreign material. When the pulp at the center of this particular burl is removed and properly treated, a liquid is produced which appears to have the ability of prolonging hu-man life-span tremendously. How about you, Born? Wouldn't you like to live twice as long?"

"I do not know," Born replied honestly. "To what end?"

"What end indeed?" Hansen murmured. "Well!" He rose and slapped both palms hard on the smooth desk. "Enough philosophy for now. Would you like to see some more of the station?"

"I'd like that very much."

Losting merely grunted his indifference.

"You two," Hansen said to Logan and Cohoma, "go back to your quarters. They've been cleared, but I'll see that your personal effects are returned immedi-ately. You've got twenty-four hours off-duty and blank credit at the commissary and cafeteria. Tell Sergeant Binder you've got an open key for your next three meals—order anything you want."

"Thank you, sir," they chorused together.

Hansen nodded toward the dense forest encircling the station. "Don't thank me till you're out there again, trying to figure out what's eating your leg off at the ankle and how to kill it. I'll take charge of your friends." He came around the desk, gave Logan's shoulder a friendly squeeze. "You've got a full shift to enjoy yourselves and a second to relax. After that, if Medical checks you out okay, I expect you to requisition a new skimmer and be back on the job."

XII

As they traveled through the place of wonders Born noted that all the other giants deferred to the Hansen person as one would to chief Sand or Joyla. From this he inferred that Logan's description of him as a hunting team leader considerably understated his authority.

Hansen showed them the living quarters inhabited by the station's staff, the communications equipment up in the polyplexalloy dome, which kept the station in contact with the swarm of skimmers that scoured the forest world, and the receiving hangar which the skimmers returned to to disgorge their cargoes of maps, reports, and new alien material.

"What of the skimmer out there?" Born asked, pointing through a thick window to the shuttlecraft platform. "Why is it so different in shape and so much bigger?"

"That's not a skimmer, Born," Hansen explained. "That's a shuttlecraft, for traveling from here to our supply ships out in space—a place above your Upper Hell. The big supply ships which visit individual worlds can only travel in nothingness."

"How can one travel in nothing?"

"By making a little artificial world out of metal—like this station—and taking food, water, and air with it."

The two hunters stoically partook of the marvels of the cafeteria, where local proteins were combined with colors and flavors and then altered to produce food more familiar to the giants.

Born's interest perked up at this explanation. "I understand, now. What kind of local foods do you use to make yours?"

"Oh, whatever's available. The instrumentation is very versatile. We send out a scoop-equipped skimmer, and it brings back the requisite number of kilos of raw material—vegetable and animal."

"Could I see where this wonder happens?"

"Sure."

He took them through the cafeteria to the processing room, showed them the hopper where plants and animals gathered from the forest were reprocessed with expensive offplanet nutrients, vitamins, and flavorings.

Born studied the bales of shrubs and bushes. The majority were herbaceous succulents, the woody material removed and discarded as scrap. None of those gathered were decayed, none were blighted or dying. These giants did not emfol—they took what they needed, efficiently, easily, blindly. His face remained an enthusiastic mask, despite his thoughts.

They moved on to the recreation chamber, where even Losting was awed by the marvels devoted to idle amusement. Eventually, after this extended tour calculated to impress, Hansen conducted them to the laboratories where research on the fruits of many skimmer trips took place.

Born and Losting were introduced to earnest teams of preoccupied men and women engaged in intense, incomprehensible tasks.

"McKay!" Hansen called to a tall, thin woman dressed in a dark lab frock, hair tied in a thick bun.

"Hello, Chief." Her voice was low, her black eyes piercing. She examined the two hunters. "Interesting—something local that is exactly what it appears to be, for a change."

"This is Born and Losting, great hunters. Gentlemen, Gam McKay, one of our very best—what was your word, Born?—shaman, yes shaman."

"I heard Jan and Kimi made it back. With the help of these two?"

"You'll see the whole report as soon as they get
173

around to making it out," Hansen declared. "Right now I'd appreciate it if you'd show our friends what you and Yazid got out of that conch bulb."

She nodded and they followed her down a narrow walkway between benches stacked high with glittering, light-catching devices, until they reached the end of a table. To one side lay three large crates made of a transparent material like the station windows. These were filled with the branches of the chaga. The bushes from which the branches had been taken, Born noted, had been in full bloom. Each branch was heavy with red-bordered, white-throated flowers, now beginning to wilt noticeably.

The woman McKay opened a small cabinet and carefully removed a tiny clear vial. "This is the distilled extract of about two thousand blooms." She unscrewed the tiny cap and offered it to Hansen. With a smile, he declined. "Born, how about you?" She extended the vial toward him and instructed him to sniff at the open top. Born did so. The scent that rose from the vial was that of the chaga, but intensified many, many times. He reeled slightly, but his expression did not change.

"I am familiar with it," he told them. McKay looked disappointed and turned to Hansen for encouragement.

"Familiar—is that all he can say?"

"Remember, Gam, Born lives among such aromatic blossoms, hunts among them daily." The chemist continued mumbling to herself as she locked the vial back in the cabinet.

"Why is this done?" Born asked Hansen as they left for the next lab.

"Properly thinned and blended with other enhancing and stabilizing chemicals, Born, the little container will serve as a base for a brand new fragrance—what we call perfume. It will be worth a great deal of . . ." Once more he tried to explain that awkward concept.

"I still do not understand. What can such a thing be used for?"

"Women will use it, Born, to make themselves more attractive, to make themselves seem more beautiful."

"They clothe themselves in the odor of death."

"Isn't that putting it a little strongly, Born?" Hansen wondered, taken aback by the grimness of the hunter's comment. He was trying to sympathize with the hunter's natural lack of understanding. However, his explanation seemed to do little to improve Born's understanding.

Born was trying to see, he honestly was. So was Losting. But the further they went through this house of strangeness, the more they saw of its purpose and intents, the harder understanding became. For example, there were the three crates filled with mutilated chaga. The branches had been taken unemfoled from the mature parent plants. Thousands more would be similarly torn to make a little concentrated chaga smell. For what? To heal the sick or nourish the hungry? No, it would be done for amusement—a kind of amusement beyond the comprehension of the two hunters.

It took Losting no longer to see these things than Born. When the bigger man finally realized, though, he was less subtle in his opinions than his companion. "This is a horrible thing you are doing!"

Hansen had already evaluated and recovered from Born's outburst. Now he fielded this second admonition accordingly. "I can sympathize with your position, but surely you can see the long-run advantages, can't you?" He looked from Losting to Born. "Can't you?"

"It is not the taking of the chaga's blooms and branches—it is the way of the taking and the time of taking that are bad," Born replied slowly. "If you had emfoled the chaga—"

"That word Logan mentioned to me. I don't know what it means, Born."

The hunter shrugged. "It is not something which can be explained. You can emfol or you cannot."

"That doesn't make it easy for us, does it?" Hansen said, somewhat testily.

"If you steal the young of the chaga it will not seed, and the parent growth itself will die."

"But there must be lots of chaga in the forest, Born," Hansen argued quietly, oddly quiet. "Surely a few will not be missed?"

"Would you miss your arms and legs?"

A look of comprehension spread across Hansen's face. "I see. It's the plant you're worried about, then. I hadn't realized you felt so strongly about such things. We'll certainly have to see what we can do about this. Naturally we don't want to pick the blooms if the plant's going to suffer, do we?"

"No," Born concurred guardedly.

"It's a minor thing, not at all necessary," Hansen continued, waving off the look of astonishment that appeared on a chemist's face. "It's a minor market we can do without."

He escorted them outside and toward the next and last lab. "There's one more thing I'd like you to see Born. This is where some local knowledge—yours—could really be of help to us. It concerns the kind of burl that produces the life-prolonging extract." They rounded a corner. "We've only been able to find two such burls so far, despite extensive searching. The tree that produces them isn't rare; the burls themselves are. My plant experts tell me the rarity is extreme. Either the trees are extraordinarily healthy, or else burling's not their usual way of combating infestations, infections. If you could find a plentiful supply of such burls, Born, I can promise you we'd listen very strongly to your opinions on which plants to leave alone and which to cut." Hansen admired his own suave professionalism and the facility with which he wielded the scalpel of deception.

They passed between two large, quiet men and entered a chamber slightly larger than the one they had just left. Like the others they had seen, this one was filled with the inexplicable devices of the giants.

Hansen's introduction of the dark, solemn Chittagong and the always agitated Celebes was perfunctory. "How's the work coming, gentlemen?" he concluded.

Celebes replied, his tone a mixture of nervous excitement and confidence. "You read our first report two days back, sir, about what we think it was that caused Wu to go over the edge?"

"I'm in the habit of reading even the meal requests that come out of this lab. They don't add up yet, but yes, I can see how a man with Tsing-ahn's habits could be affected violently by an improper interpretation of the evidence—assuming his burl displayed the same anthropomorphic mimicry this new one does."

"We think that way also, sir. It's back here."

The two white-frocked researchers led them to a broad workbench set at the back of the room. Fresh paint shone with false dampness in the overhead fluorescent lights.

This burl had been cut neatly down the middle. The halves had been separated. One lay propped up against the back wall of the lab, while the other was vised firmly to the bench. A plethora of shining instruments of metal and plastic were scattered on the table and around the halved sections like a swarm of silver spiders. Portions of the burl's interior had been excised and placed in containers of varying sizes. The scene itself conveyed the impression of a frenetic yet studious scientific activity, which had suddenly been halted.

In cross section one could easily see the outer layer of black bark, followed by the first woody layer, which was dark like mahogany. Then it lightened to a deep umber and turned eventually as light as redwood. But after the first half-meter it became something that looked like no wood born of Earth. Weaving black lines ran through a horrid reddish-yellow pulp. Peculiar nodules of gray formed where clumps of the winding black threads joined. At the center of the burl lay several ovoid lumps of brownish-pink, like the seeds of an apple. Here the concentration of jet-colored webbing grew thickest. Most bizarre were the numerous irregular lengths and humps of some pure white substance, which lay scattered throughout the interior of the burl, seemingly at random. Some appeared hard and smooth; others on the verge of powdery dissolution.

Born knew exactly what the burl was, though not its puzzling interior. So did Losting. "This is what you take your life-drug from?" Born asked.

"That's right," Hansen admitted. "Have you seen these kinds of growths before anywhere?"

"We have."

Chittagong and Celebes were immediately and

simultaneously all over the hunters with their questions. "Where . . . How many . . . You mean you've found more than one on the same tree . . . How big were the ones you saw . . . What about the color . . . You're certain they're the same shape . . . The fibrosity of the bark . . . ?"

"Easy, easy. I'm sure our friends can find such trees for us whenever they want. Couldn't you, Born?" Hansen broke in.

"We know of such trees and growths. Some have no burls, as you call them. Others have many." The two scientists whispered between themselves. "How many such burls would you wish?"

Now it was Hansen's turn to stumble in his excitement. "How many? As many as we can find! We can derive a great deal of the drug from one, but there are a lot of aging people in this galaxy, and I doubt enough burls exist to satisfy more than a fraction of them. All you can locate for us we'll make use of. You'll have just about anything you want in return, Born."

"We will not do this thing for you!" Losting shouted suddenly. He put a hand on the axe slung at his hip and took several steps backward. "Born is mad and may do anything, but not I."

"Nor I, Losting," Born muttered bitterly. "And it's true I'm subject to spells of madness. Especially with those who do not choose to think."

"What does he mean by that, Born?" Hansen asked, his manner far from fatherly now. "*You* can understand my position."

Born spun around and tried a last time to make the giant chieftain understand. "And you must understand it is we who live with this world. Not on it, but with it." He was struggling with barely comprehensible concepts. "We take nothing from this world that is not offered freely, even joyously. We take only when time and place is right. You cannot live with a world by taking when and where it suits only you, or eventually your world dies and you with it. You *must* understand this, and you must leave. We could not help you even if we wanted to. Not for all your light weapons and other wonders. This world is not a good place for you. You do not emfol it, and it does not emfol you."

Hansen sighed deeply. "I'm sorry, too, Born. Sorry because you see, this isn't your world. You didn't evolve here, despite all your carefully nurtured superstitions about emfoling and everything else. Your whole ancestral line here reaches back only a few hundred years at most. You've no more claim here than we do. No, you've less than we do. When the time comes we'll file correctly for possession and development with the proper authorities.

"As long as you don't interfere with our operations here, we won't trouble you or your people. We'd prefer to keep relations between us as friendly as possible. If that's not feasible"—he shrugged—"we're quite prepared to do whatever's necessary to ensure felicitous working conditions. I'd hoped we could work together, but—"

"You'll not find any more of these burls. Not without our help."

"It will take longer, cost more, but we'll find them, Born. They're worth whatever it takes, you see. And I'm not yet convinced we've lost your cooperation either. Some additional argumentation remains to be tried." He shook his head sadly. "More paper work, more delays. They're not going to be pleased." He turned and called back to the single doorway. "Santos . . . Nichi?" The two guards entered immediately, sidearms drawn. "There must be an empty room in the new quarters—that wing's still not up to strength. See that our two new associates are set up comfortably there. They've had a long hike and need a good rest, something to eat. Program something nice for them."

Losting had his knife out. "I am tired of this place and the giants. I'll stay here no longer." He eyed Hansen. "I'll talk to you no longer." As the knife was drawn, Born saw one of the guards point a transparent-tipped handgun at the big hunter.

"No, Losting. We must, as the Hansen-chief says, have time to think reasonably on this."

"Madman! Defiler!"

"This is not the time for muscle, Losting!" he said

sharply. "It is difficult to make decisions when dead. Consider the sky-demon and the red light."

Losting looked at the two men blocking their exit, then questioningly at Born. His expression shifted, his eyes dropped. "Yes, Born, you're right. This needs thinking on." He put the knife slowly back in its leaf-leather scabbard.

Hansen managed a grin of reassurance. "I'm sure everything will be clearer after you've had some time to consider all that's been said and shown to you. You're both excited, Born, Losting. A strange place like this station. You've seen more new things in this past half-hour than all your people have seen in the last hundred years, I'm sure! No wonder you're reacting emotionally instead of rationally! Relax, eat yourselves full." He peered hard at Born. "Then I'm sure we can talk about all this again."

Born nodded, smiled back. It was good the Hansenchief could not see into his mind as his machines could see into the Upper Hell.

The two armed giants led them to a room which was spacious and comfortable—comfortable by the standards of the giants. To the hunters the chamber and its furnishings were hard, angled, and oppressive. Born tried the bed, the chair, the single narrow desk and finally settled himself cross-legged on the floor. Losting looked up from where he had been staring at the crack under the door.

"They are still out there. Why did you stop me? Red light or not, I still think I could have killed them both and slit the fat one's throat."

"You would not have lived for a second step, Losting," Born countered softly. "You might have killed one, but—"

"I remember the sky-demon, I remember," Losting shot back irritably. "That is why I did not act as I felt though I think we are destined to go the way of the sky-demon eventually. I know this—I will die before I will aid these monsters."

"As would I," his smaller companion confessed reluctantly. "The giant called Logan was right. She could not explain this all to us. We had to see to understand. And I do understand, but not the way she and the others would have us understand. I am saddened, in a way. A part of them is missing, Losting. They are incomplete. The great pity of it is they are ignorant of their own deficiency."

"They will do great harm in their ignorance."

"Perhaps. We must think hard on this. We cannot fight the red light of the giants. Soon the Hansen-chief will desire to talk with us again. He may not be so courteous this time. The giants have strange ways of killing. The Hansen-chief hinted they have equally strange ways of persuading. If they do not persuade us—and they cannot—I cannot see them permitting us to return to the Home."

"I have held myself back out of respect for you," Losting rumbled. "And because you so often seem to be right in such matters. Why then do you hesitate now?"

"Give me some time, Losting, some time. This must be carefully and rightly done the first time."

Losting mumbled something inaudible and sat down with his back against the door. Pulling out his bone knife, he began steadily to sharpen it against the metal floor.

"Very well, thinker-tinker enemy mine. Take your time. But when they come for us again, if all your madness suggests nothing, I will kill the Hansen-chieftain first, though they make a stew of me with their red light."

Born slowly shook his head. "Can you not see beyond the first rage, Losting? Killing the Hansen-chief will do no good. When Sand and Joyla return to the world, another couple will be chosen. The giants will simply chose a new Hansen-chief." The syllables flowed sharply now. No, somehow we must kill them all and destroy this place."

Losting's seething anger was temporarily displaced by total bewilderment. "Kill them *all*? We cannot even kill one to save ourselves. How can we kill them all?"

"Kill the giants' machines and the giants will die. First we must get out of here."

"I will not dispute that," Losting snorted. "The doorway is latched and this"—he stabbed at the floor with his knife and it skidded away with a whine—"is tougher than ironwood."

"You still do not think beyond your guts, hunter." Born crossed his legs and commenced evaluation of the floor. "Give the world time and it makes its own solutions."

"Mad," whispered Losting.

It was quiet at night within the station as its occupants dreamed away the long wet night outside. Nothing moved save the security personnel who manned the scanning and detection monitors which kept the forest at bay. Outside the station proper, eight of Salomon Cargo's staff manned the gimbaled guns. With the automatic alarms quiet, these isolated representatives of corporate enforcement found nonlethal diversions to pass the time.

In one turret the crew amused itself with another round of cribbage, using a board carved from beryl wood by thranx artisans on Hivehom. Nearby, another pair lost themselves in manuals detailing the joys of vacations to be had on a certain ocean world many parsecs away. In the third, gunners of opposite sex engaged in active dereliction of duty.

While their function was quasimilitary, the station was not a military operation, though their superior, Cargo, regarded it as such. Yet no invading squadron of punishing peaceforcers was expected; no armada mounted by a sly competitor was anticipated overhead. And nothing could approach across the cleared treetops without triggering half a hundred alarms.

So the eight marksmen remained at easy readiness and enjoyed the somnolent casualness of night duty, secure in the knowledge that angels with guts of silver and copper watched over them.

From within, mechanistic atheists plotted to deny these gunners' gods the ohmage due them.

Homesickness electronically assuaged, the last idler dropped off to sleep within the station. No footfalls echoed in the corridors. Only the occasional click of a relay closing, the hum of untiring machinery, the soft sussuration of the vital air-conditioning broke the reign of silence.

There were none to grow curious when a small hole appeared in the middle of a corridor floor. Even if anyone had been passing nearby, chances were they would have passed off the noise as the echo of thunder that somehow penetrated the station's soundproofing. The gap grew larger as the metal floor was peeled up and back like foil. A close observer would have been able to see the hole that extended below the floor through a meter of ferrocrete.

Two massive paws emerged from the gap, widened it until it was big enough for more than a man to pass. A blocky, thick skull protruded, upthrust tusks gleaming in the dim nighttime illumination. Triple orbs shone like lanterns as they made a slow inspection of the empty corridor. The head vanished and a low snuffling that sounded like muffled conversation came from the cavity. It was cut off by a single grunt. Two massive, furred forms squeezed like paste from the hole into the station.

Geeliwan contemplated the alien surroundings and shivered slightly at the unaccustomed chill in the air, while Ruumahum sampled it for something other than temperature.

"Hear no giants, see no giants," Geeliwan murmured in the gentle gutteral rasp of the furcot folk.

"Many are near, behind these walls," replied Ruumahum in a cautioning tone. After a final, thorough sniff to pinpoint a very faint, but unmistakable scent, he said, "This way."

Hugging the metal walls and cloaking themselves in shadow, the furcots padded silently down the corridor they had entered, turned a corner into another. A last corner turned, and they drew back at the sight of the single giant seated before the final door. The giant was not moving.

"He sleeps," Geeliwan murmured tightly.

"Behind him the scent is steady," agreed Ruumahum.

Leaving the corner they padded toward the portal. Ruumahum located the crack at the door's base. Triple nostrils breathed in the smell of person.

Inside the door, Born had not moved from his sitting position on the floor. At the gentle snuffling from outside, his eyes came fully open again. Losting was stretched out asleep on the far side of the chamber, but came awake as Born moved.

"What is—?"

"Quiet." Born made his way to the door on hands and knees. Dropping his face to the floor, he sniffed once, then whispered cautiously, "Ruumahum?" There was an affirmative grunt from the other side. "Open the door. If possible, quietly."

The furcot growled. "There is a guard."

The low conversation finally woke the man in question. Despite the nap, the man was good at his job. He came awake instantly, already prepared for the fantasized jailbreak. What he was not prepared for was the sight of a grinning Geeliwan, massive tusked jaws opened to display a formidable array of gleaming cutlery, breathing into his face. The man fainted.

"Is he dead?" inquired Ruumahum.

Geeliwan snorted a reply. "He sleeps deeply." The furcot joined his companion in studying the doorway. "How does this open. It is not like the doors the persons have made in the Home."

Born's whisper reached them from under the sealed entrance. "Ruumahum, there is a handle near you, shaped like the grip of a snuffler. You must move it down and then pull to open the door. We cannot do so from inside."

The big furcot examined the protrusion carefully. Gripping it in his teeth, he turned his head according to Born's instructions. Born neglected, however, to mention that the handle would stop at the proper place. There was a pinging sound, loud in the quietness.

"It came off, Born," Ruumahum reported, spitting out the metal.

Losting rose and took a couple of steps toward the back of the room. "I've had enough of this place, mad-on-the-hunt. Come if you will." Giving Born no time to argue, he ordered, "Open the door, Geeliwan, now!"

Geeliwan rose on his rear feet, his head nearly touching the corridor ceiling. Falling forward, he pushed simultaneously with fore- and midpaws. There

184

was a groan, accompanied by a pinging sound like the broken handle had made only much louder. The preformed section of alloy bent at the middle and folded over into the room, hanging loosely by its bottom hinge.

Born and Losting leaped over the barrier and followed the furcots down twists and turns in the corridor neither man remembered. Distant mutters and shouts of confusion rose around them like a nest of Chollakees. All at once a man confronted them, appearing at the end of the corridor like a bad memory. He reached for his belt—even as his jaw dropped—and started to pull something small and shiny from it.

Ruumahum hit him with a paw in passing. The glancing blow lifted the man off his feet and slammed him against the wall. He was still crumpling to the floor as they passed.

The furcot rumbled terribly, "This place needs killing," and showed signs of returning to finish off the guard.

Born argued otherwise, and they ran on. "Not now, Ruumahum. These creatures kill without thinking. Let us not fall prey to the same frailty." Ruumahum muttered under his breath, but led on.

Moments later they reached the wide corridor that encircled the station. Both Born and Losting had their axes out now, but there was no need to use them. The station was still half asleep, the source of the disturbance behind them as yet unknown.

Another minute and they were at the hole Ruumahum and Geeliwan had ripped in the station floor. Ruumahum led the way. Born jumped in after, feet first, followed by Losting. Geeliwan was right behind.

Like a flotilla of fluorescent bees, lights around the station began to wink on erratically; alarms began to sound. In the outlying turrents, curses replaced idle comments as the gun crews rushed to man instruments of destruction. Alert, well-trained eyes, both human and mechanical, scanned the open area round the station, minutely examined the unchanged forest wall. Within that tensely monitored region nothing threatening moved, nothing unexpected showed itself.

Suddenly something appeared on the computer

screen, filling a fair-sized section within range of the north turret. The triggerwoman engaged her electronic sensors and let fly. The burst totally demolished a small cloud of flitters which had left the hylaea for the beckoning station lights. That had unnerved the inhabitants of the station until the central detectors report what had been destroyed.

Still blinking sleep from his eyes, a disheveled Hansen struggled to untangle robe and hair as he was conducted by a guard to the hole in the floor.

"A centimeter of duralloy over a meter-thick ferrocrete base," someone in the little crowd that had gathered muttered. The group parted as Hansen arrived. He fought to keep incredulity from his face when he saw the size of the cavity.

"I thought they weren't supposed to have any advanced tools."

"They don't." Everyone turned to see who offered the answer.

Logan joined them, pulling her hair back away from her face as she bent to examine the gap's interior. Her expression was drawn. "The furcots must have done it," she concluded tiredly.

"A singular pronouncement," Hansen declared. "What is a furcot, Logan?"

"It's an associate animal Born's people live with. A hexapodal omnivore. At least we assume it's an omnivore." She turned her gaze back to the hole. "When night came and their human companions didn't return or send for them, they must have decided to come looking on their own."

"Interesting," was all the station chief murmured.

Reports and people came and went. The population of the little crowd changed without shrinking. After a while equipment was brought and a designated "volunteer" lowered into the cavity. He was not gone too long before he had secured the information Hansen required.

Nodding and listening intently, Hansen received the explorer's report. He patted the man on the back, then returned to the edge of the hole. The group gathered around it now consisted of section heads, men like Cargo and Blanchfort.

186

"Can any of you imagine where this hole goes?" Hansen demanded. Cautious silence. Woe to the bureaucrat who volunteered inaccurate information! Besides, they would know in a minute. "Don't any of you even know where you're standing?" Puzzled glances all around. "The hole continues on downward into one of the three trunks this station is set upon. It appears this one tree isn't quite solid. It appears," Hansen continued, his expression and rising fury sufficient to make his underlings recoil, "that there's some kind of native animal that runs burrows through such trees! All these furcots had to do was locate such a burrow below the level we cleared off and walk within digging distance of this floor. *This floor,* ladies and gentlemen!"

His voice dropped slightly. "They didn't have to worry about our monitors and guns. They didn't have to worry about the charged screens encircling the trunks. The only thing that puzzles me is—how did they know they didn't have to worry about such things?"

Cohoma had joined the others. "They're a bit more than animals, sir. They can talk, a little. Enough to make conversation. I talked to them myself. They don't like talking, as I under—"

"Shut up, you idiot," the station chief said in a quiet voice that was worse than a shout. He continued muttering, "And they expect me to run a clandestine operation like this, on an inimical world like this, with a crew like this—"

"Excuse me, Chief," the head of engineering offered quietly. "Do you want me to round up some people to plug this thing?" He gestured toward the gap.

"No, I don't want you to round up some people to plug this thing," Hansen shot back, mimicking the engineer's querulous tone. "Cargo, where's Cargo?"

"Sir?" The head of station Security stepped through the group.

"Leave this opening untouched. Mount a rifle over it with a four man crew, and rotate the crew every four hours." He put hands on hips and rubbed absently at the brown robe. "Maybe they'll try and come

187

back this way. No more talk this time, not with one man already dead. We'll find this Home and start fresh with these folk."

"Sir?" Cargo hesitated, then asked, "The turret crews are a bit skittish. They're not too sure what they're supposed to be watching out for."

"A couple of short, swarthy men accompanied by—" He looked over his shoulder, snapped at Logan, "What are these things supposed to look like?"

"Six-legged," she explained to Cargo, "dark green fur, three eyes, long ears, a couple of short thick tusks sticking up from the lower jaw, several times the mass of a man . . ."

"That'll do," said Cargo drily. He nodded to Hansen, spun smartly on one heel and strode away to communicate with his people.

"Tell me," Hansen queried Logan, "did you ever get the impression that your friend Born might not approve of our aims in coming here?"

"We never went into specifics about our activities, Chief," she replied. "There were times when one could have read his questions and answers several ways. But since he was in the process of saving our lives, I didn't think it expedient to argue motivations with him. I felt our primary objective was to get back here whole."

"Yet despite this uncertainty about how he might react, you let him leave these two semi-intelligent animals free to mount a rescue."

Logan couldn't keep herself from showing a little anger of her own. "What was I supposed to do? Drag them along bodily? It seemed to me best at the time to stay on friendly terms with Born and Losting. The furcots saw what a laser cannon can do. None of Cargo's brilliant assistants located any passageways in these support trunks! How could I guess that—"

"You could have insisted he bring his pets along."

"You still don't understand sir." She fought to make it plain. "The furcots aren't *pets*. They're independent semisentient creatures with extensive reasoning powers of their own. They associate with humans because they want to, not because they've been domesticated. If they want to do something like remain behind in

188

their forest, there's no way Born or anyone else can force them to do otherwise." She glanced significantly at the hole in the floor where the metal had been peeled back like the skin of an apple. "Would *you* want to argue with them?"

"You debate persuasively, Kimi. It's my own fault. I expect too much of everyone. And those expectations are always fulfilled." He looked broodingly at the dark tunnel. "I wish there were some way of avoiding a confrontation. Not because it would make our operation here any less illegal if we have to kill a few natives."

"Not natives, sir," Logan reminded him, "survivors of—"

Hansen cocked his head and glared at her, his voice steady, hard. "Kimi, back in spoke twelve I saw a maintenance subengineer named Haumi with his face pushed in and his back broken. He's dead, now. As far as I'm concerned, that makes Born and Losting, and any of their cousins who feel similarly about our presence here, natives, hostile ones. I have an obligation to the people who put up the credit for this station. I'll take whatever steps are necessary to protect that. Now, is there any chance you could find your way back to this village, or Home?"

Logan paused thoughtfully. "Considering some of the twists and turns, ups and downs we took, I doubt it. Not without Born's help. Our skimmer must be nearly covered by fresh growth by now. Even if we were to locate it, I don't know if we could find the Home from there. You've no idea, sir," she half pleaded, "what it's like trying to move through this world on foot. It's hard enough to tell up from down, let alone horizontal direction. And the native carnivorous life, the defensive systems developed by the flora—"

"You don't have to tell me, Kimi." Hansen jammed his hands into the robe's pockets. "I helped clear the space for this station. Well, we'll still try to take at least one of them alive when they come back."

"Your pardon, sir," Cohoma said, his expression uncertain. "Come back? I'd think Born would tend to hightail it back to the Home to organize resistance to us and warn his fellows."

Hansen shook his head sadly, smiled condescendingly. "You'll never be much more than a scout, Cohoma."

"Sir," Logan began, "I don't think you're being entirely fair—"

"And the same goes for you, Logan. Goes for the two of you." His voice sank dangerously, all pretense of fatherliness gone. "You've both been guilty of underestimating your subject. Maybe their smaller stature made you feel superior. Maybe it was the fact that you're the product of a technologically advanced culture—the reasons don't really matter. You probably still think you talked this Born into making this trip. You think you kept him in the dark concerning the station's true purpose. Instead, look what's happened. Why do you think Born wanted advanced weaponry above all else? To fight off local predators? Patrick O'Morion, no! So he could eventually deal on even terms with *us!*

"Now he knows the nature and disposition of our defenses here, the station layout, has a rough idea of our numerical strength, and sees how really isolated from outside help we are. He's also divined our intentions and decided they run contrary to his own. No, I don't see that kind of man running for help. He'll take at least one crack at us on his own."

Cohoma looked abashed. "None of which would matter," Hansen went on, "if he was still sitting back in that room, under guard. It pains me to have to kill so resourceful a man. The trouble is this spiritual attitude they apparently take toward the welfare of every weed and flower. That's what you two have failed to perceive. With your Born, our announced activities here are grounds for a holy war. I'll bet my pension he's out there now, sitting on some idolized thornbush, watching us, and thinking of ways to make the blasphemer's way into hell fast and easy. Now, tell me more about these furcots of theirs." He kicked at the bent metal around the hole. "I've got the evidence of one dead man and a breach in the

190

station proper to testify to their strength. How invulnerable are they?"

"They're flesh and bone—flesh, anyway," Cohoma corrected himself. "They're quite mortal. We saw several of them slain by a marauding tribe of local killers called Akadi. The time to worry is when they throw nuts at you."

Hansen eyed Cohoma oddly, decided to press on with his questions. "What about weapons?"

"Something called a snuffler, kind of like a big blow-gun. It shoots poisonous thorns. Otherwise all we saw were the usual primitive implements—knifes, spears, axes, and the like. Nothing to worry about."

"I'll remember that," Hansen said grimly, "the first time I see one sticking out of your neck, Jan. A club can kill you just as dead as a SCCAM shell. Anything else?"

Logan managed an uneasy smile. "Not unless they've learned how to tame a silverslith."

"A what?"

"A large local tree-dweller. It's at least fifty meters long, climbs on several hundred legs, and has a face only an AAnn nest-master could love. According to Born, it never dies and can't be killed."

"Thanks," Hansen replied tartly. "That encourages me no end." He started to leave, turned back. "There's also the chance nothing at all's going to happen. So we're going to continue with normal operations under more than normal security. I can't afford to close up shop waiting for your little root-lover to proclaim his intentions. You'll both report for duty tomorrow as usual and check out a new skimmer, pick up new assignments."

"Yes, sir," they chorused dispiritedly.

Hansen took a deep breath. "For myself, I've got another report to make out, more than usually negative. Get out of my sight, the both of you."

Cohoma seemed about to add something, but Logan put a cautioning hand on his arm and drew him away. Hansen continued to hand out directives. One by one, the crowd dispersed, each to his or her assigned task. The station chief was left alone. He

191

stood staring down the hole for a long time until the rifle crew arrived.

When they began to set up the powerful, slim weapon on its tripod, he spun around and stalked off toward his office, trying to imagine the phraseology that would explain to his shadowy superiors how the station perimeter was violated by two aborigines and a pair of oversized, six-legged cats.

The director would not be pleased. No, most definitely not pleased.

XIII

Beneath a broad curved panpanoo leaf which served as shelter from the steadily falling night-rain, man and furcot rested on a wide tuntangcle and held a council of war. Hansen was right. To Born and Losting, Ruumahum and Geeliwan, the actions of the giants were grounds for a jihad.

"We can conceal ourselves in the trees below the level where they have killed," Losting suggested, his voice sharp against the constant pit-pat of rain, "and pick them off as they come out."

"In their sky-boat skimmers as well?" Born countered. "With our snufflers, no doubt."

"Gather the brethren," Ruumahum growled terribly.

Born shook his head sorrowfully. "They have long eyes for seeing and long weapons for killing, Ruumahum. We must think of something else."

It was silent then save for splash and spray and occasional shuffling below the panpanoo. Once Born's half-lidded eyes opened and he muttered to the wood, "Roots . . . roots." Other eyes gazed at him hopefully, till he turned quiescent again.

"I have an idea of how this may be begun," he finally announced without looking at anyone in particular. "It scratches at the edge of my mind like a wheep hunting for the entrance to the brya burrow. Roots . . . roots and a parable." He got to his feet, stretched. "Where is the power of the giants anchored? From whence do the marvels attributed to them come?"

"From Hell, of course," Losting mumbled.

"But which Hell, hunter? Our world draws strength from the Lower Hell. These giants, from what they say, derive theirs from the Upper. Their roots are locked in the sky, not the ground. They have cut their way into our world by digging downward. We will cut into theirs by digging up."

"How can one dig up?" Losting wondered aloud.

By way of reply Born walked to the edge of the sheltering panpanoo and stared up into the tepid rain. "We must find a stormtreader." He turned back to eye Ruumahum questioningly. "How many days till the next big rain?"

The furcot uncurled himself and padded to stand next to his person. The blunt muzzle probed the night air. As water dribbled off his face, he sniffed deeply, inhaled through his powerful mouth. "Three, maybe four days, Born."

The stormtreader was not too rare, not too common, and no two were ever found near each other. But moving on the Third Level, they had located the silver-black bole rising in the forest on the far side of the station. It was not close to the cleared area, but the long, chainlike leaves reached downward all the way to the Sixth Level. They would reach upward as easily.

There was only one way to handle the leaves of the stormtreader. By covering hands and paws, arms and legs with the sap of the lient, it was possible to safely draw up hundreds of meters of interlocked leaf and coil it in readiness.

"I still do not understand," Losting admitted, as they rubbed the sticky black sap from their hands.

"Remember, the giant-made vine web we first passed through when they took us into their station-Home? Remember the Sal-giant explaining what it ate? I once saw a cruta eat so much tesshanda fruit it exploded.

193

Its insides flew all over the branch it had been sitting on. I'll never know whether I looked as surprised as the cruta did, but I'll not forget the sight as long as I breathe. This is what we do here, I hope."

Losting was appalled. "We may only make the giants' roots stronger, firmer."

Born shrugged. "Then we will try something else."

Despite Losting's impatience and uneasiness, they waited through the storm that raged the third night. Born knew he had made the right decision the fourth evening, when Ruumahum scented the air and rasped, "Rain and wind and noise aplenty, this night."

"We must move quickly, then, before it howls at us, or even the sap of the lient won't save us." He spoke as the first big drops began to set the forest humming.

In near total darkness they started toward the station, moving beneath the cleared area covered by multiple electronic sensors and light amplifiers and the red light death. They had three of the long silvery leaves. Each of the furcots wrestled with one, Born and Losting with the third. Thickly coated with lient sap they dragged the ever-lengthening strands behind them, until they reached the dark wall formed by one of the station-supporting trunks. Born touched it, peered close. The topped tree was already beginning to die from loss of its leaf-bearing crown and infection of the heartwood.

Moving slowly they started upward, parallel to the colossal trunk. Thunder boomed down to them now, as the still distant lightning cracked the sky like drying mud beneath a summer sun. Already Born was drenched. Ruumahum had been right. Rain aplenty, this night.

The black lient also helped conceal them when they emerged into the open air. Wind still carried the rain to them, but here, directly beneath the shielding bulk of the station, it was still relatively dry. That was fortunate, since there were no friendly cubbles and creepers to mount there. They had to make their way with the heavy leaves up the vertical shaft. But though security was no less lax and those who studied the monitors and scanners no less intent on their tasks, the tiny blots that moved up the trunk were not seen. The station's defenses were aimed out, not down. Nor did Born make the mistake of trying to mount the tree Ruumahum and Geeliwan had used to rescue them. That bole, at least, still commanded plenty of attention.

Born waited till all were ready just below the metal web that prevented further ascent. Lightning split the night-rain steadily now. They had to hurry. Above him, the web crackled and sputtered with each atmospheric discharge. He nodded. Together, man and furcot carefully draped the three silver-black leaves over different strands of the web. Born held his breath as the leaf touched metal. A few tiny sparks, then nothing.

"Down and away—quickly!" he called to the furcots.

Within the sealed outpost, an unexpected movement caught the eye of the third engineer on duty at the generator station. He frowned, walked over to the dials in question. There was nothing radically wrong about the slight fluctuations in current that were registered, but there should have been no such flutterings at all. The variations were more than the most violent storm was expected to produce. For a brief moment he considered waking the chief engineer, decided against chancing that worthy's temper. Probably there was some minor malfunction in the monitoring equipment itself—the B transformer had displayed a tendency to act up from time to time. And it could hardly be due to normal shifts in the power produced by the solar collector—not in the middle of the night!

The monitoring chips checked out operational one after another. He was still searching for the source of the disturbance when a huge lightning bolt struck near enough for the sound to penetrate the station's dense soundproofing.

Several things happened simultaneously.

The ear-splitting discharge struck a tree in the hylaea to the southeast of the station. There was no shattering of wood, no brief flare of flame. The crown of this particular tree was not split or blackened. Instead, the naked apex of the stormtreader drank the lightning like a child sucking milk through a straw. The metal-impregnated wood quivered visibly under the impact, but was not damaged as the tremendous concentration of voltage was distributed by the tree's remarkable inner structure.

Momentarily, the mild defensive charge the tree usually maintained was increased a thousand million times. Under normal circumstances the entire charge would have been dissipated into the distant ground by the stormtreader's complex root system, creating oxides of nitrogen and heavily enriching the surrounding soil. But this time something else commanded the full force of that jagged disruption, diverted it through the defensive screen formed by the tree's long, deadly leaves.

The puzzled engineer would never know that his meters and dials had registered correctly, would never learn the source of those first enigmatic fluctuations in current.

Born did not know what to expect. He had hoped, as he had described to Losting, to overfeed the protective webs which guarded the station's underbelly. Instead, the three grids exploded like pinwheels a nanosecond following the deafening draw by the stormtreader. They flared like burning magnesium for long seconds before wilting and melting to slag.

Distant explosions sounded across the dark Panta, and lights flared within the station, reaching out to the tiny knot of stupefied watchers crouched in the forest wall. Modulators sparked and exploded, unable to regulate the stupendous overload. The storage batteries simply melted like ice, depriving the station of back-up power.

Thirty million volts at 100,000 amperes poured into the station's generating system, melting or shorting every cable, every outlet, every bulb, tube, and appliance within. One overriding eruption sounded from the far side of the station as the central transformer and solar plant were blown wholesale through the outside wall.

Over the steady rhythm of the indifferent nightrain, the screams and shouts of the confused, the stunned, and the burned began to sound. But there were no cries of the slowly dying. Those who had been killed, like the engineer, had been electrocuted instantly.

Losting started forward. "Let us finish it."

Born had to reach to restrain him. "They still may have the red light, which kills before a snuffler can be loaded, hunter."

Losting indicated the twisted, smoking gun turrets. Though the cannons within could still be repaired, they were momentarily useless. The turret mechanisms were thoroughly burnt out.

"Not those," Born explained. "The tiny ones the giants wear like axes may still work." He sat back on the damp branch and eyed the sky. "What will the violent and unusual noises bring by the morning, hunter? Think! What can several men shouting in unison attract?"

Losting searched his thoughts, until his eyes widened. "Floaters. Not Bunas . . . Photoids."

Born nodded. "They must be stirring already."

"But surely since they've been here, these giants have seen Photoid floaters?"

"Perhaps not," his companion argued. "Their skimmers are quiet, and Photoids are rare. Only prey large enough for a Photoid can make enough noise to attract one. I did not think of this."

Losting sat back and clasped his hands together in front of his bunched-up legs. "What will it matter, anyway? The floaters will see no prey and depart."

"They may well do just that, Losting. But think of how the giants react, how the Logan and Cohoma persons first reacted to me, how they reacted in the world. They fear without trying to understand, Losting. And they must be nervously fearful now. We will see how they react to the floaters."

Hansen kicked at the still smoking fragments of metal and polyplexalloy that speckled the buckled floor and surveyed the gaping hole where the power station had once sat. Puddles of hardened slag were all that remained of the complex, expensive installation. It was not broken—it was gone.

A very tired Blanchfort appeared. Like everyone else, he had not slept in many hours.

"Let's hear the rest of it," Hansen sighed.

"Everything which drew power is burnt out or melted, sir," the section chief reported solemnly. "There isn't a circuit, a solid- or fluid-state switch, a linked module left in the place. We're going to have to rebuild the entire system."

Hansen allowed himself several minutes to reflect on this, then asked, "Did they find out what caused it?"

"Mamula thinks so. It's . . . well, it's pretty straightforward, once you've seen it."

Hansen followed the other man through the station, passed exhausted crews working at blackened sections of walls and floor. Before long they reached the access hatch through which an open elevator lowered explorers to the roof of the cut-off forest below. The elevator, naturally, had been burnt out. Someone had cut the melted wiring and other electrical connections and rigged a makeshift winch. The elevator was in use now, suspended halfway between the station and green world beneath. Suspended right at the level where the charged grid had once been.

Hansen peered through the gap. From the point where the grid had been bolted to the tree, a ring of still hot metal ran like candlewax down the trunk. Wisps of smoke from the scorched bark still rose into the air.

"Do you see it, Chief?" Blanchfort asked.

Hansen squinted against the brightness of day, stared harder. "See what? I don't—"

"There, to the left a little and below where Mamula and his people are working. There are two more further around the trunk."

The station chief stared. "You mean that long silvery chain that extends down into the treetops?"

"That's it, sir, only it's not a chain. Not of metal, anyway. It's a leaf, or many interlocked leaves."

"What about them?"

"Mamula thinks they were laid into the grid before the storm last night. We sent a party out—I hoped our two native boys would show themselves, but they didn't—to trace it back. All three leaves go straight down into the forest for about fifteen meters, then off to the southeast. They link up to the parent tree about thirty meters back from the clearing." He turned and gestured out an uncracked window. "That way.

"It's one of the smaller emergents. Bare crown, mostly black and silver-colored—bark, leaves, everything. Very little brown or green in it, except in some subsidiary growth." He glanced down at the clipboard he always carried with him. "A woman named Stevens was in charge of the tracing party. According to her report, the tree itself maintains a lethal charge. Anything that brushes against one of its long leaves is killed instantly. Mamula theorizes that when the tree is hit by lightning, as it apparently was last night, the charge is somehow handled and carried off. Only a tiny recharge is necessary to maintain the tree's defensive system. And it's an isolated specimen, though he says if we look, we'll find more of them around."

"I see. A few of these serve as lightning rods for the whole forest, protecting the other trees from the nightly storms. Except," and he had to fight to keep from shouting, "last night that charge was directed elsewhere."

"Not directed sir—drawn."

Hansen looked grim. "No wonder it blew out every circuit in the place. And of course, nobody saw anything unusual prior to this?"

Blanchfort looked unhappy. "No, sir. Cargo is still chewing out some of his people, I'm told."

"That'll do us a lot of good. Black Horse, it's done." He quieted, kicked at a scrap of curdled acrylic. "What does Murchison say about this?"

"Murchison's dead, sir."

Hansen muttered to himself. "All right, Mamula's in charge then."

"Yes, sir. He thinks he can eventually repair some of the leads, and we've got replacements for about twenty percent of the wiring and circuitry, but we need a complete new generating facility."

"Any cretin could see that. There's a hole where the old one was big enough to fly a skimmer through."

"The big block of solar cells is cracked—that's got to be replaced. Climate control is completely gone—

that means no air-conditioning, among other things."

"Among other things," Hansen echoed disgustedly. "What have we got left?"

Another glance at the sheaf of hastily scribbled reports. "All hand weapons and four uncharging rifles intact, so we're far from defenseless. Mamula's cannibalized a fresh transformer and all the small batteries he could scavenge to keep the refrigeration units for the hospital going. And we've got plenty of prepackaged emergency rations."

"Communications?"

"Shot, of course. But the transceiver and tridee in the shuttle still work fine. All its internal systems are operating."

"Pity it's a shuttle and not a Commonwealth stingship. When's the next supply ship due?"

"Two and a half weeks, sir, according to schedule."

Hansen nodded, walked to the nearest door and strode out onto the porch that still encircled the station. "Two and a half weeks," he repeated, putting his hands on the tubular railing and studying the distant, rustling wall of green, the green-brown treetops beneath. "Two and a half weeks for a fully equipped first surface station designed to stand off anything up to and including an attack by a Commonwealth frigate to somehow survive a siege by two half-pint loin-clothed hunters—the bastard religious-fanatic offspring of a bunch of misdirected colonists!"

"Yes, sir."

Hansen spun at the voice, roared at the newly arrived figure. "Think your people can handle that, Cargo? Or do you think we're outnumbered?!"

Cargo drew himself up stiffly. "I've got to do with what I have, sir, specifically, the best personnel the company could buy." The intimation was clear: there might be certain things not even the parent corporation could purchase.

"If you wish, sir, I could assemble a pursuit force. We could scour the perimeter until—"

"Oh, come on, Cargo," Hansen muttered, "I don't need a sacrificial lamb, either. Your suicide wouldn't salve anything. You'd never be able to tell them apart from the rest of the fauna. They'd pick off your

200

people one at a time—or else just stay clear of you and let the forest finish you off." He turned back to the emerald ocean.

"I still can't figure out what prompted them to such violence, though. The desire to escape, sure. To trouble us, sure—but to counterattack? They've got to be awfully confident, or awfully angry at something. I know that Born disapproves of our intentions here, but he didn't strike me as the homicidal type. We're missing something. I'd like another chance to talk to him, just to find out how we've provoked him so strongly."

"I'd like a chance to cut his slimy little throat," Cargo responded briskly.

"I hope you get your chance, Cargo. But I wouldn't count on seeing him before he sees you."

Cargo relaxed his stance but not the stiffness in his voice. "Sir, I spent thirty years in Commonwealth forces before deciding it was thirty years wasted with no future. I've been with the company four years now as a Special Projects Security Director. If this midget gets within arm's length, you can bet your administrative certificate I'll break his neck before he can kill me."

"I'm betting more than that on it, Sal." He looked skyward. "Going to be another hot—mother of god, what are those?"

Cargo's head turned and he looked into the faint blue-green of the southern sky. Three drifting shapes were slowly nearing the station. Each of them was half the size of the structure.

"Have we any turrets operational?"

"No, sir," Cargo told him, still staring at those apparitions. "But we've still got the rifles."

"Set them up in the dome. Leave a few people to watch the three support trunks and get the rest of your people up there, too. Leave the guard on the tunneled trunk, also. I don't want any surprises from that direction while we're occupied with *those*. Move."

Shouts and orders resounded throughout the damaged outpost. Anyone with an operational handgun was directed to report to the dome. No one had to question

201

why—the three Photoid floaters made no attempt to camouflage their approach.

Logan and Cohoma were among those who found themselves clustered beneath one of the now retracted polyplexalloy panels. Three laser rifles were also set up there, the long tubes aimed skyward now.

Hansen saw the two scouts arrive, beckoned to Cargo and stalked over to them. "Ever see anything like those before?"

Logan studied the bloated monsters, fascinated. "No, Chief, never. I don't recall Born ever discussing anything like them."

"Any chance your pygmy might be controlling them, somehow?" asked Cargo.

Logan considered. "No, I don't think so. If they're dangerous but manipulatable, I think Born would have summoned them to protect us when we were traveling along the treetop level."

The floaters were gigantic gas bags, roughly ovoid and showing rippling, saillike fins on their backs and at the sides. The steady fluttering of the body-length protuberances propelled them lazily through the air. The gas sacs themselves were a pale, translucent blue through which the sun shone clearly. Beneath each bag lay a mass of rubbery-looking tissue that folded and refolded in on itself like knotted cables. Suspended from this was a series of short, thick tendrils which shone like the mirror vines Logan remembered from weeks in the forest. Colors flashed from turning, spinning organic prisms, giving the whole creature the appearance of a balloon trying to hatch a rainbow. Longer tentacles dangled well below this glittering, polished conglomeration. These had a more natural appearance, in hue a light blue like the gas sacs, and seemed to be coated with a dully reflective mucuslike substance.

They continued to drift toward the station while a little knot of scientists huddled by the ruined deep space transceiver debated whether they were primarily plant or animal.

"Ready on those rifles!" Hansen commanded. So far the creatures had made nothing resembling a hostile move. But their sheer bulk was making him jittery.

The eerie silence with which they approached did nothing to improve the state of his nerves.

"If they approach within twenty meters, fire," he told Cargo, "but not before." The security chief nodded.

One of the floaters shifted toward them, those trailing cablelike tentacles twitching in the air. It stopped outside Hansen's critical perimeter and hovered there. Despite the fact that it displayed nothing resembling an organ of sight, Hansen could not escape the feeling that it was studying them. It continued hovering there, long fins rippling rhythmically to hold it steady, while the tension within the dome and the rest of the station rose unbearably.

Someone shouted and all eyes went down and out. The other two floaters were drifting over the shuttlecraft—the last remaining contact with the company, with the rest of the universe, with help. One long tentacle dipped, to curl around the shuttle's bow. The tentacle pulled curiously, effortlessly. There was a screech as the shuttle slid a little within its flexible moorings.

A pencil-thin beam of intense red light reached across the intervening space to strike the curious floater. Cargo spun and yelled at the rifle crews. "Who fired? I gave no order to—!"

The beam contacted the gas sac and seemed to pass straight through at an angle. The floater dropped slightly at the strike, then regained its altitude and position. On impact a slight wisp of smoke had risen from the point where the laser had struck. There was a faint, barely audible whistling sound, that might have been a sigh. The floater started to rise, forgetting momentarily to release the shuttle. Distant pings sounded clearly across the cleared treetops as one mooring cable after another snapped like piano strings.

Someone fired a pistol then, and the other rifles opened up. Cargo raged among his people, but the rising panicky cries within the station all but drowned him out. Burst after crimson burst lanced out to strike at the massive floaters. Whenever one struck a gas sac the injured floater would drop slightly, then puff itself up and regain its former height. Bursts which landed among the forest of tentacles glanced off the reflective stubs and mucus-covered tentacles.

From their position behind a tangle of singing comb vines, Born whispered, "They are very patient, for floaters."

"Perhaps they will not chose to fight," Losting worried aloud.

Behind him, Geeliwan growled. "Floaters' anger comes slow, lasts long."

Whether stimulated by the irritating, persistent stings of the lasers or by the noisy milling of the tiny shapes in the station, the floaters finally began to react. Their shorter, almost quartzlike tendrils shifted, forming complex patterns, instinctive defensive alignments—even as the red light from below continued to stab at them. The sun was high and hot. But within the newly arranged complex of short tendrils the sunlight was internally concentrated, reconcentrated, magnified and remagnified, shuttled and focused and jimmied around through a farrago of organic lenses, intricate enough to put the human eye to shame.

From the two nearest floaters beams of immensely concentrated sunlight struck the station. By and large the walls of the outpost were honeycomb aluminum and not duralloy. Where the angry sunlight struck, it melted away, to burn what lay within.

Hansen fled the dome. So did Cohoma and Logan and most of the other personnel. Cargo stayed with his crews, cursing their inaccuracy and ineffectiveness. He did not realize that the gas sacs of the floaters were compartmentalized, did not recognize the speed with which they were replaced, with which fresh gas was generated in the newly rewalled cells. He failed to recognize the futility of the laser rifles, which could bring down a shuttle or major aircraft; failed to even as the ultraintensified light projected by the third floater struck the dome, melted away the tough polyplexalloy, melted away the rifles themselves, melted or ignited chairs, consoles, flooring, and instrumentation. He realized the failure, however, just as he and the last rifle crew were carbonized.

The angry floaters remained for half an hour, drifting back and forth across the station. They continued

204

playing energy into the ruins long after the last flicker of desperate red rose from the smoking wreckage.

Eventually they tired, whatever they possessed for minds finally sated. Leaving the station pockmarked with gaps and scorched slashes, fires consuming its innards, they drifted off to the south whence they had come.

"Now, let us finish it," rumbled Losting.

"There may be some left," Born argued. "Let us wait until the flames have finished their work and the sun has begun its dying."

As happened now and again, the night-rain began before evening that day. It was still light enough to see as they entered the ravaged hulk of the station, water dripping around them. Droplets sizzled and hissed where they struck the still superheated metal. In places the corridor walls had run like butter under the floaters' assault. Recooled metal leaped and plunged.

The hunters entered the outside corridor with snufflers loaded and ready, though neither expected to find anything alive within the smoking structure.

"Even necessary death is unpleasant," Born observed solemnly, sniffing the penetrating odor of carbonized flesh. "This is not a place to linger long."

Losting agreed, pointing down the curving pathway. "I will take this half and meet you on the other side. The sooner we conclude this and start Home, the better I'll feel." Born nodded agreement and started off in the opposite direction.

The big hunter waited until his companion was out of sight before following Geeliwan. He did not encounter many corpses. Most had either been buried beneath rubble and slag, or else burned beyond recognition.

Losting considered the annihilation wrought by the floaters. Once he had watched while a curious one prodded with a tree-thick tentacle at a sleeping hunter, only to leave the dreamer in peace and proceed amiably on its way. He had also seen one of the normally gentle scavengers have a tentacle bitten in half by a startled diverdaunt. The floater had proceeded to tear the carnivore's tree apart and reduce its upper trunk to splinters before trapping and roasting its attacker.

He wished there had been another way. They were passing through the far end of what had been the big skimmer hangar. The swift exploratory disks it had housed were hardly recognizable now. Most had their transparent domes crushed in, their hulls reduced to slick lumps of fused alloy. One uptilted fuselage held the melted remains of two giants still in the small circular cockpit, their bones welded whitely to the metal. Had the surviving giants not pressed the fight as long as they had, the floaters probably would have grown bored and eventually drifted off to their nesting grounds in the south. Instead, these bulky, panicked assassins had fought to the last, their weapons of red light pathetically useless against the nervous systems of the translucent Photoids.

Geeliwan suddenly growled and leaped ahead. The furcot had smelled the smell—too late. It had been masked by the miasma of the burning station. The light caught him above the eyes in midjump. He fell to the floor, a silent, crumpled heap.

Losting had the snuffler up and was firing before the furcot fell. There was the distinctive soft phut of the tank seed bursting. In the near dark, someone screamed. Then it was quiet.

From behind a twisted, bent section of floor an unsteady figure rose—Logan. Swaying, she dropped her pistol and reached down with both hands to pull the jacari thorn from her right breast. A tiny blot of red appeared, staining her tunic. She stared at it dumbly. Losting had reloaded when the second beam caught him in the side, ripped through skin, bone, nerves, and organs. Usually the shock of such extensive, abrupt destruction was enough to kill instantly. Losting, however, was not a normal man. He dropped to his knees, then toppled onto his left side. Still alive, he clutched with both hands at his side. The snuffler clattered to the damp metal floor.

Logan staggered forward a couple of steps and tried to say something to the hunched-up figure on the floor. Her mouth worked but nothing came out. Then her eyes glazed over as the potent nerve poison

took hold, and she fell like a tree. She lay there unmoving, a broken toy doll, one arm bent grotesquely
under her.

From a black tunnel nearby two figures rose cautiously. Cohoma walked to the still form of Logan
and knelt beside her. Hansen continued past with
barely a glance at her, toward Losting. Behind him,
finding neither pulse nor heartbeat, the scout pilot
muttered bitterly, "He's got you there, Kimi."

The station chief kept his pistol trained on Losting
as he approached. In the hollowness of the death-
filled corridor, the hunter's breathing sounded loud.
Hansen had lost much of his clothing and all of his
bureaucratic demeanor. He was panting heavily. Kinky
gray hair formed a mat over the bulge of his stomach.

"Before I kill you, Losting, why?"

"Born knew," the hunter gasped painfully. A pro-
found numbness slowly blanketed him, creeping over
his body from the burned side. "He told you. You
take without giving. You take without asking. You
borrow without returning. You do not emfol. Our . . .
world."

"It's not your world, Losting," Hansen said tiredly.
Behind them, Cohoma suddenly looked thoughtful.
He murmured something about empathetic foliation
and forced evolution. Hansen didn't hear him. "But
you refused to accept that. Too bad." Hansen turned
and called. "Muerta . . . Hofellow . . . check his
animal."

A man and woman, one armed with a pistol and the
other with a machete, emerged from the side access-
way. Taking no chances, the woman put another
burst into the head of the supine furcot, but Geeliwan
was already as dead as he would ever be.

"Damnation and hell!" Hansen roared, anger and
frustration finally coming together within him at the
same time. "No reason . . . no reason for any of
this!" He gestured around, then looked back down at
Losting, his voice full of sorrow at the waste. "Don't
you see—you didn't stop us! I've got four people—"
He glanced back at Logan's motionless body. "No—
three people left."

Every word caused a sharp pain to shoot through
207

Losting. Each one was a new surprise. "You are all dead. All your little sky-boats are broken and so is the big . . . shuttle. Your little weapons are dead and so are your walls and webs. The stormtreader beat the life from them. The forest will come for you, now."

Hansen wore an expression of pity. "No, Losting. It was a good try you made. You almost did it. But we've plenty of food, and water from the sky every night. I know how fast this hylaea grows. It may very well obscure the station before our next relief ship arrives. It's true our shuttlecraft can't fly again. But its internal systems check out operational, including communications. I don't believe those gas-bag prisms will come back, and I don't think we'll be attacked by anything else capable of penetrating a ship hull. This forest can bury us under an avalanche of green, but our distress signal will still be picked up.

"You've managed to cost some people a lot of credits and a lot of trouble. They won't be pleased. But they'll rebuild this station, start over again—because of the immortality extract, Losting. You can't begin to imagine what ends people will go to to secure it.

"We won't make the same mistakes again. We'll rebuild halfway around this planet, far from your tribe. The new outpost will have aerial patrols, three times as many guns and bigger, with independent power-up systems. And we'll make a clear space four times as wide and twice as deep.

"No, we won't make the same mistakes again. You're a brave man, Losting, but you've failed. A great pity. I'd rather have been your friend."

"Grv . . . rbber . . ." Losting whispered.

Hansen leaned close, the muzzle of the pistol never wavering. "What's that? I didn't hear—?"

"You would steal everything," the hunter rasped, "even a man's soul, even a flower's smell."

Hansen shook his head slowly, sadly. "I don't understand you, Losting. I don't know if we could ever understand one another."

He was still shaking his head when the jacari from Born's snuffler punctured the side of his neck.

It was over quickly. Ruumahum brought down the

pair bending over Geeliwan's corpse. Born's axe stopped Cohoma before the bigger man could pull his pistol.

The hunter cut at the fallen giants more than was necessary. He was still hacking away at the bodies long after most of the blood had drained away, until his fury had done likewise. Exhausted, he stumbled over to slump down by the body of the man he had hated most in all the world. Ruumahum was sniffing at Geeliwan's flank, but there was no hope for the fallen furcot. That remarkable system was not invulnerable. Logan's beam had cut the brain. A slow trickle of dark green seeped from a severed vein in the skull and stained the olivine fur.

The face of the fallen hunter was twisted with a pain that was more than physical. "No luck . . . not for Losting. You always . . . win, Born. Always one branch ahead of Losting, one word, one deed. Not fair, not fair. So much death . . . why?"

"You know why, hunter," Born muttered awkwardly. "There was a disease, a parasite come new to the world. It fell upon us to cut it out. It would have killed the Home. You saved the Home, hunter." His voice cracked. "I love you, my brother."

Born sat there and conjured solemn images while Ruumahum squatted on hind legs and mourned with the weeping sky. They remained like that until time brought a new day and light.

The first wave of unchallenged cubbles, creepers, fom, and aerial shoots was already pimpling the once smooth edges of the clearing when Born and Ruumahum set on their way.

Two bodies—one human, one furcot—were secured to Ruumahum's broad back. To think of returning all the way Home with such a burden was absurd. It would slow them, hinder them, endanger them. But neither Ruumahum nor Born for a moment thought of returning without them.

Born remembered the words of the Hansen-chieftain as he had crawled near enough to kill him, last night in the darkness and rain. The words were false. He

209

did not think the giants would try another station elsewhere on the world—not now. Not with all their work here swallowed up whole, wordlessly, inexplicably. Even if they did, they could not find the burls they wanted. Not on the other side of the world. If they tried here, they would never get their light weapons and metals in place. The tribe would see to that. Other tribes would be told. The warning would be spread.

Brightly Go was the first to greet him on their return, when they staggered into the village exhausted and half dead many seven-days later. She did not stay with him for long after she saw Losting's body. To his mild surprise, Born found he didn't care.

Then he slept for two days, and Ruumahum a day longer.

The tale was told to the council.

"We will guard against their coming. We will not let them set their sickness in the world again," Sand declared when the relating was finished. Reader and Joyla agreed.

Now there was only one last thing to be done.

The next night the people took their torches and children and moved into the forest with the bodies of Losting and Geeliwan. For this Longago they sought out the greatest of They-Who-Keep—the tallest, the oldest, the strongest. This tree was the final resting place for the Home's most honored returnees. Ignoring the greater danger from nocturnal sky-demons and marauding canopy-dwellers, the procession climbed up to the First Level.

The ceremony was chanted then, the words recited in tones more solemn than any could remember. Then the bodies were treated with the oils and herbs and interred in the cavity, side by side. The humus and organic debris were set in place over them.

Losting would have enjoyed that eulogy. His prowess and skill as hunter, his strength and courage were expanded upon and praised. By his fellow hunters, by Sand and Joyla, by Born, especially by Born. So much so that the madman had to be led away by two others.

It was done.

The ceremony concluded, the double file of men and women and children began the long spiraling journey back to the Home, flanked on either side by their silent furcots.

The towering They-Who-Keep stood beneath wailing clouds as the last trailing torch was snuffed out by the all-encompassing dark greenery. Dark forest, green and unfathomable—who knew what thoughts arose in those malachite-colored depths?

Two days later a bud that grew near the base of the They-Who-Keep ripened to maturity. The tough skin shattered, and a small emerald shape spilled out, its bristling wet fur reaching for the faint streamers of sunlight. Three tiny eyes blinked open and small ivory tusks peeped out from the still damp edges of an as yet unopened mouth. Then the thing yawned and struggled to preen itself.

Fighting and twisting, the last green rootlets on its back pulled free from the lining of the seed-bud. They lay back and became fur, drinking in the sunlight. Photosynthesis began within the small body.

Mewling at the enormity of the world, the infant furcot looked around to see bright orbs gleaming at it in the day-shadows.

"I am Ruumahum," the mind behind those eyes announced. "Come with me to the brethren and the people."

The adult turned. Weakly, but with increasingly confident steps, the cub followed the elder up into the light.

Far above, a newborn child squalled at its mother's breast.

Forces stirred within the greatest of the They-Who-Keep at the new intrusion. The tree reacted, secreting a tough woody sap around the two forms to isolate and shield the vulnerable organic material. The sap hardened quickly, forming an impenetrable barrier to bacteria, mold, and insects.

Within the high branch, sap and strange fluids flowed and worked, dissolving and adding, reconstructing and preserving, reviving and reconstituting. Minute derivatives of the new intrusion were distributed throughout the whole seven-hundred-meter-high growth while tiny portions of other, older intrusions were carried to the new addition from other branches.

Bones were dissolved and carried off, flesh and needless organs disappeared. They were replaced by a network of patient black filaments—woody neurons. Old neural links of human and furcot were plugged into this vast network. New nutrients energized the metamorphosed cellular structures.

The process of blending Losting and Geeliwan into the soul-mind of the They-Who-Keep took forever and not long at all. The world-forest was unceasingly efficient. New sap moved, chemicals that should not have been were produced. Stimulus was applied to the new area. Catalyzation occurred.

Losting and Geeliwan became something more, something greater. They became a part of the They-Who-Keep matrix-mind, which in turn was only a single lobe of the still greater forest-mind.

For the forest dominated the world with no name. It evolved and changed and grew. It added to itself. When the first humans had reached it, the world-nexus saw their threat and their promise. The forest had strength and resilience and fecundity and variety. It was adding to its intelligence now, slowly, patiently, in the way of the plant.

Losting, feeling the last faint trace of no-longer-needed individuality fading away, feeling himself flow into the greater mind formed of dozens of human and many They-Who-Keep minds, all linked through the minds of the tree-born furcots, rejoiced.

"You didn't win, Born!" he cried triumphantly as the greatness swallowed him. Then envy vanished and he was a part of the greater whole, such human moods and emotions sloughed off like a dead crysalis. The forest-mind grew a little more. Soon it would add Born and Ruumahum and the others. Soon it would reach the end of its Plan. Then humans and any others would not be able to come and kill and cut with impunity. Eventually, it would reach out across the vast emptiness it now was starting to sense dimly, and then . . .

In the forest, Born emfoled a struggling sprout and smiled with it at the goodness of the day. He glanced upward at his beloved strange sky and was unaware he was looking beyond it.

Universe! Beware the child cloaked in green bunting.

SENSATIONAL SCIENCE FICTION
from

BALLANTINE BOOKS

WHO? Algis Budrys — **$1.50**

TALES OF KNOWN SPACE Larry Niven — **$1.50**

STAR TREK LOG FIVE Alan Dean Foster — **$1.25**

MARUNE: ALASTOR 933 Jack Vance — **$1.50**

THE BEST OF CORDWAINER SMITH
Cordwainer Smith, with an
INTRODUCTION and NOTES by J. J. Pierce — **$1.95**

WORLD OF PTAVVS Larry Niven — **$1.50**

ICE & IRON Wilson Tucker — **$1.50**

THE PATH OF UNREASON George O. Smith — **$1.50**

SLAVE SHIP Frederik Pohl — **$1.50**

▼ **Available at your local bookstore or mail the coupon below** ▼

BB 58/75